DEATH
BY
KILLER
MOP DOLL

ACCLAIM FOR *ASSAULT WITH A DEADLY GLUE GUN*

"Crafty cozies don't get any better than this hilarious confection
. . . Anastasia is as deadpan droll as Tina Fey's Liz Lemon, and
readers can't help cheering as she copes with caring for a host of
colorful characters."

—*Publishers Weekly* (starred review)

"Winston has hit a home run with this hilarious, laugh-until-
your-sides-hurt tale. Oddball characters, uproariously funny situ-
ations, and a heroine with a strong sense of irony will delight fans
of Janet Evanovich, Jess Lourey, and Kathleen Bacus. May this be
the first of many in Winston's Anastasia Pollack Crafting Mystery
series."

—*Booklist* (starred review)

"North Jersey's more mature answer to Stephanie Plum. Funny,
gutsy, and determined, Anastasia has a bright future in the
planned series."

—*Kirkus Reviews*

"A comic tour de force . . . Lovers of funny mysteries, outrageous
puns, self-deprecating humor, and light romance will all find
something here."

—*ForeWord Magazine*

"Fans of Stephanie Plum will love Lois Winston's cast of quirky,
laughable, and loveable characters. *Assault with a Deadly Glue
Gun* is clever and thoroughly entertaining—a must-read!"

—Brenda Novak, *New York Times* best-selling author

AN ANASTASIA POLLACK CRAFTING MYSTERY

DEATH
BY
KILLER
MOP DOLL

Lois Winston

MIDNIGHT INK
WOODBURY, MINNESOTA

First Edition
First Printing, 2012

Book design and format by Donna Burch
Cover design by Lisa Novak
Cover illustration © Marc Tobin
Editing by Connie Hill

Midnight Ink, an imprint of Llewellyn Worldwide Ltd.

Library of Congress Cataloging-in-Publication Data
Winston, Lois.
  Death by killer mop doll : an Anastasia Pollack crafting mystery / Lois Winston. — 1st ed.
     p. cm.
  ISBN 978-0-7387-2585-7
1. Single mothers—Fiction. 2. Periodical editors—Fiction. 3. Television producers and directors—Crimes against—Fiction. 4. Television programs—Fiction. 5. Handicraft—Fiction. I. Title.
  PS3623.I666D43   2012
  813'.6—dc22   2011031199

Midnight Ink
Llewellyn Worldwide Ltd.
2143 Wooddale Drive
Woodbury, MN 55125-2989
www.midnightinkbooks.com

Printed in the United States of America

For Zack, Zoe, and Chase

ACKNOWLEDGMENTS

To Terri Bischoff, Midnight Ink acquisitions editor, for offering Anastasia a home, and to all the other members of the Midnight Ink team, including Connie Hill, Steven Pomije, Courtney Colton, Courtney Huber, Donna Burch, and Lisa Novak, for the various roles they've played in making Anastasia look her best and giving her such incredible support when they sent her off into the world.

To Carolyn and Ashley Grayson for believing in my abilities.

To Denise Dumars for introducing Anastasia to Midnight Ink.

To my extremely talented son Scott Winston who, even though nominated for an Emmy Award, still has time to design my website and bookmarks and deal with my various computer problems.

To my other incredibly talented son Chris Winston, even though he hasn't helped me with anything related to Anastasia, but who would be very upset to see his brother mentioned in the acknowledgments and not him.

To Jennifer and Megan, the daughters I didn't have to raise through adolescence and therefore got the good without the grief.

Special thanks to DorothyL member Pattie Tierney for lending her name to Zack's ex-wife.

To my fellow founding members of Liberty States Fiction Writers: Gail Freeman, Melinda Leigh, Caridad Pineiro, Kathye Quick, Michele Richter, Rayna Vause, and Anne Walradt, for their amazing friendship, their constant support, and their ability to keep me sane.

And finally, to my husband, Rob, who has weathered many a storm with me over the years, both figuratively and literally.

ONE

Upstairs, the front door slammed with enough force to register a five on the Richter scale. Dust dislodged from the exposed basement rafters and drifted down like polluted snow, settling over the basket of clean laundry I'd been folding. The ensuing shouting, barking, and yowling drowned out my muttered curse of choice and yanked my attention away from the now Dalmatian-spotted white wash.

"*Once more unto the breach, dear friends,*" squawked Ralph, the Shakespeare-spouting African Grey parrot I'd inherited when Great-Aunt Penelope Periwinkle died two years ago. "*Henry the Fifth*. Act Three, Scene One." He spread his wings and took flight up the basement stairs to check out the action. I raced after him, eager to prevent World War III from erupting in my living room.

"Muzzle that abominable creature, or I'll have the pound haul him away," shrieked Mama. "He's traumatizing Catherine the Great."

1

"So shove some Prozac down her throat," said my mother-in-law, Lucille. "What the hell are you doing back here? And don't you ever bother to knock? Just barge right in like you own the place."

"I have more right to be here than you. This is my daughter's house, you ... you *pinko squatter*."

As I hurried through the kitchen, I glanced at the calendar tacked next to the telephone. Mama wasn't due back from her Caribbean cruise for another three days. Damn it. I needed those three days to steel myself for the inevitable explosive reaction that occurred whenever Flora Sudberry Periwinkle Ramirez Scoffield Goldberg O'Keefe, my mother and the former social secretary of the Daughters of the American Revolution, locked horns with Lucille Pollack, my mother-in-law and current president of the Daughters of the October Revolution. I'd been swindled out of seventy-two hours.

By the time I entered the living room, Mama and Lucille's voices had reached glass-shattering decibel range.

"Crazy communist!" yelled Mama. She stood in the middle of the room, cradling Catherine the Great, her corpulent white Persian with an attitude befitting her namesake.

Manifesto, my mother-in-law's runt of a French bulldog, stood inches from Mama's Ferragamos, his bark having switched to growl mode as he glared up at his nemesis. With a hiss and a yowl, Catherine the Great leaped from Mama's arms. Showing his true cowardly colors, Mephisto, as we always called him behind his back and often to his snout, scampered to safety behind my mother-in-law's ample girth.

Lucille barreled across the room, waving her cane at Mama. "Reactionary fascist!"

"How dare you threaten me!" Mama defended herself with a French-manicured backhand that would have done Chris Everett proud. The cane flew from Lucille's grasp and landed inches from Mephisto's nose. Demon dog yelped and dove between Lucille's orange polyester-clad legs.

My mother-in-law's rage multiplied into Vesuvian proportions. Her wrinkled face deepened from a spotted scarlet to an apoplectic heliotrope. "You did that on purpose!"

Mama jutted her chin at Lucille as she rubbed the palm of her hand. "You started it."

"And I'm stopping it." I stepped between them, spreading my arms to prevent them from ripping each other's lips off. "Knock it off. Both of you."

"It's her fault," said Mama. She jabbed a finger at Lucille. Her hand shook with rage, her gold charm bracelet tinkling a dainty minuet totally incompatible with the situation. "And that vicious mongrel of hers. She sic'd him on us the moment we walked through the door."

Highly unlikely. "Mephisto's all bark and bluster, Mama. You should know that by now."

"*Manifesto*!" shrieked Lucille. "How many times do I have to tell you his name is *Manifesto*?"

"Whatever," Mama and I said in unison. It was an old refrain. *Mephisto* better suited demon dog anyway. Besides, who names a dog after a Communist treatise?

Behind me, Ralph squawked. I looked over my shoulder and found him perched on the lampshade beside one of the overstuffed easy chairs flanking the bay window. A chair occupied by a cowering stranger, his knees drawn up to his chest, his arms hugging his head. I glanced at Mama. Glanced back at the man. "Who's he?"

"Oh dear!" Mama raced across the room, flapping her Chanel-suited arms. "Shoo, dirty bird!"

Ralph ignored her. He doesn't intimidate easily. Mama was hardly a challenge for a parrot who had spent years successfully defending himself against Aunt Penelope's mischievous students. "Anastasia, I told you that bird's a reincarnation of Ivan the Terrible. Do something. He's attacking my poor Lou."

Her Poor Lou? Okay, at least the man had a name and someone in the room knew him. I stretched out my arm and whistled. Ralph took wing, landing in the crook of my elbow. Poor Lou peered through his fingers. Convinced the coast was clear, he lowered his hands and knees and raised his head.

"Are you all right, dear?" asked Mama, patting his salt and pepper comb-over. "I'm terribly sorry about all this. My daughter never did have the heart to turn away a stray." She punctuated her statement with a pointed stare, first in Lucille's direction and then at Ralph.

Lucille harrumphed.

Ralph squawked.

Mephisto bared his teeth and rumbled a growl from the depths of his belly.

Catherine the Great had lost interest in the family melodrama and dozed, stretched out on the back of the sofa.

Before Mama could explain Poor Lou's presence, the front door burst open. Fourteen-year-old Nick and sixteen-year-old Alex bounded into the living room. "Grandma!" they both exclaimed in unison. They dropped their baseball gear and backpacks on the floor and encircled Mama in a group hug.

"Aren't you supposed to be on a cruise?" asked Nick.

"Who's this?" asked Alex, nodding toward Poor Lou.

Poor Lou rose. He wiped his palms on his pinstriped pants legs, cleared his throat, and straightened his skewed paisley tie. "Maybe I should be going, Flora. The driver is waiting."

I glanced out the front window. A black limo idled at the curb.

"Yes, of course." She walked him to the door without bothering to make introductions. Very odd behavior for my socially correct mother.

"I'll call you tomorrow," Poor Lou told Mama.

She raised her head, batted her eyelashes, and sighed. Poor Lou wrapped his arms around my mother and bent her backwards in a clinch that rivaled the steamiest of Harlequin romance book covers. His eyes smoldered as he met her slightly parted lips. Mama melted into his body.

I stared at my etiquette-obsessed mother, my jaw flapping down around my knees, and wondered if she had eaten any funny mushrooms on her cruise. Out of the corner of one eye, I saw my two sons gaping with equally bug-eyed expressions. Behind me, Lucille muttered her disgust. Even Ralph registered his amazement with a loud squawk.

Over Mama's shoulder, Poor Lou stole an anxious glance toward Ralph, broke the kiss, and darted out the door.

Mama fluffed her strawberry blonde waves back into place, smoothed the wrinkles from her suit jacket, and offered us the most innocent of expressions as we continued to ogle her. "Is something wrong?"

"Wrong? Why? Just because my mother was doing the Tonsil Tango with a total stranger?"

Lucille stooped to retrieve her cane. "I suppose this means that trashy hussy is moving back into my room."

"*Your* room?" asked Mama.

"Hey, it's *my* room!" said Nick.

Poor Nick. He was none too happy about having to give up his bedroom to his curmudgeon of a grandmother. He didn't mind the occasional upheaval when Mama came to visit because he knew it was temporary. Besides, the boys and Mama had a great relationship. Lucille was another story. When she moved in with us to recuperate after a hit-and-run accident and subsequent hip surgery, none of us had expected a permanent addition to the household. Then again, I had suffered from quite a few delusions back then.

Lucille scowled at me. "You should teach those boys some respect. In my day children knew their place."

"Don't you speak to my daughter like that."

Lucille scoffed. "Look who's talking. A fine example you set."

"What's that supposed to mean?" demanded Mama.

"Strumpet." Lucille pounded her cane once for emphasis, then lumbered from the living room, Mephisto following at her heels. Lucille habitually pronounced judgment with a pounding of her cane, then departed.

"At least I'm getting some," Mama called after her. "Unlike a certain jealous Bolshevik who hasn't experienced an orgasm since Khrushchev ruled the Kremlin."

"Mama!"

Nick and Alex grabbed their middles and doubled over in hysterics.

Mama brushed my indignation aside with a wave of her hand. "For heaven's sake, Anastasia, I'm a grown woman."

"Then act like one. Especially in front of your grandsons."

She winked at the boys. "I thought I did. Besides, if they don't know the facts of life by now, they've got a lot of catching up to do."

I glanced at my sons, not sure how to interpret the sheepish expression on Alex's face or the feigned innocence on Nick's. After the initial shock of seeing their grandmother in the throes of passion, both seemed quite amused by the drama playing out in our living room. "They know all about the facts of life. What they don't need is a graphic demonstration from their grandmother."

The corners of Mama's mouth dipped down. "Honestly, Anastasia, just because I'm over sixty doesn't mean I'm ready for a hearse. When did you become such a stick-in-the-mud, dear?"

I suppose right around the time she morphed from Ms. Manners into Auntie Mame. Other sixty-five-year-old women might behave this way in front of their daughter and grandsons, but up until today, Mama wasn't one of them. Was Poor Lou's last name *Svengali*?

Alex spared me from defending myself. "So who's the stranger dude, Grandma?"

"Lou isn't a stranger. He's my fiancé."

"Your *what*?" Surely I hadn't heard her correctly. Had some of that rafter dust settled in my ears? "What about Seamus, Mama?"

"Seamus?"

"Yes, Seamus. Remember him?"

Mama heaved one of those sighs reserved for children who need repeated instruction and explanation. "Seamus died, Anastasia. You know that."

Of course I knew Seamus had died. He'd suffered a cerebral aneurysm while kissing the Blarney Stone. "But he *just* died. Three months ago." Within days of losing my own husband, Mama had lost hers.

"Well, it's not like we were married very long. He died on our six-month anniversary. Besides, I'm not Merlin. I don't grow younger with each passing year."

Ample justification for getting herself engaged to a total stranger, no doubt. "Where did you meet this man?"

"On the cruise, of course."

"So you're engaged to a man you've known for all of one week?"

Mama shrugged. "Time is meaningless when soul mates connect."

Soul mates? The now-departed Seamus had been soul mate number five for Flora Sudberry Periwinkle Ramirez Scoffield Goldberg O'Keefe. When Mama finally met her maker, she'd have a line of soul mates waiting for her at the Pearly Gates. She'd better hope St. Peter allowed polygamy up in Heaven.

"Besides," continued Mama, "at my age, I have to grab happiness when it presents itself. Advice you'd do well to heed." She glanced down the hallway toward the bedrooms. "Unless you want to wind up like *her*."

"No, not that!" Nick grabbed his throat and made gagging noises. "Not my mom!"

Alex fell to his knees in front of Mama, his hands clasped in supplication. "Please, Grandma, save our mom!"

Comedians. I tossed them a mom-scowl. "If the two of you have so much time on your hands, you can vacuum and do a load of wash before dinner." Nearly seven and I still had to prepare a meal, finish a project for a photo shoot tomorrow, and figure out a way to rob Peter to pay Paul before the bill collectors came knocking. Again.

Alex grabbed his backpack. "Sorry, Mom. Got an economics paper due tomorrow."

"Bio test," said Nick, retrieving his backpack from the floor.

"Dibs on the computer," called Alex as he sped down the hall to the bedroom they now shared. The boys used to have their own computers, but Nick's died last month. A replacement would have to wait until I won Mega Millions or Powerball.

Nick raced after Alex. Neither bothered with the baseball gear they'd dumped on the carpet. Apparently, it had become invisible to all but me.

I stooped to pick up the discarded duffels of sports paraphernalia. "I'm still in mourning."

Mama snorted as she followed me into the kitchen. "For a no-good gambling addict who left you without two nickels to rub together?"

"Karl and I were married eighteen years," I said softly as I hung the duffels on pegs in the mudroom off the kitchen. "He's only been dead three months."

Mama regarded me with an expression that hovered somewhere between pity and skepticism. "You don't still have feelings for him, do you?"

I grabbed the leftover chicken and broccoli casserole from the fridge. There was barely enough left for four, let alone five people. "Not exactly," I said, reaching for a box of mac and cheese to supplement the casserole. Not after what Karl Marx Pollack had done to his kids and me. I mourned for my former life. Before lies and deceit and death shattered the illusion of our perfect middle-class world.

I brushed my desperately-in-need-of-a-styling-but-can't-afford-it hair out of my face and turned to confront Mama. "Besides, I don't have time for romance. I'm too busy paying off Karl's debts."

Three months ago, my husband of eighteen years had permanently cashed in his chips at a Las Vegas roulette table—after also cashing in his sizable life insurance policy and 401(k), maxing out our home equity line of credit and numerous credit cards, *and* draining our teenage sons' college accounts.

Besides the mountain of debt, my dearly departed had saddled me with both Ricardo the Loan Shark and Comrade Lucille, the communist mother-in-law from Hell. Karl had also stolen his mother's life savings, thus leaving Lucille and Mephisto ensconced in Nick's bedroom where they'd remain—short of an act of God. Considering Lucille didn't believe in God and I had the luck of an excommunicated leprechaun, chances of her leaving anytime soon were slim to none.

At least I no longer had to worry about Ricardo. He now resided at a federal facility. Permanently. No chance of parole, thanks to a trail of dead bodies three months earlier.

"A life without romance isn't worth living," said Mama. "Which reminds me, how's that sexy tenant of yours?"

"Zack?" asked Nick, bounding into the kitchen. He opened the refrigerator and began to survey the contents. "He's cool. Don't you think he and Mom—"

I cut him off before he could finish his sentence. "I thought you had a test to study for." I yanked his head out of the fridge and closed the door.

My sons shadowed Zachary Barnes like unweaned puppies. More often than not, I arrived home from work to find Zack sitting at my kitchen table, regaling Nick and Alex with his latest adventure. Lucky for me, the too-sexy-for-my-own-good photo journalist traveled frequently.

"I'm hungry."

"You'll have to wait until dinner."

He glanced at the clock over the sink. "Jeez, Mom, it's after seven. When are we going to eat?"

I tossed the box of mac and cheese at him. "If you're so hungry, you can help."

He tossed the box back. "Can't. Have to study." He snagged an apple from the bowl on the kitchen table and hustled out of the kitchen.

"So what's with you and Zack?" asked Mama as I filled a pot with water and placed it on the stove.

When Mama first met Zack, she tossed her hair, batted her eyes, and preened in front of him like a svelte Miss Piggy trying to woo Kermit the Frog. When Zack didn't take the bait, she decided I should have him. This all took place within days of both of us entering the ranks of widowhood.

I handed her a half-empty bag of carrots and a vegetable peeler. "Nothing."

She raised an eyebrow as she began scraping carrots. "He's a very handsome man, Anastasia. Unattached. Good job."

"Forget Zack. Let's talk about you. Why are you home three days early?"

Mama had a knack for marrying grasshoppers—men who lived life to the fullest without any regard for tomorrow. When they died, as each of them had, they left her with fond memories of a good time and little more than pocket change. So between husbands, she camped out at *Chez Pollack*. Although also a grasshopper, Seamus O'Keefe had had the foresight to purchase a small life insurance policy prior to his and Mama's Irish sojourn—a life insurance policy Mama had discovered only by chance weeks after returning from Ireland. Behind my back she paid off twenty thousand dollars of my inherited debt, then treated herself to a post-Seamus first-class cruise with the remaining five thousand dollars.

Mama waved a raggedly peeled carrot in the air. She was as useless in the kitchen as the rest of my brood. "The ship had some sort of mechanical problem in Antigua. Since there were severe storm warnings, Lou and I decided to fly home before the storm hit."

"And just who is this Lou?"

A dreamy look settled over her face. The corners of her mouth turned upward into a beatific smile as she exhaled a long sigh. "Lou? He's the answer to my prayers. And yours."

"Want to run that by me again?"

Mama rose from the table and tossed the carrot scrapings into the sink. "Lou is Louis Beaumont, Anastasia."

I waited. And waited. I crossed my arms, tapped my foot, cocked my head, and waited some more. "And?"

Mama's eyes grew wide. "Surely you've heard of Louis Beaumont."

"Can't say as I have."

"He produces *You Heard It Here First with Vince and Monica*."

That explained so much. I offered Mama a blank stare.

"The morning talk show with Vince Alto and Monica Rivers? Surely you've watched it."

"Television?" I laughed. "Right. Every morning while I loll around at the spa. In the afternoon I sip champagne, eat bonbons, and watch the soaps."

"There's no need for sarcasm, dear. It's a popular show. Even if you haven't watched it, I'd expect you to know about it."

"In case you hadn't noticed, Mama, I'm a single parent. I'm juggling a full-time job, two teenage kids, a house, a parrot who thinks he's the reincarnation of William Shakespeare, a semi-invalid mother-in-law, and her spawn of Satan dog.

"*And* when I'm not dealing with all of that, I'm trying to figure out ways to earn extra income because I'm up to my patootie in debt. I've never heard of Louis Beaumont. And you've heard *that* here first."

"Well, you'd better make an effort to watch *You Heard It Here First*, dear, because you're going to be a regular on the show."

TWO

I laughed until tears streamed down my cheeks and I couldn't catch my breath.

"What's so funny?" asked Mama. She scowl-stared at me as if trying to determine whether I was making fun of her or had gone completely *non compos mentis.*

"You are." I swiped at my face and broke into another chortle-athon. I had little enough to laugh about these days, and besides, sometimes a girl just has to bow to the absurd and let it all hang out. "Come on, Mama. Be serious. Me on TV? Not unless *You Heard It Here First* is a reality show for middle-aged, pear-shaped, financially strapped single parents."

"I *am* being serious," she said, hands planted on her hips. "Lou thinks it's a marvelous idea. Just what the show needs, he said."

That sobered me up. I tossed the chicken casserole in the oven and turned to her. "Forgetting that I have absolutely no acting experience, *what's* what the show needs?"

"Fresh blood."

I wasn't sure I liked the sound of that. "So *You Heard It Here First* is a daytime *Buffy* rip-off? And Vince and Monica are the resident vampires?"

"I don't know about anyone named Buffy," said Mama. "The stars are Vince Alto and Monica Rivers. I told you that already. And they're certainly not vampires."

"And now I'm one of the stars?"

"Well, you and some of the others."

"What others?"

"The other people from the magazine, of course."

"Of course." Silly me. The sound of boiling water drew my attention back to the stove. I dumped the dry macaroni into the pot, gave it a stir, and lowered the flame. Then I turned my attention back to my mother. "Let's start from the beginning, shall we, Mama?"

"I don't know why this is so difficult for you to grasp, dear. Lou wants to revamp his show. Ratings are down. I suggested he think about switching from the sordid gossipfest he's got now to one of those makeover shows that are so popular."

I glanced at my body. As much as I could use a makeover, I wasn't about to engage in one on national television. Even *I* wasn't that hard up for money. Well, actually I was, but I still maintained *some* principles, and making a public laughingstock of myself wasn't even at the bottom of my list of ways to earn extra cash to pay the bills. *Queer Eye for the Frumpy Middle-Aged Widow*? "No way. I'm not going to be a guinea pig for a group of fairy godfathers."

Mama's scowl-stare returned, her perfectly arched eyebrows knitting together over the bridge of her nose. "What on earth are you talking about? I never said anything about anyone using you as a guinea pig."

"Then what?"

"You're not getting a makeover, dear; you're giving them. You and the rest of the staff at *American Woman*."

American Woman was a second-rate monthly magazine sold on the racks at supermarket check-out lines. In my glamorously titled but poorly paid position, I created the various craft projects featured in each issue. "I'm the magazine's crafts editor," I reminded her. "I have nothing to do with fashion or beauty."

"I know that."

So why did I get the feeling I was reasoning with a rutabaga?

She exhaled a long-suffering sigh, as if I were the rutabaga—and a mentally challenged one at that. Then she spoke in a carefully modulated tone, the kind one might use to explain something to a mentally challenged rutabaga. "The fashion and beauty editors will deal with personal styling. You and the decorating editor will deal with home projects."

Okay, so maybe *I* was the rutabaga after all, considering Mama was beginning to make sense. "What about Trimedia?" I asked. Trimedia was the conglomerate that owned *American Woman*, and a stingier group of pecuniary tightwads had never walked the face of the earth. My paycheck could attest to that. I couldn't see them kicking in the moolah to support such a venture.

Mama issued forth another exasperated sigh. "Don't you know anything about the company you work for, dear?"

I knew they had instituted a hostile takeover last year, wresting control of the family-owned company out of the hands of former publisher and now meaningless figurehead Hugo Alsopp-Reynolds.

Once in control, the bean-counting suits had reduced our benefits and upped the employee contribution for what little remained. Then they moved us from our easy-to-commute-to Lower Manhattan offices to a cornfield in the middle of Morris County, New Jersey. I'd say I knew more than I wanted to know about Trimedia.

When I didn't answer her, Mama continued. "Trimedia owns the network that produces *You Heard It Here First*. Lou already pitched the idea while we were on the cruise, and they love it. They're going to hold a press conference at the end of the week. At a cocktail party." Tapping her lips with the opalescent pink nail of her index finger, she graced my bleach-stained jeans and faded New York Mets sweatshirt with a critical once-over. "You do have something nice to wear, don't you, dear?"

————

An hour and a half later, I was back in the basement, tossing the rewashed whites into the dryer. Before pushing the start button, I offered up a prayer to the gods of household appliances that my sixteen-year-old Kenmore would live through yet another load. It had recently begun making ominous noises. I wondered if I should also burn some incense or set up a little shrine to further appease the laundry gods. Couldn't hurt. I needed all the help I could get. I didn't have money for a repair bill, let alone a new dryer. And I certainly didn't have the time to hang wet laundry on a clothesline.

I searched around for the makings of a shrine. No incense, but I did have a half-melted, strawberry-scented candle and a bottle of Mr. Clean. The muscle-bound bald guy looked enough like a Buddha to pass as a laundry god. I draped the bottle with a strand

17

of Mardi Gras beads, lit the candle, and offered up a prayer. Then I turned my attention to the half-finished craft project spread out on the card table in the middle of the room.

Because staff meetings, photo shoots, and mounds of paperwork often gobbled up my day, I did much of my designing at home in the evenings and on weekends. Up until three months ago, I worked out of a comfortable home studio housed in the apartment above our detached garage. Now Zachary Barnes occupied the apartment, and I worked beneath the spastic flickers of a fluorescent strip light, shivering in the cold basement with my craft supplies spread atop an abandoned ping-pong table wedged between the hot water heater and the washing machine. One stumble to the left were assorted tools and a plethora of sports equipment. To the right were cartons of Christmas decorations and shelves of cleaning supplies.

Did I mention I've got the luck of an excommunicated leprechaun?

Even though it was the first week of May, the makings of a Halloween centerpiece, faux fall foliage and resin pumpkins, covered my work space. A monthly magazine's biological clock runs five to six months ahead of the calendar. Come October, I'd be knee-deep in fuzzy Easter bunnies and cellophane grass.

As I worked, I mulled over Mama's bombshell announcements. I'm not sure which bothered me more—yet another stepfather in a continuing parade of short-term stepfathers, or the fact that I would soon be wielding my glue gun in front of a few million television viewers.

The first disturbed me; the second terrified me, thanks to my one and only on-air experience. As a very young child, I had wet my pants on *Bozo the Clown*.

Don't ask.

Besides, I didn't need any additional responsibilities to cram into my already over-extended life. During the past three months I had come to the conclusion that juggling family, career, and homemaking duties as a single parent ranks up there with having a root canal, an ingrown toenail, and a colonoscopy—all on the same day.

However, Mama had said the television show was the answer to my prayers. Lately those prayers had centered around learning I was the long-lost sister of Bill Gates or daughter of Warren Buffett. Apparently God saw otherwise. I'd settle for an extra weekly paycheck, despite the additional work.

"I need a wife," I groused, gluing a silk burnt sienna oak leaf into position.

"*Heaven witness,*" squawked Ralph. "*I have been a true and humble wife. Henry the Eighth.* Act Two, Scene Four."

I glanced to my left to find him perched on a shelf above the washing machine, between a box of Tide and a package of Ty-D-Bowl. "No offense, but parrots don't count." Ralph might have an uncanny knack for uttering circumstance-appropriate quotes from the Bard, but like the rest of my household, he was useless when it came to domestic assistance.

———

At work the next day, I found myself the center of attention—anything but a common occurrence except for that one occasion three months ago when I was the suspect of a murder investigation.

A hierarchy existed at *American Woman*. Fashion and beauty reigned, garnering the most number of pages per issue. Crafts maintained Bottom Feeder status. Ad space—or more accurately, lack of it—determined my monthly page allotment. Ads equaled revenue. An issue with lots of crafts projects meant the sales force hadn't done a very good job that month. Thus, the bean counting shirts who resided upstairs were exceedingly unhappy when I wound up with more than a page or two of editorial content per issue.

And when the bean counters were unhappy, they made life miserable for the rest of us. Consequently, even though I had nothing to do with generating sales, I wasn't the most popular person around *American Woman*.

However, when I entered the break room and dropped Mama's bombshell news, I became Miss Popularity. Everyone demanded details. "That's all I know," I told them after providing the information I'd garnered from Mama. "I guess we'll have to wait until the press conference tomorrow."

"I wonder if Naomi knows more," said Cloris, munching on a chocolate glazed donut with pink sprinkles. Cloris McWerther was the magazine's food editor, a few rungs above me in Bottom Feeder Land, and my closest friend at work—even though she possessed a metabolism that enabled her to inhale calories, yet maintain a size 2 figure. I, on the other hand, merely had to glance at a chocolate glazed donut with pink sprinkles to blow up another dress size.

Normally, I'd hate someone like Cloris, but she had also played Doctor Watson to my Sherlock Holmes a few months ago when Ricardo the Loan Shark tried to frame me for murder, so I forgave her that enviable metabolism of hers.

"Know what?" asked Naomi. Our editorial director entered the break room and helped herself to a cup of java. With her aristocratic features, the elegant Naomi Dreyfus reminded me of Grace Kelly. She wore her silver hair pulled back into a tight chignon and always looked like she had stepped off the pages of *Vogue*, circa 1955.

Kim O'Hara, Naomi's half-Chinese, half-Irish, ever-present assistant, stood several paces behind her boss. As usual, Kim clutched a phone between her cheek and shoulder while jotting notes on a pad balanced atop a stack of file folders. Every once in a while she offered an "uh-huh" as she jotted another detail from the caller.

"About all of us doing a television show," said Jeanie Sims, our decorating editor.

Naomi frowned. Mutual animosity existed between her and upper management. Some of it, no doubt, stemmed from her long-time relationship with Hugo. Except for a brief period when Hugo fell under the spell of former fashion editor Marlys Vandenburg, he and Naomi had been an item for years. They got back together after Ricardo dispatched Marlys to the great catwalk in the sky. The rest of the hostility between Naomi and the guys upstairs dealt with her ongoing battle over control of editorial content. "No one has said anything to me about a TV show," she said.

I told her what I knew.

She turned to Kim, who had ended her call and was now helping herself to a cup of coffee. "You hear anything?" In order for

Naomi to control her blood pressure and keep ulcers at bay, she used Kim whenever possible to run interference for her against the tightwad suits.

Kim shook her head, her blunt cut sweeping across her face like a silky auburn curtain. "Not a word. You want me to talk to some of the girls upstairs?"

"See what you can find out," said Naomi.

Kim grabbed her files, her phone, and her coffee and headed for the elevator.

"I hope it's true," said Tessa Lisbon, Marlys's replacement. She bent her knees to check her perfectly applied make-up in the reflection from the toaster oven on the Formica counter. As fashion editors went, Tessa was not much of an improvement over the self-absorbed Marlys, a *prima donna* personality seeming to be a prerequisite for fashion editors. "I'd kill to be a big-name TV star," she added.

"That's probably the only way you'd gain a name for yourself on that show," said Cloris.

"What do you mean?" asked Tessa. She removed a lipstick from her pocket and began repairs to a collagen-enhanced pout that already looked perfectly painted to me.

"I caught it once when I had the flu and was channel surfing," said Cloris. "Once was enough. They really scrape the bottom of the tabloid barrel."

"How so?" asked Janice Kerr, our health editor.

"Mama did say it was one of those sleazy gossip shows," I said.

"We're not talking Regis and Kelly here, ladies," continued Cloris, reaching for another donut. "Even the show's hosts are washed-up B-listers. The day I watched, one guest was a Hollywood has-been who'd recently completed a few hundred hours of community service."

"Drugs?" asked Jeanie.

"Uncontrollable sticky fingers on Rodeo Drive," said Cloris. "The other was some right-wing radio pundit who'd served mandatory time at Betty Ford."

Tessa wrinkled her nose. "And we're supposed to give *them* makeovers?"

"Sure," said Jeanie. "You educate them on how to accessorize orange jumpsuits, and I show them how a few yards of chintz can transform a prison cell into a cozy abode."

We all laughed. "Maybe the craft segment will be considered art therapy," I said. "Something they can do to keep busy while in rehab or prison."

"And Cloris can teach them how to bake a cake with a file hidden in it," added Janice.

"Frankly," I said, "I really don't care who the hosts or guests are. I'm just happy for an opportunity to increase my bank account."

"Ditto," said Cloris. "My daughter's tuition is going up again next semester. Nearly ten percent this time."

I groaned. If I remembered correctly, this was the third tuition increase for Cloris's daughter, and she was only a sophomore. Alex was two years away from college. I had no idea how we'd manage tuition, even the more reasonably priced state schools, no matter how much extra I earned from the television show. *Thank you from the bottom of my penniless heart, Karl Marx Pollack.*

Frown lines settled at the corners of Naomi's mouth. She cleared her throat. "I hate to be the bearer of bad news," she said, "but chances are none of you will be seeing anything extra in your paychecks from this. If there actually is a show in the works."

We all stared at her. "What do you mean?" I asked.

"I'm not taking on more responsibilities without adequate compensation," said Tessa. Only periodic Botox injections prevented her from frowning the displeasure evident in her voice.

"Read the fine print in your contracts," said Naomi. "We all have a clause that requires us to perform any public relations duties Trimedia deems necessary to the success of the publication. The contracts specifically mention television, radio, and public appearances."

"But this isn't an occasional three-minute holiday stint on *Good Morning America*," said Cloris.

"Right," said Jeanie, her head bobbing in agreement with Cloris. Even the smattering of freckles across the bridge of her nose seemed to scowl her displeasure. No Botox for Jeanie. No Miss Clairol, either. She believed in the natural aging process. Her gray-streaked hair proved she practiced what she preached.

"Doing a television show would be like taking on a second job," I said. "Surely Trimedia needs to compensate us for that. Besides, according to Mama—"

"Maybe we shouldn't jump to conclusions until we know all the facts," suggested Naomi. "Right now all we have is what your mother told you. Nothing official."

What Mama told me. I chewed on my lower lip and admitted what had nagged at me from the beginning. "Mama isn't always the most reliable source of information."

Except that this time she was. Kim returned a few minutes later waving a sheet of paper. "This is a copy of the memo going out to all of us via e-mail later today."

Tessa snatched it from her hand and read out loud, "All staff members are required to attend a cocktail party Friday evening, seven-thirty sharp, at the Marriott Marquis where the launch of a joint venture between two of Trimedia's highly successful properties, *American Woman* magazine and our morning talk-show *You Heard It Here First with Vince and Monica,* will be announced."

"*Highly successful?*" Janice raised both eyebrows. "Wasn't it just last week they were threatening to fold us if retail sales didn't improve?"

"That was a ploy to keep from handing out annual raises," said Kim. We all stared at her. She shrugged. "Hey, you hear things upstairs."

Cloris turned to Naomi. "Is that true? No raises this year?"

Crap. Besides my huge husband-induced debt, Westfield had announced school tax increases for the coming year. Then there was the recent rise in everything from postage stamps to gasoline to milk. "Not even a cost-of-living adjustment?" I asked.

Naomi frowned into her coffee cup. "Don't look at me. I'm on a need-to-know basis when it comes to those guys."

"Hugo hasn't said anything?" I asked. After all, Hugo had an office upstairs, even if it wasn't more than a broom closet and situated as far away from the action as the big boys could stash him without actually shoving him out a window.

"Hugo knows even less than I do."

Naomi had always remained semi-aloof when it came to relations between herself and her editors, but the problems of the past few months had shattered the wall that separated the drones from the queen bee and created a bond between us. I suppose murder will do that to people. Especially when the police finger you as one of the suspects. Naomi and I had both been singled out for extra scrutiny during the investigation into Marlys's murder.

I exhaled a sigh of disgust. My problems were my own and not Naomi's fault. "That's it?" I asked Kim. "We don't get any other information about the show until tomorrow night? Like whether or not we're getting paid?"

Kim turned to Naomi. "They want to see you upstairs."

"That sounds ominous," said Cloris.

"Should I bring my shovel?" asked Naomi.

Kim nodded.

"This is not looking good," muttered Tessa, biting off all her carefully applied lipstick.

———

When Naomi returned an hour later, Kim called all eight editors into the conference room.

"I want you to know I did my best," Naomi began.

"Here comes the big *but*," Cloris stage-whispered.

Naomi sighed and nodded. "But I couldn't sway them. They've consulted with the corporate attorneys who have concluded editorial participation on the show falls within the parameters of your existing contracts."

"Shit!"

Everyone turned to stare at me. Thermonuclear heat jettisoned up my neck and into my cheeks. I hung my head and mumbled, "Sorry."

"Don't apologize," said Naomi. "I used far more graphic language a few minutes ago. To no avail." She went on to feed us the company line. "They believe this is an excellent opportunity for all of us."

"How do they figure that?"

"The show is being renamed *Morning Makeovers*. It will run Monday through Friday from 9 a.m. to 10 a.m. Each editor will be responsible for a fifteen-minute segment once a week—one each for fashion, beauty, decorating, crafts, food, travel, finance, and health—two segments per show."

"The math doesn't add up," said finance editor Sheila Conway.

Naomi shrugged. "They didn't outline the remainder of the programming to me, and frankly, I wasn't interested. My only concern is the magazine's involvement."

We all nodded in agreement as Naomi continued. "Anyway, each of your segments will relate to the makeover of a lucky viewer participant. The magazine, as well as each of its editors, will gain tremendous national exposure. Or so they believe."

"Silly me," I said, slapping my forehead. "I had no idea the utility companies were now accepting exposure credits in lieu of checks for payment. How many minutes of air time equals a dollar's worth of electricity or gas? One-for-one like mileage awards? There aren't any blackout periods, are there?"

Naomi winced. "The exposure could lead to product endorsements or other offers."

"Don't try to put a positive spin on this," said Cloris. "Let's face it. The only winner here is Trimedia. Think of the increased advertising revenues. Corporate stuffs their pockets on our slave sweat."

"So, we won't be compensated at all for these weekly appearances?" asked Tessa.

"They expect you to honor your contracts. Their attitude is that they're only asking for an additional fifteen minutes of your time per week. And due to the new format, the show will now be taped, so none of you will have to leave home before dawn to arrive at the studio on time."

"Their benevolence knows no bounds," Jeanie grumbled.

"Wait a minute," I said. "Fifteen minutes? What about the additional hours it takes to prepare that fifteen-minute presentation? I don't pull craft projects out of a magician's butt, you know. And each completed project I show in the magazine requires several step-by-step models."

"Same here," said Cloris. "When I bake a cake, I actually bake half a dozen."

"And what about the commute in and out of Manhattan?" asked Tessa. "In case you've forgotten, we're stuck in the middle of a New Jersey cornfield."

"Add to that the time we'll have to spend in make-up prior to taping and you've killed an entire day," said Nicole Emmerling, our beauty editor. She panned the room, a scowl plastered across her face, as she waited for the rest of us to chime in our agreement.

"Fifteen minutes, my ass," grumbled Sheila.

"Unless they want us to appear *au natural*," suggested Jeanie.

Cloris laughed. "Are you kidding? We'd frighten the hell out of women waking up all over America."

"Which might not be such a bad idea," I said.

"What?" Nicole's perfectly shadowed, lined, and mascara-ed eyes widened with horror. "I'm not appearing on television without make-up. Are you crazy?"

"Like a fox," I said. "Can you think of a quicker way to turn off the public? No viewers, no show."

"I didn't hear that," said Naomi. "However, before you plan a mutiny, bear in mind that Trimedia keeps an office full of barracuda attorneys on retainer. Don't do anything that might set you up for a lawsuit."

"So you're saying we have no choice?" Janice asked.

Naomi raised her hands in defeat. "I did my best. They refuse to budge. The only concession I could wheedle out of them was a verbal hint of a *possible* bonus if the show is successful."

"Any chance of getting that in writing?" asked Cloris.

"From those guys?" I tossed her a smirk. "When armadillos fly."

"What if we refuse to participate?" asked Tessa.

"People who don't meet their contractual obligations get fired," said Naomi. "If you want to keep your job, you have no choice."

Tessa crossed her arms over her silk-clad, silicone-enhanced cleavage. "Well, I'm not going to stand for this. I'll hire my own attorneys to fight them. No one takes advantage of me and gets away with it." She stormed out of the conference room, her Jimmy Choo heels clicking a quick staccato beat on the terrazzo floor.

Tessa wasn't one of my favorite people at the magazine, but I had to give her points on this one. The last thing I needed was another uncompensated responsibility egg to juggle. Problem was, I also didn't have any excess cash to hire a contract attorney, and I doubted any pro bono flunky at Legal Aid would stand much of a chance against the Trimedia barracudas.

"Just like Marlys," said Cloris to Tessa's retreating backside.

"I hope not," I said. "Finding a dead fashion editor in my office was one experience I'd rather not repeat."

———

The next evening, minutes before the press conference, the *American Woman* editors were ushered into a small meeting room next to the reception room. Mama's Poor Lou, looking fully recovered from his traumatic encounter with Ralph, bobbed his head in silent response to Alfred Gruenwald, the Trimedia CEO speaking to him. Naomi, regal in pearls, basic black, and a tight smile, stood beside Gruenwald. I scanned the room but saw no evidence of Hugo.

To my surprise, Mama, decked out in a two-piece Pierre Cardin plum-colored jacket dress and acting the perfect corporate wife—or fiancée in this case—hung onto both Poor Lou's arm and every word spouting from our pompous CEO. She had given no indication that she'd be attending the press conference when I mentioned it to her yesterday, and she hadn't been home when I popped in to change clothes before catching the train into Manhattan. Then again, Mama hadn't divulged much of anything after dropping her bombshell two nights ago.

Halfway across the room, a man and woman watched Mama, Lou, Naomi, and Gruenwald. They made no attempt to conceal their murderous expressions as they whispered to each other.

"Vince Alto and Monica Rivers," said Cloris, following my gaze.

Vince Alto appeared to be in his mid-fifties, a man who spent too much time either in the sun or in tanning beds, judging from the deep crow's feet and laugh lines engraved into his bronzed skin. His way-too-jet-black wavy hair made me wonder if he owned stock in Grecian Formula. His slight paunch strained the gold buttons of the blue serge blazer he wore with a pair of khaki pants, lemon yellow dress shirt, and blue gingham checked silk tie. A matching silk handkerchief peeked from his breast pocket. He looked like he'd taken a wrong turn on the way to his yacht.

In contrast, his co-host had dressed for New Year's Eve at the Ritz—more than seven months early. Monica Rivers wore a long-sleeved crimson sequined gown with plunges front and back that required at least a roll of double-sided tape. Otherwise she'd run the risk of arrest on charges of indecent exposure. Her deep chestnut teased hair was piled high on her head. Strategically placed tendrils cascaded over her face and kissed her shoulders.

I pegged her at around my age, maybe a few years younger. The tight pull of her facial skin suggested someone who lived fast and hard but had the money to camouflage it. Plastic surgeons live for such women.

I had dressed in a conservative black silk suit with pearl buttons, the same outfit I'd worn three months earlier to Karl's funeral. Most of the other editors were similarly garbed except for Jeanie, who hadn't bothered to change from the flared denim patchwork skirt, matching jacket, and Birkenstocks she'd worn to work. Only Tessa had donned a cocktail dress, but her shocking pink chiffon baby doll chemise looked like a nun's habit compared to Monica's almost-a-dress.

The two hosts interrupted their whispering long enough to dart a quick once-over in our direction. The homicidal set of their jaws and dagger glint in their eyes remained in place. "They look about as friendly as a pair of porcupines with hemorrhoids," I said.

"Get a load of those baubles," said Cloris. A pair of multi-diamond and ruby earrings dangled from Monica's lobes. "I'll bet they're worth enough to cover a few years of college tuition."

"If they're real," said Tessa. "Hard to tell from this distance. Or they could be on loan. The dress, too."

"Yes," said Cloris, "your predecessor used to take advantage of that little perk quite often. Got herself killed for the Cartier trinkets she was wearing."

Well, not exactly. I raised an eyebrow ever so slightly. Cloris ignored me. We both knew Marlys's borrowed diamonds were a bit of serendipity for Ricardo the Loan Shark, but Cloris liked to yank the newbie's chain a bit from time to time. Having few perks of our own, we Bottom Feeders took whatever advantage we could get.

Jeanie continued to stare at Vince and Monica. "I'm feeling like the poor relation no one really wanted to invite. Do you get the sense they don't want us here?"

"They don't."

We all turned. A shocking pink and lime green floral muumuu-draped woman stood behind us. I pegged her as early-to-mid fifties. She wore a Dorothy Hamill helmet of peat-brown hair and a smile that stretched between a pair of plump, splotchy red cheeks. Raising her hand, she wiggled her fingers in greeting. "Welcome, ladies. I'm Sheri Rabbstein, otherwise known as the power behind the throne." She giggled.

We stared at her.

"Lou Beaumont's indispensable assistant producer," she explained. "Nothing gets done around here unless I do it. And I am *so* happy to meet all of you." She reached out and pumped our hands, one after the other. "I've been after Lou for ages to give this show a swift kick in the gluteus maximus. 'Bout time he listened to me." She darted a quick frown toward Poor Lou.

Then, her face-filling beam somersaulted back into place, and she cocked her head in the direction of Vince and Monica. "Those two are *so* yesterday. They were killing us. We were about to be canceled, you know." She spoke this *sotto voce*, her hand cupping her mouth. "But you gals are tomorrow. Between my ideas and your know-how, this show is going to rock and roll."

"We don't do music," said Cloris.

Sheri offered up another giggle. "Here." She handed us each a sheet of paper. "This will explain all the changes in case any members of the press buttonhole you during the reception."

"Buttonhole us?" I asked, glancing down at three paragraphs of black type on a pink page.

"Don't worry," she said. "After they hear about the changes, they'll be all over Vince and Monica. I doubt anyone will ask you any questions. If you do get trapped and need rescue, I'll be circulating, ready to bail you out of any jam." She darted another quick frown toward Poor Lou. "That's what I do best." Then with her smile pasted in place, she wiggled her index finger at us before bouncing toward the exit. "Remember," she sing-songed over her shoulder, "I'm here if you need me."

"That woman missed her calling," said Cloris. "She belongs on *Sesame Street*."

"Too sweet." Janice wrinkled her nose. "She's more like that obnoxious, obese purple dinosaur."

The others grunted in agreement as I bowed my head over the pink sheet of paper. "Oh. My. God."

THREE

"Wнат?" My fellow editors stared at me staring at the paper in my hand. Too flabbergasted to speak, I responded by jabbing at the words on the page. As they read from their own copies, I stole a glance at Vince and Monica. I swear I saw angry puffs of steam rising from the tops of their expertly coifed heads.

"No wonder they look ready to tear us limb from limb," I said.

"Hell hath no fury like a celebrity snubbed," muttered Cloris.

Vince Alto and Monica Rivers had been screwed. Big time. Not only had *Poor Lou* stripped their names from the show's title, he'd yanked those plush host seats right out from under their celebrity derrieres. Naomi was the new host of the show, with Vince and Monica demoted to sidekick status.

"Looks like Mama was right," I said.

"About what?" asked Cloris. "Your mother said we were all going to make money on this gig, remember?"

An awkward silence fell between us. I bowed my head and contemplated the press release. Each month the producers would choose one lucky person for a total makeover of herself and her home with the various editors taking charge of their areas of expertise. Jeanie and I would do a trash-to-treasures transformation of her home.

"*Queen for a Day* meets *Extreme Makeover*," said Sheila.

"What's *Queen for a Day*?" asked Tessa.

Sheila sighed. "Showing my age again, huh?" In her early sixties, Sheila was the oldest among us. "A TV show from my childhood. One lucky contestant each show was granted her fondest dream."

"Like a mansion with live-in help or a first-class trip around the world?" asked travel editor Serena Brower.

"More like a washing machine or new refrigerator," said Sheila.

Tessa snorted. "That's what people dreamed about back then? Appliances?"

"I suppose they pre-selected contestants whose dreams corresponded with the show's sponsors," said Sheila. "After all, this was back in the days of rigged game shows."

"Stop prattling," said Jeanie, waving her press release. "Did any of you really read this? *A total transformation of her home*?" Her voice rose several octaves. "We don't do this much work for each issue."

"What happened to fifteen minutes once a week, taped ahead of time?" asked Cloris.

"It's obvious," said Tessa. "The boys upstairs lied to Naomi." She paused for a moment, eyeing us one at a time. "Or Naomi lied to us."

"Naomi wouldn't lie to us," said Sheila. "This show means lots of extra work without additional pay for her, too."

"Does it?" asked Tessa.

"What are you implying?" asked Cloris.

Tessa shrugged. "I think it's obvious. After all, we don't really know whether or not Naomi negotiated a hefty raise for herself at our expense, do we?"

"Naomi wouldn't screw us," I said. "If you weren't so new, you'd know that."

"Why do you keep defending her?" asked Tessa. "Look at her hobnobbing over there with the kingpins. It's every woman for herself in this world. She wouldn't agree to hosting the show without adequate compensation. I say she took care of herself at our expense."

I glanced at Cloris. She nodded. "It certainly looks like Naomi's sold us out."

I had always admired and respected Naomi. I didn't want to believe that I was such a bad judge of character. But then again, I had married Karl, hadn't I?

"We should go on strike," said Tessa.

"Easy for you to say." Tessa had mentioned on more than one occasion that she came from money. Old money. And lots of it. "The rest of us have financial obligations."

"They can't run the magazine and TV show without us," she said. "That gives us leverage."

Cloris laughed. "Trimedia could replace all of us within a day."

"More like an hour," said Janice. "Look how quickly they filled our dead fashion editor's chair."

An involuntary shudder skittered up my spine. To force the image of Marlys's dead body from my mind, I gestured toward Vince and Monica. "I don't know what they're so annoyed about.

We'll be doing all the work for *bupkis* while they continue to collect their weekly paychecks for doing nothing more than showing up and smiling."

"Nice work if you can get it," said Jeanie.

Cloris waved the press release. "According to this, they're supposed to assist us. Along with guest celebrities."

"Right." I said. "Can you see Monica Rivers and Jack Nicholson donning smocks to faux finish a second-hand chest of drawers?"

"Let alone trolling suburban garage sales to find that chest of drawers?" added Jeanie.

Considering Mama's role in precipitating our current situation, I wondered if my coworkers would eventually blame me for our new status as indentured servants. I had to hope they never found out.

At that moment the culprit in question, still arm-in-arm with her newest catch, joined us, and I was finally formally introduced to my stepfather-to-be.

"Isn't this exciting, Anastasia?" asked Mama, her charm bracelet and an assortment of gold bangles tinkling as she stroked Lou's forearm. "We're all going to be famous."

"We?" I asked.

"Well, after all, it was my idea," said Mama, puffing out her chest. "I'm even going to have my name in the credits." She raised her chin and batted her eyes at Lou. "Isn't that so, dear?"

He smiled down at her. "Of course, my sweet. It's the least I can do to honor your creative genius."

Mama turned to me. "It's going to say..." She glanced back up at Lou. "How exactly did you word it, dear?"

"Based on an original idea by Flora Sudberry Periwinkle."

She nodded as she beamed a megawatt Pepsodent smile at all of us. "Yes, that's right."

Cat out of the bag. My fellow editors glared at me. "Sheri claimed she came up with the idea," I said, hoping to keep seven murderous editors from drawing and quartering me on the spot.

When I had told Mama I wouldn't get paid extra for the television show, she assured me that everything would work out for the best. So in typical Mama fashion she had moved on, fixating on what was important to her.

"Sheri who?" she asked.

"An assistant," said Lou with a pat to Mama's arm. "No one important."

"Just another one of the overworked, underpaid Trimedia minions?" I asked.

Lou's balding pate under the comb-over grew crimson. "I heard about your contract situation," he said. "I'm sorry. I have no control over that."

The editorial gaggle raised a collective eyebrow at each other.

"Why would this Sheri person take credit for my idea?"

Lou stooped to kiss Mama's cheek. "She's not, my sweet. Don't worry. The credit goes to you."

"I should think so," said Mama with a jut of her chin. "People have no right stealing other people's ideas. Is she here? Someone needs to set her straight."

At that moment the lights blinked, signaling that it was time to move into the other room for the start of the press conference. I now understood the earlier malevolent look Sheri had cast toward Lou. Or maybe her glare had been aimed at Mama. Somewhere between Fort Lauderdale and Antigua, Mama had mesmerized

Lou Beaumont. As he regaled her about his show, Mama had stolen claim to Sheri's ideas. Sheri may have originated the reformatted show, but apparently Lou hadn't considered it worth pursuing until Mama pushed it.

If Lou knew what was good for him, he'd keep two oceans and a continent between the show's staff and his fiancée. If Sheri, Vince, or Monica didn't kill Mama, my fellow editors surely would.

———

Two hours later I had crammed myself full of enough mini quiches, potato puffs, and crab balls to qualify as a tummy tuck candidate. Too bad Trimedia's munificence stopped with free carbs and didn't extend to offering a week at a fat farm before sticking us in front of blubber-enhancing cameras.

Since liposuction was out of the question, I headed for the nearest ladies' room, only to find a queue of women stretching out the door and halfway across the lobby. Leave it to Trimedia to book a reception on the same floor as the Marquis Theatre and schedule a press conference that ended right before an eight o'clock curtain.

I decided to hop the escalator and find an empty facility one flight up. Apparently, Monica Rivers had the same idea. As I stepped onto the escalator at the bottom, I noticed her stepping off at the top.

As the moving stairs ascended, a man sprinted past me, taking the steps two and three at a time. His shiny blue-black ponytail bounced between shoulder blades broad enough to threaten the integrity of his jacket seams. By the time I reached the top, he'd nearly caught up with Monica. I ducked behind a column and watched as he grabbed her by the arm and spun her around.

What can I say? I have a dominant nosey gene. Anyone else in my position would have done the same.

"What are you doing here?" she demanded.

"I think that's obvious," he said.

"Stop following me, you suspicious bastard."

"I know what you're doing," he said.

"What I'm doing is going to take a piss. Since you're so paranoid, maybe you'd like to watch?"

Monica winced as his grip tightened around her arm and he shook her. "I've had enough of your sneaking around. Do you think I don't know what's going on behind my back? It's Alto, isn't it?"

Monica jerked free. "Oh, please! Give me credit for better taste than that."

"Then who is it? Beaumont? You've always had a thing for diddling old geezers. As long as they're fat in the one place that counts. Isn't that so, sweetheart?"

Instead of answering him, she hauled back and clipped him across his two-day stubble. As he staggered backwards, she twirled on her four-inch designer stilettos and marched into the ladies' room.

Since I couldn't be sure the man wouldn't follow her, I decided to head for a restroom on the floor above. I wasn't worried about Monica. With that left hook of hers, she could take care of herself.

———

The following Monday we had our first official production meeting with Sheri Rabbstein. "Could be an ethnic statement," whispered Cloris as we eyed Sheri's outfit, another muumuu but this time a turquoise, navy, and purple geometric print. "Maybe she's Hawaiian."

I helped myself to a cup of coffee while we waited for the others to arrive. "Only if the lost tribe of Israel wound up on Waikiki Beach," I said.

One by one, the other members of the *American Woman* team trickled in. Twenty minutes after the scheduled start of the meeting I checked my watch for the eighteenth time, mentally running through a checklist of the tasks awaiting me back at the office.

"What are we waiting for?" asked Naomi.

"Vince and Monica," said Sheri.

We waited. And waited. And waited. Fifteen minutes later, Vince called in sick. Ten minutes after that, Monica did likewise.

"Sick my ass," muttered Sheri, disconnecting from the call. Then she flashed us a tight smile. "Vince and Monica have both come down with Blue Flu. They won't be joining us today."

"What about Lou?" asked Naomi.

"Lou isn't hands-on. He deals with the big picture. I handle segment production." She grabbed a stack of thick presentation books sitting on a chair and dealt them out along the makeshift conference table set up in the *You Heard It Here First* studio. Around us, workmen dismantled the former stage set.

"This is the first month's shows broken down into segments and taping schedules," said Sheri. She raised her voice above the din of hammers, drills, and grunting carpenters. "We begin rehearsals a week from today. Five days for everyone to learn the ropes, then we begin taping."

"Doesn't give us much time," grumbled Jeanie.

"Sorry about that," said Sheri. "Lou wants to kick off on Labor Day, so we have no choice." She waved her arm at the chaos surrounding us. "We're broadcasting reruns now in order to get ready for the premier show."

I flipped open my book. "You've chosen the makeover candidate already?"

Sheri's normally ruddy cheeks flamed to near-vermilion as she grinned sheepishly and spoke around a giggle. "You're looking at her."

"You?" asked Tessa.

"Uhm ... isn't that a bit unethical?" asked Sheila.

"Not at all," said Sheri, a puzzled expression settling across her brow. "Given our time constraints, this was the most expeditious solution. We have no intention of misleading our viewers. We plan to use staff members to start things rolling and will have a disclaimer to that effect at the end of each show. Once the shows begin to air, viewers will be invited to send videotaped resumes from which we'll select future candidates."

"Nice little perk," said Cloris. "Do you get to take the vacation, too?"

Sheri graced her with one of her flush-cheeked, perky smiles. "Of course. Each month's segment ends with a video diary of the vacation."

"I don't suppose we get any such perks," said Sheila.

"You'll get to meet and work with lots of celebrities."

"Like Vince Alto and Monica Rivers?" asked Tessa. "Whoop-de-fucking-doo."

Sheri's buoyant attitude deflated like a punctured dirigible. "Look," she said. "I know how you're all feeling about getting roped into this show—"

Naomi placed her palms on the table and leaned forward. "With all due respect, you can't possibly know how my editors feel."

Cloris and I made eye contact, silently acknowledging to each other that Naomi hadn't included herself in her statement. Reluctantly, I concluded my coworkers were right about our editorial director. She'd sold us out.

"Unless you've agreed to forego your salary and work for free," Serena added. Two angry splotches appeared on either side of her café latte complexion, and her eyes narrowed into tight slits.

Sheri blinked. "Why would I do that?"

"Exactly," said Cloris. "However, we weren't given a choice."

I stared at Sheri's confused expression. "She doesn't know," I said.

"Know what?" she asked.

"That our contracts with Trimedia have trapped us into taking on what amounts to a second full-time job without getting an extra cent."

"But we have a huge budget," she said.

"Except we're not a line item on it," said Naomi.

We? I glanced at Cloris. Maybe Naomi hadn't screwed us after all.

Sheri slumped back in her chair. "I'm sorry. Really. I had no idea." Then she inhaled a deep breath, settled that perky smile back on her face, and tapped the presentation book in front of her.

"Then I guess none of you will be offended that I've taken the liberty of planning out all your projects for you."

———

"What a control freak," said Cloris. The eight of us were on the train, returning to our New Jersey office. Naomi had remained in Manhattan.

"Who, Sheri?"

"Of course, Sheri. This show's a farce." She pummeled the presentation book resting on her lap. "And we're nothing more than unpaid drudges."

"Maybe you shouldn't be so hard on her," I said. "After all, she's actually made our lives easier."

"True," said Jeanie, leaning over from her seat across the aisle to join in the conversation. "I'm just relieved to learn the press release exaggerated concerning the total home makeover." Instead, Jeanie and I were responsible for finding ways to jazz up the existing residence using lots of imagination and limited cash. Sheri wanted the show to reflect decorating tips viewers with modest budgets could incorporate into their own homes.

"She's saved us hours of planning," I said. "But I doubt she'll bother going to all this trouble for future shows."

"Why would she?" asked Cloris. "She won't be the recipient of your labors."

I fanned through the pages of my book. "She may be a control freak, but she's also a dynamo. Look at the amount of work she put into this. And in only a few days."

"How do you know she organized this in a few days?" asked Jeanie.

"Mama met Lou less than two weeks ago. Except…" I chewed on the inside of my cheek for a moment. Something didn't add up. "Mop dolls?"

"Come again?" asked Cloris.

"Sheri wants mop doll crafts for the first taping. I haven't seen mop dolls around in well over a decade. No crafts store I know even carries mop heads anymore."

"Meaning?" asked Cloris.

"Meaning, I'll bet Sheri worked up this pilot program years ago when mop dolls were popular. Friday night she said she'd been trying to get Lou to change the show's format for ages, remember?" No wonder Sheri seemed so pissed at Lou. And Mama. Sheri had finally gotten her way, but Mama was getting all the credit.

"What exactly is a mop doll?" asked Tessa from the seat behind us.

"A doll made from a cotton string mop."

"Am I supposed to know what that is?"

"The kind of mop the janitors use to swab the floors at work."

"Eww! Gross! Why would anyone want a doll made of something like that?"

I turned to confront her. "Actually, they're quite cute and easy to make. Very folksy."

Tessa scrunched her nose. "If you say so." She turned her head to study her reflection in the window. "Mop dolls and muumuus," she muttered. "This woman doesn't need a makeover; she needs a taste transplant."

"Not to mention a perky-ectomy," added Janice. "The woman is too Mary Sunshine giggly for my taste."

"Must be the Karo syrup running through her veins," said Cloris.

"Personally, I think it's in our best interests not to make an enemy of Sheri Rabbstein," said Sheila. "I have a feeling we're going to have enough problems with Vince and Monica."

"Too late for me," I said. "Your mother didn't kidnap Sheri's baby and pass it off as her own idea."

"So what are you going to do about it?" asked Cloris.

"Damned if I know." But somehow I had to get Mama to relinquish ownership of the new programming. I'd seen the way Sheri looked at Mama and could read between the lines, no matter how many giggles punctuated Sheri's perky chatter. I didn't want her taking out her resentment for Mama on me.

BASIC MOP DOLL

Materials: 24 oz. mop head (available in the cleaning section of most hardware stores, discount centers, and supermarkets), 4" Dylite® (smooth craft foam) ball, 5" x 5" natural muslin, wooden craft stick, 3/16" black half-round beads, rubber bands, tacky glue, glue gun (optional), blush or pink powdered chalk.

Directions: (NOTE—all gluing can be done with either tacky glue or a glue gun except for attaching the muslin to the Dylite® ball. This step must be done with tacky glue.) Cut a 4¾" diameter circle from muslin for the face. Snip ¼" cuts around the perimeter of the muslin circle. Using tacky glue, glue the muslin to the front of the Dylite® ball, smoothing out any wrinkles.

Poke a hole in the bottom of the Dylite® ball directly under the muslin face. Glue the craft stick into the ball, allowing approximately 3½" of the stick to extend.

Spread the mop apart on a table. Randomly pull 26 strands from the mop. Set strands aside. With the bottom of the doll head adjacent to the top of the mop, glue the craft stick centered over the mop tape. Glue several strands of mop closest to the head down over the craft stick and mop tape to conceal them. Flip the doll over and repeat the previous step to conceal the mop tape on the reverse side. Wrap one of the set-aside mop strands around the doll's neck, gluing in place.

At both the left and right sides of the doll, take the top 18 mop strands. Trim 3" from length, saving trimmed pieces to use for hair. Braid strands for arms, securing each wrist with a rubber band.

Tie the body together under the arms with one mop strand to form a waist. Trim ends even with bottom of mop.

Set aside 8 mop strands for pigtails. Cut remaining 16 strands into 3" lengths. Run a line of glue around the edge of the muslin for hairline. Fold strands in half, gluing folded edge to the muslin. Run a second line of glue in front of the hairline. Glue a second row of folded strands in front of the first row. Place the doll face down. Working in even horizontal rows from the base of the neck to the top of the head, continue gluing hair in place.

Cut remaining 8 lengths of mop strands in half. Tie each half in the middle with one strand. Glue tied section to each side of head for pigtails.

Glue beads in place for eyes.

Use blush or chalk to color cheeks.

Mama claims to descend from Russian royalty. I didn't doubt it, considering her stubborn streak was as long as the Volga and as deep as Lake Baikal. Later that evening, as I began work on a group of mop dolls, I confronted her about the show. She refused to relinquish credit for the new format.

"It was my idea!" she insisted as I tried to convince her otherwise. "Lou said so, and he's the boss. If that woman doesn't like it, she can quit." She pounded her fist on my makeshift work table, releasing a cloud of mop doll lint. "Who needs her?"

I batted at the white fuzz flying in front of my face. I had forgotten the one drawback to crafting mop dolls: they shed more than Catherine the Great. "Lou needs her, Mama."

"Lou could replace her like that." She snapped her fingers under my nose, then crossed her arms over her chest and jutted out her lower lip. Full Flora Sudberry Periwinkle Ramirez Scoffield Goldberg O'Keefe sulk mode.

I secured a braided mop doll arm with an elastic band, took a deep breath, and played my trump card. "If you won't do it for her, do it for me." Then for good measure, I dug deep into my childhood repertoire and conjured up a pair of hang-dog Hush Puppy eyes. "Please?" How could she resist?

Mama wasn't falling for it. "I don't understand. How does this concern you?"

So much for hang-dog Hush Puppy eyes. I sighed. "I have to work with the woman. It's bad enough I'm not getting paid for all this added responsibility, I'd at least like to work in a no-combat zone."

Mama thought this over for a moment, then patted my arm. "Don't worry, dear. If she makes life difficult for you, I'm sure Lou will fire her."

Not the answer I'd hoped for.

———

The remainder of the week passed in a cyclonic tumult of magazine deadlines, photo shoots, and mop dolls. In-between, I sandwiched the standard mom duties of laundry, cooking, carpooling, and nagging. Not to mention dousing the spontaneous combustion that flared up at least once a day when a proud Daughter of the American Revolution and an equally proud Daughter of the October Revolution faced off.

Friday morning, I packed the trunk of my bottom-of-the-line, eight-year-old mud brown Hyundai, and with a quick prayer to the God of Rattletraps, I headed for midtown Manhattan to drop off the models and supplies for Monday's rehearsal.

Prior to widowhood, I drove a two-year-old Camry, but finances—or more precisely, a lack of them—had forced me to trade comfort and car payments for a free-and-clear clunker that wheezed like a three-pack-a-day emphysema victim. However, for the past three months the Hyundai had managed to provide dependable, if noisy, transportation and—fingers crossed—would continue to do so.

Eighteen miles and an hour and a half of bumper-to-bumper traffic later, I pulled into a parking garage a block from the studio. Lugging one carton with me, I left the other five in the car for additional trips.

Ever since 9/11, visitors have to show photo ID and sign in at all New York office buildings. On top of that, any unattended packages immediately raise suspicion. I was hoping I could convince the security guard to let me stack the cartons in the lobby while I made trips back and forth to the car, but I wasn't holding my breath. He could just as soon decide I was a new breed of middle-aged suburban soccer mom terrorist and call in the bomb squad to blow up my mop dolls.

Once at the security desk, I placed my first carton on the counter while I hunted in my purse for my driver's license. "I have five more cartons to bring in from my car," I said, handing over the license. "I'm headed up to the *Morning Makeovers* studio. Is it okay if I pile the cartons somewhere instead of making six separate trips upstairs?"

The guard, a middle-aged Hispanic man with a baby face and a Hulk Hogan body, studied my ID, glanced down at a list in front of him, then stood up. The next thing I knew, he was pushing a hand truck around from the back of the counter. "Ms. Rabbstein had this sent down for you, Ms. Pollack. She said you'd be bringing in a bunch of cartons."

He parked the hand truck in front of me and handed back my license, along with a card. "This here's your temporary ID until you're issued a permanent one. I'll keep an eye on this carton while you get the rest. I'd do it for you, but I can't leave my post."

Definitely not the reception the cynic in me had expected, either from the security guard or Sheri. I glanced at his name badge. "Thank you, Hector."

He tipped his cap. "Not a problem, ma'am."

I headed back toward the parking garage, hand truck in tow. Ten minutes later I returned, panting from the effort of maneuvering the carton-laden hand truck against the tide of New York City pedestrians. I really needed to start exercising. I'd even added it to my to-do list, right under finding a cure for cancer and a solution to the Israeli-Palestinian conflict.

Carcinomas, the Middle East, and aerobic workouts would have to wait, though. I needed to deal with Sheri. This would be our first one-on-one encounter, and I didn't know what to expect. However, her thoughtfulness regarding the hand truck gave me hope.

Once upstairs, I parked the hand truck in the hallway, took one last deep breath and headed for her office. Finding the door slightly ajar, I rapped a quick knock-knock before stepping inside. Sheri stood at the window, talking on the phone, her back to me. Her free hand twisted the hem of a black cardigan that covered the top half of a yellow, peach, and mint green diagonally striped muumuu.

"Yes, we had an agreement," she told the caller, "but you have to understand … No! How can you think that? I've told you. I wouldn't—"

I cleared my throat. "Sheri?"

She spun around, her eyes wide, her cheeks glowing fire hydrant red. Without releasing her death grip on the sweater, she help up her index finger, then turned back to the window and dropped her voice to a whisper. "Look, Max, I have to go. Someone's here. Can we discuss this later? Over dinner? I'm sure we can work something out." She paused for a moment, nodding her head as she listened. "All right. Tonight. I love you, too."

I watched as she took a deep breath, her shoulders rising and falling, before she hung up the phone and turned to me. "Anastasia, I was beginning to think you'd forgotten our appointment."

Great. She's already pissed over Mama stealing her idea. Now I'm late for our appointment, and I get caught eavesdropping on a lover's quarrel. *Nice work, Anastasia.* Hand truck thoughtfulness aside, for someone who didn't want to make an enemy, I'd certainly gotten off to a slam-bang start.

"Sorry about being late." I shrugged. "Traffic. No matter how much time you allow yourself, it's never enough." Without pausing, I launched into damage control. "Look, I didn't mean to intrude. Your door was open, and I—"

Sheri held up her hand. "No need. It was nothing. Really. Don't worry about it." She smiled as she rounded her desk, but the smile didn't mask the hurt and worry in her eyes. "Come see the set," she said, grabbing my arm. "You'll love what we've done."

The generic talk-show desk and chairs with a faux New York city skyline backdrop had been replaced by a country great room, complete with gas fireplace and overstuffed leather sofas. A kitchen-to-die-for took up a sizable section to the left. "We'll do the craft demos here," she said, pointing to the granite-topped island that separated the kitchen from the seating area. "What do you think?"

"Very nice." A heck of a lot nicer than my own humble abode with its chipped Formica countertops and worn upholstery. "When can I move in?"

Sheri giggled. "We have a storage closet set aside for all your supplies and models." She led me back out of the studio, grabbed the hand truck and headed down a hallway past the dressing rooms, unlocking a door at the far end. The closet was more a room, nearly as large as my bedroom. Floor-to-ceiling metal shelving units stood along one wall. A counter with cabinets underneath ran the length of the opposite wall. Additional cabinets hung above the counter. Along the back wall were several wheeled clothing racks holding an assortment of outfits. No muumuus.

"The other editors came by yesterday, but there's still plenty of room for you," she said, indicating the empty shelves with a sweep of her arm.

"I had a photo shoot yesterday and didn't finish the mop dolls until last night." Why did I feel compelled to offer her an excuse? After all, we weren't taping for another week.

"Not a problem," she said. "I'll help you unpack. I can't wait to see what you've come up with."

An odd comment, I thought, considering she had specified each project. I ripped the packing tape from the first carton. Sheri reached in and removed a mop doll witch attached to a woven grapevine wreath. Her eyes sparkled; her mouth stretched into a wide grin. "For my front door?"

I nodded. "As you requested. One for each holiday."

Sheri gingerly fingered the witch. I had dyed the mop black, dyed the strands used for the hair orange, and dressed the doll in a black witch's hat with a purple felt cape. Yellow felt stars embellished both. She carried a straw broom and a jack-o-lantern. Black plastic spiders climbed over the vines of the wreath.

"Oh, I love it! Thank you!"

And then she did something that knocked the Cynicism Gene right off my DNA helix: she hugged me. So maybe she didn't blame me for Mama's credit hijacking, after all.

When she had finished oohing and aahing over each mop doll wreath, Sheri locked the storage room and handed me the key. "See you Monday," she said with a wiggle-wave of her index finger.

I wiggle-waved back and headed for my car.

By the time I arrived at the office, the day was half over, but I still had at least ten hour's worth of work ahead of me. I fired up my computer, stared at my to-do list, then did the only sensible thing under the circumstances. I headed for the break room in search of coffee and a chocolate anything. Nothing was so bad that it couldn't improve with an infusion of caffeine, carbs, and calories.

———

Or so I thought until Monday morning when I arrived back at the studio to find the proverbial caca had hit the proverbial fan.

FOUR

Mornings at *Casa Pollack* are never pretty, not when two hor-
monally driven teenage boys and their bodily function-obsessed
grandmothers vie for the same bathroom. Call me selfish, but I
refuse to share the master bathroom with any of them. I have little
enough privacy in this madhouse as it is. And given that I'm the
sole pumpernickel-winner, I like to think of my actions as more
practical than selfish. I can't afford to be late for work. Which is
why I installed a lock on my bedroom door.

Not sharing my bathroom has its drawbacks, though. Invari-
ably, someone runs late. This morning it was Mama, thanks to Lucille staking claim after the boys departed.

I exited my bedroom to find Mama still in her lilac robe and
matching fuzzy mules, pounding her fist on the hall bathroom
door. I checked my watch. "Mama, we've got fifteen minutes to
catch the train."

"We'll have to take the next one," she said. "The commie
pinko's hijacked the bathroom again."

I sighed. Then capitulated. "Use my bathroom."

"I can't. She's holding my make-up hostage."

Needless to say, we missed the train. By the time we arrived huffing and puffing into the studio reception area, we were forty minutes late, but I didn't think forty minutes warranted the reception that greeted us.

Vince looked annoyed.

Monica looked antsy.

Naomi looked frustrated.

Lou looked apoplectic.

Sheri looked fit to kill.

"What's wrong?" I asked as Mama inserted herself between Sheri and Lou. She tipped her head, awaiting a lip-lock, but Lou appeared too distracted to even notice she'd arrived.

Naomi cleared her throat. "We have a slight problem."

"*Slight* problem?" Vince snickered. "A regular master of the understatement, isn't she?"

Monica curled her lip. "The hostess with the mostest."

"Lou, aren't you even going to say hello to me?" demanded Mama, one hand on her hip, the other tucked around his arm.

Sheri's already crimson face deepened three shades darker than her pink carnation print muumuu. Her narrowed eyes targeted Vince and Monica. "The two of you are enjoying this, aren't you?"

Monica stared her down. "What if we are?"

"God works in mysterious ways," said Vince. He clasped his hands in front of him and glanced ceiling-ward, as if expecting divine acknowledgment to rain down on him from the fluorescent fixture. "Maybe the good Lord isn't happy with the way you've railroaded us."

"And maybe you're trying to railroad me," said Sheri, her voice seething with unrestrained rage.

Vince placed his hand on his chest, his eyes growing wide with surprise. "*Moi*? Surely you don't think *I'd* stoop to anything so ..." He wrinkled his nose and enacted a fake shudder. "So messy."

"Of course not, darling," said Monica. "You'd never do anything to jeopardize your manicure."

Vince held his hands up to study his buffed nails. "So true."

"Would someone please tell me what's going on?" I asked.

Lou disentangled himself from Mama and turned to me, his face the ashen pallor of a man on the verge of a coronary. Mama might not make it to the altar with this one, I thought. "We canceled today's rehearsal," he said.

That's when I noticed the lack of hustle and bustle. The reception area had taken on the aura of a funeral parlor.

"Honestly, Lou, you could have called," said Mama. "I rushed to get here."

She wasn't the only one annoyed. I had plenty of work to do back at the magazine and certainly didn't need to waste half a day in the city. "Why?" I asked.

"*Why*?" Sheri's strangled voice pitched higher. "I'll show you why." She grabbed me by the hand and dragged me toward the studio. The others followed behind us. "This is why," she said, kicking open the door.

I stepped inside and stared bug-eyed, my gaze sweeping the formerly pristine stage set. "My God!" Someone had let loose the Tasmanian Devil, and he'd done one hell of a makeover to *Morning Makeovers*.

Clumps of stuffing pulled from slashed cushions lay in cumulus nimbus-like piles across the floor. Deep gashes had been sliced into the wood cabinets and shelves. Splatters of blood red paint covered every horizontal and vertical surface. And in the midst of all the chaos, sitting propped against a paint bucket on the granite-topped island, sat my Christmas angel mop doll, looking proud as punch nestled in her gumdrop-decorated wreath. However, instead of a candy cane in her arms, she held a blood red acrylic-soaked paintbrush.

"Oh dear!" said Mama.

"Who did this?" I asked.

"Someone out to sabotage my program," said Sheri through gritted teeth. She stood hands-on-hips, her glare encompassing Naomi, Vince, Monica, and me.

"*Your* program?" asked Mama, getting in Sheri's face. "It's *Lou's* program and *my* idea."

"Mama, don't." I pulled her away from Sheri. "We've been over this," I hissed in her ear. "Sheri came up with the idea way before you met Lou. Now drop it. We've got more serious problems here."

"Hmmph!" She exhaled a classic Flora pout. "We'll see about that."

Lou eyed Mama, eyed Sheri, then shook his head before wrapping a shaky arm around Sheri's shoulders. Mama stiffened. "We don't know that it's sabotage directed specifically toward this show," Lou said to Sheri. "You know the network has had union problems ever since Trimedia refused to give in to their latest contract demands. We may have been a random target of organized labor high jinks." But he sounded like he was trying to convince himself.

"Like hell," she said, jerking out of the fatherly embrace. Mama stepped back between them, hip-bumping Sheri out of the way and latching on to Lou's arm once more.

"What do the police think?" I asked. "And speaking of police, where are they?"

Lou's ashen pallor grew paler. "No police!"

"You mean you haven't reported this?" I asked.

"No, and we're not going to."

"But a crime's been committed."

"No," said Sheri. "Lou's right. We can't afford the negative publicity."

I glanced at Naomi. Surely she'd see the absurdity of this. But if she did, she wasn't agreeing with me. "Trimedia already knows what happened. They want to keep this contained. No police. No press."

"What about security tapes? Can't you at least look at those without bringing in the police?"

"We only have security cameras at the building entrances," said Lou.

"This had to have been committed by someone with access to the building," I said. "Someone who probably came back long after everyone else left on Friday or sometime over the weekend. You should at least have security review the tapes."

"That's not a bad idea," said Lou.

"I'll take care of it," offered Sheri.

Lou nodded in agreement.

"It still makes no sense not to file a report with the police," I said.

"Whether it makes sense or not, that's the ruling from the suits," said Naomi.

I shrugged. "Fine. What happens now?"

"Our schedule gets pushed back a day," said Sheri. "We'll condense rehearsals. Taping still begins next Monday."

"Only a day?" I asked. "To clean up and construct a new set?"

Mama turned to Lou. "As long as you're changing things, dear, you know I didn't like those leather sofas. They were much too masculine. We should go with a nice floral damask. In soft pastels, I think. Or maybe a peach and mint stripe. And stainless steel appliances look so industrial. Classic white is best, don't you agree, Anastasia?"

I groaned.

To her credit, Sheri ignored Mama's prattling and answered my question. "We'll have a new set by tomorrow morning even if we have to pay the crew triple-time to work through the night. They're already tracking down replacement furnishings. It may not be as nice as this one, but—"

Naomi broke in. "You probably need to make another model, Anastasia." She nodded in the direction of the angel wreath. "Unless you can repair that one."

I walked over to the island and lifted the doll wreath to examine it. Definitely not salvageable. Same old rotten luck. I turned to Sheri. "I don't suppose I get paid triple time, too?"

She offered me a tight smile. "Not unless you're unionized."

"If I were unionized, I'd be getting paid for all the work I'm putting in on this show." *Nada* times three still equaled nothing more than a huge goose egg, no matter how you did the math.

"That certainly sounds like a pretty good motive for vandalism to me," said Vince. He offered a malicious smile.

Mama spun around to confront him. "How dare you accuse my daughter of anything illegal!"

Monica waved an index finger at the paint-drenched angel wreath. "Vince is right," she said. "She even left a calling card of sorts. Just like the Pink Panther did when he stole the jewels. Only Peter Sellers left a glove, not a mop. Although, a mop would have made more sense, don't you think?"

We all stared at her.

"How do you figure that?" asked Vince.

"Well, he was cleaning out safes, wasn't he?" She laughed at her own joke, a laugh that came out too loud and coarse.

Vince snorted. "Not bad."

I glared at the two of them. No way would I stoop to vandalizing the studio to get out of my contractual obligations, but at the moment I wasn't beyond strangling both of them for insinuating as much. "Rumor has it neither of you is happy about the format change. How do we know the two of you aren't behind this?

"And by the way," I said to Monica, mimicking her sneer, "Peter Sellers played Inspector Clouseau. David Niven played the jewel thief. And he was known as The Phantom. The Pink Panther was the diamond he stole." For someone in show business, she had an abysmal knowledge of classic films.

Monica waved her hand, dismissing me along with the dust motes floating in the air around us. "Whatever."

Sheri stamped her foot. "Who the hell cares about *The Pink Panther*?"

"Not me," said Vince. "I'm outa here. See you all tomorrow. Unless *The Pink Panther Strikes Again*."

Monica spun on her Manolos. "I'm right behind you," she said, following him off the set.

"Did anyone check the room with the models and supplies?" I asked Sheri after Vince and Monica left.

"Why?"

"Isn't it obvious? The doll wreath was locked up. Whoever took it, either broke into the room or had a key."

"So you think maybe the vandal struck elsewhere?" asked Lou, wringing his hands. Perspiration beaded on his brow. "Jeez, what if he destroyed everything in that room? All the models, the props, the wardrobe."

A lump of dread settled in the pit of my stomach. I didn't want to think about having to make all those mop doll wreaths over again. "What I meant was, if there's no damage to the door or lock, we can narrow the suspects down to whomever had a key to that room."

The five of us headed down the hall, Mama clinging to Lou. "It's locked," said Sheri as we arrived at the door and she jiggled the knob. "My keys are in my office."

After digging around in my shoulder bag, I produced my key ring, selected the correct key, and inserted it in the lock. The key turned; the tumblers clicked. With a twist of the knob, I pushed the door open.

Lou ducked his head in for a cursory examination. "Thank goodness," he said. "No vandalism." He mopped his brow with his sleeve and exhaled a sigh of relief.

I stepped inside. The room looked exactly as I had left it Friday. Minus one mop doll wreath. "Who else has a key besides you and me?" I asked Sheri.

"The other editors. Some of the crew. The janitor."

"Any recent problems with anyone?"

She pierced me with a penetrating stare. "Other than all you editors who don't want to participate?"

Ouch. Not looking good for the *American Woman* contingent. "I meant with the crew and janitor. Lou mentioned union problems."

She shook her head. "Not here."

"What about Vince and Monica?"

"What about them?" asked Lou.

"Do either of them have a key?" I wasn't ready to believe any of my coworkers would resort to criminal activity to get out of a work assignment. File a lawsuit? Maybe. Trash a studio? Highly unlikely. "There doesn't seem to be much love lost between you," I added.

"Vince and Monica have it too good here," said Sheri, "and they know it. They get paid an obscene amount of money to work a few hours a day. If the show gets canceled, they'd be lucky to score a gig playing dinner theater in Peoria. For scale. Neither their wallets nor their egos could afford that."

Lou grimaced. "Not exactly."

Sheri snorted. "You think with our ratings some other network's going to grab them up? Everyone in the industry knows what a joke they are."

Lou swallowed hard. Avoiding eye contact with Sheri, he spoke to the floorboards. "Actually, they have a clause in their contracts that pays them in full if the show is cancelled."

"What?" Sheri's voice rose to glass-shattering level. "Recreating Versailles for their dressing rooms wasn't enough? What idiot signed off on that?"

Lou cleared his throat. "There were extenuating circumstances at the time. The negotiations were rather complex."

Sheri threw her arms up. "I don't believe this! How could you? Why?"

"*Why* doesn't matter," I said. "You two can argue about that some other time. The point is Vince and Monica have good reason to sabotage a show that neither one of them wants to take part in, and they'd walk away with their pockets lined."

I paused for a moment to let that sink in. "So I'll ask you again, Sheri, do either Vince or Monica have a key to this room?"

She grimaced. "They both do."

"Then I suggest you concentrate your efforts investigating them and stop trying to blame me and my fellow editors. We may not be happy about getting roped into doing this show, but we don't behave like juvenile delinquents when things aren't going our way." I turned to leave.

"Where are you going?" she asked.

"To work. I have a magazine deadline to meet. And thanks to some hooligans, another mop doll to make. Coming, Mama?"

"You go on without me, dear. I'll stay to help Lou." She smiled up at him. "Besides, I think a nice long, relaxing lunch is in order, don't you?"

Lou smiled down at Mama, patting her hand. "An excellent idea, my darling. We have some things to discuss."

"And afterwards we can go shopping for furniture for the set," she suggested.

Lou waylaid me as I was about to step into the elevator. "I need to speak with you." He glanced up and down the hall to make sure we were alone before continuing, his voice lowered to a near-whisper. "I just wanted to let you know I'll straighten things out with your mother and Sheri."

"Good luck," I said.

He winced. "Flora's such a delicate creature, you know, and I'm afraid I got a bit carried away trying to impress her on the ship."

My mother? A delicate creature? The Steel Magnolias of way down yonder in the land of Dixie couldn't hold a candle to the Titanium Flora of the North. Mama had survived widowhood five times and was brave enough to be planning another plunge into matrimonial waters. Besides, she went nose-to-nose and toe-to-toe with Comrade Lucille on a daily basis. She could survive not getting her way once in her life.

"Mama can be very headstrong."

"And I can be very persuasive." He reached into his pocket and removed a small robin's egg blue velvet box. No mistaking that trademark color. Tiffany & Co. With a flick of his thumb, he flipped open the lid, revealing a chunk of ice the size of Cleveland. "By this time tomorrow, Sheri will have her credit, Flora will have her ring, and all will be right with the universe."

"We still don't know who trashed the set."

He snapped the box shut and shoved it back in his pocket. "There is that."

"You don't really believe this has anything to do with Trimedia's union problems, do you?"

"No." Lou scowled for a moment before something clicked inside him, and he broke out in a broad grin. "Your mother told me you're a bit of a detective."

"Hardly. In case you haven't noticed, Mama tends to exaggerate."

"She said you solved a murder."

"I got lucky."

"So maybe you'll get lucky again. What do you think?"

"I think everyone has a motive except you and Sheri." But I didn't believe any of my coworkers were involved. My money was on Vince and/or Monica. Who knew how far they'd go to avenge the slight their celebrity egos had suffered? But right now I was leaning more toward Monica. She was the only person who hadn't seemed upset by the vandalism. Everyone else acted angry—or in Vince's case, annoyed. Only Monica appeared fretful. Like she had something to hide. And what was with the nervous chatter about *The Pink Panther*?

There was also the melodrama outside the ladies' room at the Marriott Marquis the evening of the press conference. I described the scene I had observed to Lou.

"That's Ray Rivers," he said. "Monica's husband and agent. He's always accusing Monica of two-timing him. At least once a week he bursts in here hurling accusations. One week it's Vince, the next week me. As if either of us would want to get involved with that nut job."

"But if he's accusing Monica of having an affair with either Vince or you, and Monica gets paid whether the show proceeds or not, then—"

Lou slapped his forehead. "Then Ray's the vandal. Of course! I should have known. The man's been a thorn in my rump for years.

I'd love to nail him. Too bad Trimedia refuses to let the police get involved."

"Hold on. I'm only conjecturing here," I reminded him. "Thinking out loud. We have no proof. Ray could have an alibi. For that matter, so could Monica and Vince."

"But it looks like you're on to something," said Lou. "Pursue it. See what you can find out."

"I told you, I'm no detective."

"What if I offered to pay you?"

The man had found my Achilles heel. "How much?"

He named a figure that would take care of the upcoming school and real estate tax bill—even with the increase. "I suppose I could snoop around, ask a few questions."

"Good. It's settled then. I'd better get back to your mother before she thinks I've gone AWOL."

He hustled back down the hall before I remembered to ask him about those extenuating circumstances in Vince's and Monica's last contract.

———

The next morning Mama and I returned to the studio, Mama sporting her Cleveland-sized diamond and Sheri all nervous energy and giggles as she rushed around the new set powwowing with the director and various techies. Looked like Lou had succeeded in smoothing out the credit wrinkles.

"What's this?" asked Mama, indicating the replacement leather sofas and the same stainless steel stove and refrigerator. "I said damask upholstery and white appliances. Where's Lou?"

"Probably in his office," said Sheri, all smiles.

Mama spun on her heels and headed off in search of her fiancé. Twenty minutes later she returned, all flustered. "I can't find Lou. No one's seen him."

"I'm sure he's around somewhere, Mama."

She grabbed my arm. "What if something's happened? What if he's had a stroke or heart attack?" Given Mama's track record with men, this was certainly a possibility, except that her men always waited until after she married them to croak. She turned to the nearest crew member. "You. Check the men's room."

But Lou wasn't in the men's room. Lou didn't seem to be anywhere. "He probably left the building for a few minutes, Mama. Maybe he had a meeting."

But Mama wasn't buying it. She gripped my arm so tightly that I had to pry her fingers loose. I led her to a chair and sat her down. "Look, if he isn't back by the time I'm finished, I'll help you track him down, but right now I have to rehearse my segment. They're waiting for me, and I haven't even collected my models and supplies yet."

She jumped out of the seat. "Let me help you."

Mama followed me out of the studio and down the hall to the models and supply room. I unlocked the door and pushed it open.

Mama screamed.

FIVE

"Lou!" Mama dropped to the floor. "Anastasia, do something! Get help!"

But Lou was beyond help. His body lay sprawled on the floor, my Valentine mop doll wreath sitting on his chest. The knitting needle I planned to use to demonstrate making curly hair for one of the mop dolls was impaled through both the doll and Lou's heart.

Mama reached for the knitting needle. I grabbed her wrist. "What are you doing?" she shrieked. "We have to save him!"

"He's dead, Mama." I lifted her to her feet and wrapped my arms around her. "You can't touch anything. This is a crime scene."

"Dead? Nooooo! You don't know that."

I figured Lou's open-eyed, blank stare was a dead giveaway— no pun intended—but I didn't say anything, just held firm to Mama. She struggled to break free, throwing her head back and letting loose a blood-curdling scream that echoed off the walls. Within seconds the doorway was crammed with the curious.

"What's going on?" asked Sheri, pushing her way through the jaw-gaping crowd. But before anyone could answer, she saw for herself. "Ohmigod! Is he …?"

"What do you think?" answered Vince.

"As a doorknob," said Monica. She wrinkled her nose at Lou's prostrate body.

"Ever seen a live doorknob?" asked Vince.

Sheri glared in disgust at the two of them. "The man was murdered. How can the two of you make jokes?"

Vince raised his eyebrows and offered us a smile that was more sardonic than apologetic. Then he placed his hand on the small of Monica's back and elbowed the two of them out of the storeroom.

Sheri stared after them for a moment before whipping out her cell phone and punching in 911. In a voice choked with tears she reported the homicide.

The finger-pointing began before the police arrived. While Lou's corpse lay in state in the storeroom, accusatory whispers assailed every corner of the studio, the hallways, and the reception area. No techie, clerk, or gopher was without a theory, and none was too shy to voice them.

"Had to be Alto."

"My money's on Monica."

"Could be one of them editors. Hell, I'd probably kill, too, if someone forced me to work without pay."

"What about Ray? He's always accusing Lou of boinking Monica."

"Ray's certifiable. He accuses everyone of getting it on with Monica."

"I heard Sheri really ripped a new hole into Lou the other day."

"Can't say as I blame her. Seems like Lou dumped his common sense overboard on that boat trip. What do you think he saw in that harebrained dimwit he took up with?"

"Beats me but at least with Lou gone to the great TV studio in the sky, we won't have to put up with that old bat and her silk damask demands."

"Maybe she killed him."

"If she did, she's dumber than I thought. Rumor has it Lou was loaded. A smart broad would've waited until after the *I do*'s."

I could understand people suspecting Monica, Vince, and Sheri. I could even conceive of them darting suspicious glances at the *American Woman* editors. But Mama? I hurried back to where I had parked her on a couch in Lou's office.

I found her staring glassy-eyed at her engagement ring as tears streamed down her cheeks and plopped onto the skirt of her nubby linen Pierre Cardin suit. "Mama, I want you to take this." I sat next to her and handed her a glass of water and a Xanax I'd coaxed from Naomi. One dose wouldn't turn Mama into a happy pill junkie, but it might calm her enough to get her through the police interview.

She took the pill without question. After a few sips of water she heaved a deep sigh and turned to me. "Everything's ruined, Anastasia. For me. For you. The boys. Lou was the answer to our prayers." She hiccupped a sob. "A man to take care of us. No more money worries."

"Are you telling me you planned to marry Lou for his money? That you didn't love him?"

"I was doing it for us, dear. Lou had more money than he knew what to do with. What's so wrong with helping him spread the wealth a bit? And I *was* fond of him. Besides, look where marrying for love has gotten me? Five dead husbands and hardly two nickels to rub together. I thought I'd try something different this time around." She heaved another sigh, held her hand at arm's length, and inspected the Cleveland-sized chunk of ice on her third finger. "Do you think Tiffany's will give me a refund on my ring?"

Great. Mama, the Queen of Romance, had become Goldie the gold digger in her dotage.

The police kept us for hours as two homicide detectives questioned all of us one at a time. I don't know what Mama told them when it was her turn, but she was with them a good deal longer than anyone else. And when they escorted her from the office they'd commandeered for interviews, they looked like they'd been the ones to undergo the grilling.

Mama, on the other hand, had resorted to her natural busybody self, all signs of her emotional breakdown gone. Whether it was the effect of the happy pill or her own stoic resilience, I couldn't say, but she did have more than her share of experience dealing with death.

"Now, you dear boys will keep me informed about your progress in capturing my poor Lou's killer, won't you?" She craned her neck to face the two men who were both well over six feet tall.

"Of course, ma'am," said one.

Mama patted his arm. "If you need any help, you be sure to give me a call. I started watching *CSI* and *Law & Order* after that nasty business I told you about. Believe me, getting tied up with a Ruskie in a bathtub for hours certainly changed my perspective on life, not to mention my television viewing choices. I could be a big help to you boys."

"Yes, ma'am."

Apparently Mama had regaled them with her tale of how Ricardo the Loan Shark broke into my house three months ago, hog-tied her to Lucille, and dumped them in the bathtub. I don't know how the detectives managed to remain straight-faced. I reached for Mama's arm and nudged her along. "Come on, Mama. We need to let these gentlemen continue with their investigation." I turned to them. "We can go?"

They nodded. "For now," said one of them.

Mama and I had only taken a few steps down the hall when she stopped short and turned back to them. "And you won't forget what I told you about you-know-who," she said in a conspiratorial whisper that could be heard halfway down the corridor.

"No, ma'am. We'll check into it," said the detective standing to the left.

"What was that all about?" I asked as we stepped into the elevator.

"What was what, dear?"

I eyed Mama with skepticism, not about to fall for her Miss Innocent act. "Who's you-know-who and what did you tell the detectives?"

"I told them the truth, of course."

I silently counted to ten on a swiftly exhaled rush of exasperation and balled my fists, fighting the urge to grab her by the shoulders and give her a good shake. "The truth about what?"

The elevator came to a stop, and we stepped out into the street level lobby. Turning to face me, Mama exhaled her own breath of annoyance before answering in a tight, clipped voice. "I told them all about that nasty Sheri and how she tried to steal my idea. As far as I'm concerned, she's the prime suspect. She had motive, opportunity, and method."

Who said network television isn't educational? Thanks to her nightly diet of police dramas, Mama had police jargon down pat. I resisted the urge to say, "Ten-four, good buddy," but since she seemed to be challenging me, I decided to play along. As we exited the building and headed down the street, I asked, "And exactly what was Sheri's motive, Detective Sudberry Periwinkle Ramirez Scoffield Goldberg O'Keefe?"

Mama stopped in the middle of the crowded sidewalk and turned to face me. As pedestrians darted around us, she lifted her chin and puffed out her chest. "Jealousy, of course."

I raised both eyebrows. "If that's the case, why didn't she kill you?"

With a roll of her eyes, a click of her tongue, and a shake of her head Mama said, "Oh, don't be ridiculous, Anastasia. Why would anyone want to kill me?"

———

We didn't arrive home until after seven. Lights blazed from every window of the house even though we were well into Daylight Savings Time, and the sun was just beginning to lower in the sky. Time for another mom lecture on how pennies saved on electricity grew into dollars for college.

As I opened the front door, classic rock assaulted my ears. Across the living room, Catherine the Great leaped from her throne atop the sofa and sauntered over to greet Mama with a loud purr and a rubbing of fur against stockinged legs.

Mama stooped to pick up her oversized Persian and hugged the white fur ball to her chest. "I'm afraid there won't be any caviar for you now," she said, nuzzling her face into Catherine the Great's long-haired coat. After some cooing and cuddling, Mama lifted her head to speak to me. "Lou promised nothing but the best for my Catherine the Great."

Caviar for a cat? I eyed the corpulent feline in my mother's arms and wondered about the witchcrafting skills Mama must have acquired during her Caribbean cruise. She'd certainly cast a spell over the recently departed Lou Beaumont. "She'll survive."

Mama sighed. Her shoulders sagged. I wasn't certain whether from the weight of her emotions or her cat. "As will we all, I suppose."

I draped my arm around her shoulders and pecked her cheek. Poor Mama. She'd had the best of intentions, and as badly as she felt now, I was glad she wasn't marrying Lou. Not that I wanted him dead, but I hated to think Mama the Romantic had planned to marry a man she didn't love in order to provide financial security for herself and her family.

She slipped out from under my arm and began walking toward the bedroom she shared with Lucille. "I hope you don't mind, but I need to rest a bit from all the excitement of the day. Be a dear and call me when dinner's ready."

"Sure, Mama."

Dinner. I sniffed. The pungent aroma of herbs and spices assailing my olfactory glands told me someone had beaten me to that task. Surely not Lucille. She never lifted a finger in the kitchen. And Nick and Alex limited themselves to nuking leftovers in the microwave. I followed the tantalizing scent in search of the Dinner

Fairy and found my too-sexy-for-his-own-good tenant standing at the kitchen sink. His arms were submerged to the elbows in sudsy water, my emerald green *Kiss the Cook* apron looped over his neck but left untied at the waist. Black jeans cupped a pair of steel buns that swayed to the sounds of the Rolling Stones coming from the boom box on top of the refrigerator as Zack sang along about getting no satisfaction.

I sucked in my lips, stifling the groan that had skyrocketed from an area south of my belly into the back of my throat. *Propriety, Anastasia. Propriety. You're supposed to be in mourning.* But mourning a louse wasn't easy, especially when an Adonis was scouring my frying pan. Besides, my resistance was down. Stumbling over dead bodies tends to do that to me.

Zack's deep baritone shifted to singing about being on a losing streak.

Story of my life lately.

And as if that weren't enough, the Adonis, who must also be a reincarnation of the magical Merlin, had somehow cast a spell over my sons. Both sang backup while Alex loaded the dishwasher and Nick swept the floor. Ralph held court on top of the boom box, bobbing his beak from side to side like a feathery metronome.

Oh, no, no, no.

Hey, hey, hey.

Nick spied me first. "Hi, Mom! We were too hungry to wait, so Zack made dinner."

The cook in question turned at the sound of his name. "Hope you don't mind. There's leftover beef stir-fry and couscous with roasted pine nuts in the microwave for you and Flora."

Mind? Why should I mind my very own personal chef-hunk? I collapsed into a chair and waved away his concern. "Hey, feel free to take over KP any time." As long as he didn't demand a rent reduction. I needed every penny of that monthly rent check he wrote me.

Alex removed a still-steaming plate of food from the microwave and set it in front of me. Nick brought me a napkin and silverware. "Time to hit the books," said Alex with a wink to his brother before the two of them dashed from the kitchen. Subtle my sons are not.

"Tell Grandma Flora dinner's ready," I called to their departing backs.

After lowering the volume on the boom box, Zack poured two glasses of wine from a half-empty bottle of Merlot sitting on the kitchen counter. I raised an eyebrow. I hadn't been able to afford wine in months, and Zack wasn't irresponsible enough to have served Nick and Alex.

Handing me a nearly full glass, he answered my silent question. "Nick said he found it hidden in the back of his closet while searching for a missing sneaker."

I should have known. "Lucille. No wonder she's always tripping over her cane or walker. She's not supposed to mix alcohol with her medication." Not that Lucille has ever followed orders from any authority figure. My mother-in-law answers to no man. Or woman. I paused for a moment and listened to the relative quiet of the house. No senior citizen bickering coming from the bedroom wing. "By the way, where is our resident Comrade in Arms?"

"Haven't seen her."

I shrugged. "Out fomenting revolution, no doubt. If she winds up in jail this time, she's out of luck. I no longer have the money to bail her out, and the house is mortgaged up the wazoo."

Nick darted through the kitchen on his way to the basement. "Grandma says she's too tired to eat. Have you seen my cleats, Mom?"

I quoted my standard response. "They're wherever you last left them," then added, "I thought you had homework."

"I'm doing it."

I had no idea what kind of homework required cleats, but I was too tired to don my Grand Inquisitor's hat.

Zack took the seat opposite me. "Lucille's done time? Tell me you're kidding."

Nick bounded up the basement stairs, cleats in hand. "Found 'em." As he raced out of the room, he said, "Yeah, and every time she gets locked up, Alex and I get stuck taking care of Demon Dog."

I shook my head. "She's slowed down a bit since her accident. Inciting political upheaval is physically challenging when you're an arthritic eighty year old who's recently undergone hip replacement surgery."

"Eighty? Then she was barely out of her teens back in the early fifties."

"So?"

"The heyday of communism in this country was in the thirties, and most of the people enamored of it back then grew disillusioned with it well before the fifties and the McCarthy hearings. How'd she become such a die-hard Commie?"

"You'd have to ask her. But don't hold your breath. Lucille isn't very forthcoming about her past. Even Karl knew nothing. Or so he claimed." I leaned back in my chair, closed my eyes, and savored the wine. "I needed this."

"Rough rehearsal?" Zack had ridden into the city on the same train as Mama and I that morning. Between what the boys told him and Mama's non-stop prattle on the ride from Westfield to Manhattan, Zack knew as much about my life as I did. Maybe more.

"We never got around to rehearsal."

"More vandalism?"

I shook my head. "Worse. Murder."

"Jeez!" Zack finished his wine in one gulp. "Who?"

I told him about Poor Lou. Poor *dead* Lou.

"That makes you two for two," he said.

"What do you mean?"

"Two Trimedia murders. And you discovered them both."

I winced. He had a point. How many other women's magazine editors find themselves in the middle of not one but two company murders? "And both times the killers have implicated me. First with my glue gun, now with my mop dolls." Not a pattern I wanted repeated.

"Murder! Murder!" squawked Ralph, still atop his perch on the boom box. "*You have done well, that men must lay their murders on your neck. Othello.* Act Five, Scene Two."

I scowled. "You call one step ahead of the bill collectors doing well?" I asked the buttinsky parrot.

Zack refilled his wine glass and topped off mine. "You know, I'm no expert on the subject, but maybe you should consider a safer line of work. I know Navy SEALs who don't stumble across dead bodies as often as you do."

"And how many Navy SEALs do you know?" Before he could answer, the phone rang. Zack grabbed the handset and handed it to me.

"Hello?"

"Anastasia, this is Naomi. I have some news."

SIX

I LEAPED UP, NEARLY toppling my chair to the floor. "The police caught Lou's killer? Is it Ray?" During my interview with the detectives I'd told them about the incident I'd observed at the press conference and my conversation with Lou the day before his death.

"No, they haven't. This isn't exactly good news."

Unlike some editorial directors, Naomi respected her editors' private lives and wasn't in the habit of calling us at home. The downy hairs on my arm stood at attention; my stomach executed a triple flip-flop. "Then what?"

She took a deep breath and expelled it with a rush. "Trimedia has decided to go ahead with the show. Once the police finish going over the crime scene, we're all to report back to the studio."

"But how—?"

"Corporate handed full responsibility for the program over to Sheri. I wanted to give you enough warning because you'll have to make another Valentine mop doll. The police will hold onto the original as evidence."

As well as the knitting needle. And they could keep it. That was one tool I never wanted to see again. As a matter of fact, I was seriously considering tossing out all the knitting needles I owned. I'd buy some dowel rods the next time I needed to make curly doll hair. I even contemplated calling Goodwill to pick up all my knitted sweaters and scarves. I wanted nothing that could remind me of poor Lou impaled by a Susan Bates size 11 aluminum needle.

"When do you think they'll let us back in the studio?" I asked, glancing at Zack. His eyebrows raised in question.

"Sheri seems to think within a day or two."

"Before Lou's even buried?"

Naomi's voice took on a bitter edge. "Business is business, and the show must go on."

I hung up from Naomi and filled Zack in on the part of the conversation he hadn't overheard. "So if the killer knocked off Lou to get the show cancelled, he hasn't succeeded."

"Which also means the killer might strike again."

And that meant none of us was safe. Not Mama. Not the *American Woman* editors. Not even Sheri. Who knew to what lengths the killer would go? With shaky hands, I reached for my wine glass and chugged the remainder of the Merlot. "Someone has to find Lou's killer before he strikes again."

Zack's lips tightened as he stared at me for a minute without saying anything. When he finally spoke, he sounded more like a father reprimanding an errant teenager than my tenant. "You'd better leave that to the police. The way I hear it, only dumb luck kept you from getting killed last time you played Sherlock Holmes."

Dumb luck, an X-Acto knife, and a cell phone, actually. But I like to think that I learn from my experiences, and being locked in the trunk of a killer's Mercedes was certainly an experience I'll never forget.

This time I'd be more careful. No need to tell Zack, though. After all, steel buns to drool over or not, he was still only my tenant. Not my husband. Not my boyfriend. Hardly more than an acquaintance, really. What right did he have to lecture me and order me around?

I tamped down the urge to bristle. "You're right. This time the case is in the hands of New York's finest, not some inexperienced rural county detectives. I'm sure they'll have the killer locked up before we go back to the studio for rehearsals and taping."

CURLY DOLL HAIR DIRECTIONS

You can create curly doll hair for any size handmade doll, not just mop dolls. Choose a yarn, crochet cotton, or embroidery floss that suits your doll. Bulky yarns work best for bigger dolls; worsted weights for medium sized dolls; and finer yarns, crochet cottons, and floss for small dolls.

Tie the yarn to the end of a knitting needle and wrap tightly, tying off the yarn at the opposite end of the needle. The smaller the knitting needle, the tighter the curls. You can also use shish kabob skewers or dowel rods of varying diameters.

Soak the wrapped needles in hot water, then remove and use a towel to blot up the excess water. Allow the yarn to air dry thoroughly before removing from the needles. You can also place the needles on a cookie sheet and heat in a 225 degree oven to speed up the drying process.

When the yarn is dry, carefully remove it from the needles. Cut into pieces twice the desired length. Apply to doll's head in the same manner described in the basic mop doll directions.

A hot hunk in tight-fitting black jeans had me in his arms. We were dancing a barefoot samba on the pink sands of Bermuda. He drew me closer and whispered in my ear, "Anastasia?"

"Hmm?"

"Anastasia! Wake up!"

Poof! My eyes sprang open. Good-bye hot hunk. Hello Mama. She stood over me, shaking my arm.

"Mama, what's wrong? Are you sick?"

"Only if heartsick counts." She nudged me over and plopped down on the edge of the bed. Catherine the Great bounded up after her and with a purr of contentment, settled herself onto my pillow, her tail across my face.

"We need to talk," said Mama.

I brushed aside the tail and glanced at the clock. Ten minutes past six. Mama had better have a damn good reason for robbing me of a precious twenty minutes before the alarm was set to go off. Not to mention robbing me of that hot hunk. Although I suppose I was partially to blame since I'd obviously forgotten to lock my bedroom door last night.

"If this has anything to do with having to share a room with Lucille, I don't want to hear it. Your only other option is the sofa in the den. I'm not sharing my bed with you."

We'd been through that before. Call me selfish but as the only breadwinner in the house, I needed a decent night's sleep, and that wasn't possible with Mama camped out next to me. Been there. Done that. Not doing it again.

"This has nothing to do with that commie pinko. Wake up and focus, dear. We need to plan poor Lou's funeral."

I rolled to my side and propped my head up with my fist. "We?"

"Well, of course. Who else will do it? That incompetent, idea-stealing assistant of his? She can't even decorate a set properly. I'm certainly not letting her have anything to do with poor Lou's funeral arrangements."

"Mama, you barely knew the man. Surely he has family that will be handling his funeral. Besides, it may be some time before the coroner's office releases his body."

"They have to release him immediately. Lou was Jewish."

"Lou *Beaumont* was a Jew?"

"Yes, dear, and the coroner is going to have to respect his religious beliefs. It's up to me to see to that."

"I think a murder investigation trumps the Talmud, Mama."

Mama learned all about Jewish funereal law when Arnie Goldberg, Husband Number Four, lost his footing and plunged off the edge of the Grand Canyon during their honeymoon. Jews are supposed to be buried within twenty-four hours after death. By the time Arnie's body was retrieved and shipped back to New Jersey, he made it with only minutes to spare.

Of course, being Mama, she ignored the "buried" part of the law because she insists on having all her husbands close to her. So, like Husbands Number One, Two, and Three before him and Number Five after him, Arnie was cremated and now resides with the rest of Mama's deceased husbands in a row of bronze urns on a shelf in my dining room. Nothing speaks to an enjoyable dining experience like Flora's Dead Husbands Shrine staring down at you from above while you eat.

"I'm sure his family will handle the arrangements, Mama."

"Lou had no family."

"None?"

"None that he ever mentioned. He would have told me, dear. We were very close."

"You knew the man for three weeks, Mama. I'm sure he didn't tell you everything about himself in that time."

"Well, if he didn't tell me, he didn't tell anyone else, either."

"What do you mean?"

"The detective asked if I had contact information for his next of kin, and when I told him he had none that I knew of, he said the others had said the same thing."

"What others?"

"Shake the cobwebs from your brain, dear! The other people the police questioned at the studio, of course."

I thought for a moment. There had to have been someone else in Lou's life that he'd been close to before Mama came along. Someone who would have been notified of his death. "His will would mention beneficiaries and an executor," I said. "And Trimedia offers a small life insurance policy as part of our benefits package. He'd have a beneficiary named on that. I'm sure the police have already taken steps to secure those documents and notify the appropriate people."

"And I'm telling you there was no one, dear. Why do you find it so hard to believe me?"

I bit my tongue on that one. "Mama, I need to get ready for work. We're going to have to continue this discussion later tonight."

"Later tonight will be too late."

"There's nothing you or I can do about it."

"There's plenty we can do. I made a list." With that she pulled a piece of paper out from the pocket of her robe and shoved it in my face. Under the heading of *Lou's Funeral*, Mama had written:

1. Have Anastasia take the day off.
2. Arrange with funeral home to pick up Lou's body.
3. Decide on specifics of service.
4. Pick out Lou's clothes and deliver to funeral home.
5. Invite guests.
6. Arrange for after service catering.

I suppose by now I shouldn't be surprised by her organizational skills when it came to planning funerals. After all, Mama had enough funeral planning experience to open up her own funeral home. "Why do I need to take the day off?"

"How else am I going to get around? I need you to drive me. Besides, I'd think you'd want to help."

"Why is that?"

"Honestly, Anastasia! How else are you going to snoop around Lou's apartment to find clues to his killer?"

I bolted upright, knocking a startled Catherine the Great from her pillow perch. "You have a key to Lou's apartment?"

"Of course, dear. We *were* engaged."

Too bad I didn't have any personal leave days left for the year. Or sick days. I'd have to come up with some work-related reason for a trip away from the office and into Manhattan. Under the circumstances, Trimedia should consider a trip to Lou's apartment as job-related. After all, until his killer was caught, none of the magazine staff was safe. If nothing else, I'm sure they didn't want to see their premiums skyrocket when all their murdered employees' heirs cashed in our life insurance policies.

———

Naomi didn't exactly agree that sleuthing out clues at Lou's apartment qualified as a job-related activity, but neither did she want herself or any of her magazine staff targeted as the killer's next victim. "Be careful, Anastasia."

"There's one more thing," I told her.

"Yes?"

"I don't have any days off left."

Naomi sighed into the phone. "I'll cover for you with Human Resources, but you'll have a much bigger problem with me if this issue isn't ready to put to bed on time."

"I'll meet my deadline," I promised. I didn't add, *just don't ask me how*. I'd worry about that later.

———

"Where to first?" I asked Mama. The boys had already departed for school. Ralph and Catherine the Great were both fed. Mama and I were finishing up breakfast, having already both showered and dressed. Lucille and Mephisto were camped out in the hall bathroom and would probably remain there for some time. Don't ask. I was happy to duck out of the house without having to face either of them this morning.

"Campbell's," said Mama.

"Campbell's? In Manhattan?"

"Of course, dear. Where else? Lou was an important man. He should have a funeral befitting him."

The Campbell Funeral Chapel, located on the Upper East Side of Manhattan, catered to celebrities, dignitaries, and the filthy rich. People like Jackie Kennedy Onassis and John Lennon had lain in state behind their polished mahogany doors. Lou Beaumont hardly made the cut.

"And who's going to pay for this?"

"Don't worry about such minor details, dear. I'll have them bill Trimedia."

Trimedia? The skinflint corporate entity that scrutinizes every receipt I submit for reimbursement, down to the last pompom and glue stick? If Mama could pull that off, I'd nominate her for Fed chairman.

But damned if she didn't.

An hour later I stood by in amazement as she fluttered her teary eyes and beguiled the funeral director into billing all the funeral expenses directly to Trimedia. No questions asked. I wondered why instead of having inherited Mama's stubby legs, I couldn't have been blessed with her ability to charm any two-legged creature with a Y chromosome. Such a talent would have come in handy at many times in my life, especially three months ago when I faced down a killer.

———

After Mama chose everything from a string quartet and the music it would play at the funeral to the coffin Lou would rest in for all of a few hours before doing the ashes-to-ashes thing, we headed over to his apartment in the Murray Hill section of the city.

"Are you sure you have the right address?" I asked Mama. We stood in front of a narrow, five-story walk-up sandwiched between two towering condo complexes.

Mama led the way up a set of crumbling concrete steps. "Of course, I'm sure. Why?"

"This isn't exactly what I pictured, given Lou's wealth." Then again, maybe Lou's net worth had been greatly exaggerated by either the corpse in question or the woman who'd set her sights on him. Exactly how much money did the producer of a Grade Z morning talk show make? I'm sure Lou hadn't commanded anywhere near the number of zeros in his contract as the producers of the A-list talkfests he competed against for morning viewers.

Mama choked back a sob as she unlocked the outer door to the building. "Lou and I planned to go apartment shopping this weekend. He said he never saw the point in moving before because he spent so little time at home."

She pulled a tissue from her pocket, dabbed at her eyes, and blew her nose. I wrapped my arm around her shoulders. Poor Mama had the worst luck with men. If only she'd find someone who'd stay alive for once.

After she composed herself, we trudged up the dimly lit staircase to Lou's third-floor apartment. Mama unlocked the three deadbolts and pushed open the door.

I stepped inside and did a quick survey of a living room that looked more like a frat house. "With all his money, he couldn't hire a cleaning lady?" I asked.

Mama stared at the mound of soiled laundry piled on the floor just inside the front door, the dirty dishes stacked on the coffee table, the empty bottle of Glenlivet sitting on the end table, the newspapers and mail strewn across the sofa. "I don't understand. This apartment was spotless the last time I was here."

"When exactly was that?"

"Monday. After Lou proposed. We came back here to celebrate and—"

"Stop! I get the picture." Even though I wish I hadn't. "No need for details."

"Honestly, Anastasia, you're such a prude. I'm a red-blooded woman with a healthy sexual appetite."

"You're my mother!"

"Yes, dear, and how do you think you got here? The stork?"

"That's right. He dropped me in the cabbage patch." The last thing I wanted to hear were details of my mother's sexual exploits.

A change of subject was in order. "Why don't you find some clean clothes for Lou while I search through his desk?" And figure out why he went on a bender the night before he met his maker.

Mama headed for the entertainment unit, instead. She chose a CD from Lou's enormous collection, inserted it in the CD player, and pushed the power button. The room filled with Tchaikovsky's *Symphony No. 4.* "I need something to soothe my nerves while I tackle this task," she said by way of explanation.

I kissed her cheek. "I know." Mama may not have loved Lou the way she loved her husbands, but her grief was genuine. She adjusted the volume to a decibel below blaring, then crossed the room to the bedroom.

"Oh, before I forget." She turned back toward me. "See if you can find the receipt from Tiffany's for my ring. I'll need a copy for the insurance company."

"Sure, Mama."

I cleared a stack of *Variety* magazines off Lou's desk chair and sat down to survey the contents of his desk. The bottom drawer served as a filing cabinet. Given the mess surrounding me, I was surprised to find his files so well-organized. It took me no time to extract a copy of his will, filed under W, and a copy of his life insurance policy, filed under I.

For once Mama was correct. If Lou had any family, he certainly wasn't close enough to any of them to bequeath them anything. "You were right," I called to her. "Both Lou's will and his life insurance policy list the American Heart Association as his beneficiary." I didn't comment on the irony, given that Lou had been stabbed right through the heart.

"That's understandable," Mama called back. "He told me both his parents and his four grandparents all died of heart disease. And quite young. He said that's why he walked to and from work every day. No matter how bad the weather, he always made sure he got his exercise." I heard her choke back another sob. "A lot of good it did him."

I glanced over at the empty bottle of Scotch. Men concerned with heart health don't usually down 750 milliliters of Glenlivet in one sitting. Of course, I had no way of knowing how full the bottle had been before Lou emptied it. Out of curiosity, I headed for the kitchen. There on the counter next to the sink stood the empty cardboard carton. I've never known anyone to put an opened bottle of booze back in its packaging. Under the circumstances, I drew the only logical conclusion. Lou Beaumont had gotten himself soused sometime after bringing Mama home Monday evening.

But why? Had Lou been a closet alcoholic? Or was there some other reason for his night of binge drinking?

I walked back to the desk, returned the will and insurance policy to their proper folders, and pulled out the file marked IN-VESTMENTS. It contained only one statement. Back when we had investments, Karl simply added each month's statement to the front of the folder. I suppose Lou employed a different system. At any rate, the American Heart Association was going to be very happy. According to the statement, Lou's portfolio was greater than the GNP of many a small third-world nation.

Something just didn't add up.

Mama poked her head out from the bedroom and held up a hanger holding a white dress shirt, a necktie draped over each shoulder. One was a royal blue with a small white dot pattern, the other a navy with a red stripe. "Which do you think, dear? The suit is a navy single-breasted."

I quickly closed the investment folder and shoved it back into the file drawer. Mama didn't need to know how close she'd come to filthy rich status. No point upsetting her further.

"The red stripe is more stately," I said. Not that it mattered. Jewish funeral law dictated a closed casket, but this was hardly the time to remind Mama of that fact. Better to humor her.

She nodded. "That's what I thought."

"See if you can find a wheeled overnighter for the clothes in one of Lou's closets. And don't forget shoes and socks." That should keep her busy a little longer. I wanted to search through the rest of Lou's papers to see if I could determine what had happened Monday night.

I found no clues on Lou's desk or by rifling through the remaining desk drawers. The other files contained nothing beyond standard household utility and credit card receipts and a stack of bills awaiting payment. What I didn't find was the receipt for Mama's ring.

I walked over to the bedroom. Mama held a pair of tighty-whitey briefs in one hand, a pair of navy silk boxers in the other, and a perplexed expression on her face.

"I don't think it matters which you choose," I told her. Did funeral parlors even bother to dress the deceased in underwear?

"Why would Lou have both boxers and briefs? Don't most men prefer one over the other?"

"That's more your area of expertise," I reminded her. "I had only one husband, remember?"

"Of course, dear, but you have that nice Zachary Barnes waiting in the wings. Which is he? Boxers or briefs?"

"Mama! How should I know?"

"Well, if you don't know yet, I'm sure you'll know soon." She folded the boxers and placed them in the garment bag she'd opened on the bed, then tossed the briefs into an open bureau drawer.

An image of Zack parading around in nothing but a pair of silk boxers, the iconic Rolling Stones red tongue graphic splashed across the front, filled my brain. I shook my head and tried to focus on why I'd entered the bedroom. "Did Lou seem upset or nervous at any point Monday?"

"Of course, dear. He was upset about the vandalism to the set."

"Yes but beyond that. Did he mention anything else?"

"I don't think so."

I walked back into the living room. Maybe Lou's mail held a clue. I collected the strewn sections of Monday's *New York Times* and set it aside. Then I gathered up the mail and began to sort through the pile. Lots of junk. A cable bill. An empty white business envelope with no return address. I sifted through the remaining mail in search of the envelope's contents. Nothing. Could whatever had come in that envelope be what caused Lou to hit the Glenlivet bottle?

I closed my eyes and tried to imagine the scene, putting myself in Lou's place. I've had a stressful day. I come home and open the mail. Something in one of the envelopes upsets me. Or angers me. Upsets or angers me enough that I start drinking. What would I have done with the contents of that envelope?

My eyes sprang open, and I jumped to my feet, nearly toppling the coffee table. I scanned the room, searching for what I knew must be hiding somewhere, but I couldn't find it. I ran into the kitchen and started opening drawers until I found a flashlight. Returning to the living room, I got down on my hands and knees and systematically checked behind and under each piece of furniture. Nothing.

But I knew it had to be somewhere in this room. I sat back down on the sofa and pretended to crumple a piece of paper and hurl it across the room. A large entertainment unit sat on the wall opposite the sofa. Books filled shelves on either side of the flat screen TV. I bounded back up, this time careful not to knock into the coffee table, and headed for the shelves on the left. And there it was, wedged into a shadowy corner, resting on top of a well-worn copy of Melville's *Moby Dick*.

I carefully uncrumpled the sheet of paper, holding only the edges with the very tips of my fingers and nails. No point adding my fingerprints to those already on the paper. Just as I finished reading the short note, the door to the apartment flew open.

"Freeze!"

SEVEN

I froze. Except for my adrenaline, which was pumping so fast I thought my heart would explode. The two detectives from the day before, guns pointed and ready to fire—at me—stood inside the entryway.

"You!" said one by way of recognition. He holstered his gun. His partner did likewise. "What the hell are you doing here?"

"Can I move?" I asked, barely opening my mouth to speak.

The first detective nodded.

Before I could answer his question, Mama poked her head out from the bedroom. "I thought I heard someone." Then recognizing the detectives said, "Oh hello, boys. Have you caught my poor Lou's killer already? Was it that nasty you-know-who, like I suspected?"

"No, ma'am," said the one on the left. The two were pretty much interchangeable, except for a few pounds and even fewer inches. They both sported graying buzz cuts that screamed *marine sergeants*, right out of central casting, the ones from World War II-era movies. Only these guys wore off-the-rack navy gabardine instead of khakis or camouflage. For the life of me, I couldn't remember their names, although I'm sure they had introduced themselves prior to questioning me yesterday.

"What are the two of you doing here?" asked the shorter one, short being a relative term since both towered over six feet.

Although he'd directed the question to me, Mama answered, "We came to pick up some clothes for poor Lou's funeral. And maybe find some clues to the identity of his killer."

"Why didn't you open the door when we knocked?" Again, addressed to me, but this time by the taller, slightly thinner detective, and this time Mama didn't answer.

Instead, she turned to me. "Why didn't you answer the door, Anastasia?"

I nodded toward the entertainment unit. *Symphony No. 4* had long since ended, replaced by the *1812 Overture*. "May I?" When the shorter detective waved his consent, I reached for the volume control and lowered Mr. Tchaikovsky's volume down to that of background music.

I wanted to roll my eyes and exclaim, "Duh!" but decided sarcasm directed toward men with guns wasn't the brightest move. Instead, I simply said, "I'm sorry, detectives, but I didn't hear your knock over the rockets and cannon fire."

"Where are my manners?" exclaimed Mama with a clap of her hands. "Would you boys like some coffee or tea?"

The two detectives exchanged a quick glance. Then the shorter one said, "That would be great, ma'am. Coffee. If it's no trouble."

"No trouble at all."

Mama bustled off to the kitchen, and the two detectives turned their full attention to me. "Clues?" asked the taller one.

"Or destroying evidence?" asked the shorter one.

I glared at both of them. They'd certainly established good cop/bad cop pretty quickly. "Clues. I have nothing to hide, and neither does my mother. Frankly, it never occurred to me that you hadn't already searched Lou's apartment. I was hoping to discover something you might have overlooked, given my mother knew Lou and you didn't."

"The way we understand it," said the shorter detective, "your mother only met Lou a few weeks ago. How intimately could she have known him?"

"If you're inferring what I think, detective, you're not only way out of line, your skills are questionable. What would be her motive? Wouldn't it make more sense to kill Lou *after* they'd married? Not to mention *after* he'd had a chance to change his will?"

"How do you know he hadn't already changed it?" asked the taller detective.

I pointed to the desk. "Bottom drawer. Filed under W. And while you're checking, his life insurance policy is also there. Filed under I. When you're through making sure I'm not lying, there's something I found that might interest you."

The taller detective strode across the room to the desk, opened the file drawer, and thumbed through the folders until he found both documents. After checking them out, he turned to his partner, "She's right. The vic left everything to charity."

"As I could have told you," I said.

"What else did you want to tell us?" asked the shorter one.

I still held the uncrumpled sheet of paper between the tips of my thumb and index finger. "Something either angered or frightened Lou Monday night."

"What makes you think that?" asked the taller detective.

I told him what Mama had said about the state of the apartment and pointed to the empty bottle of Scotch. "He downed the entire bottle. The cardboard packaging is still on the kitchen counter."

"Pardon me for saying so, ma'am," began the taller detective, "but maybe the guy was just having second thoughts about—" He cocked his head in the direction of the kitchen where Mama was still puttering around with the coffee.

"Or maybe after he came back from bringing my mother home, he opened his mail and found this." I extended my arm and dangled the paper in front of him. "I found the empty envelope on the sofa with the other mail. He'd balled the contents up and hurled it across the room."

The detective withdrew a plastic evidence bag from his pocket. Grabbing the typed message by the corner, he dropped it into the bag before reading it, then passed the bag to his partner. "We'll need to fingerprint you to eliminate your prints," he said.

"No need. I made sure not to leave any."

Before either of them could say anything further, Mama returned to the living room. She carried a tray laden with a coffee pot and all the necessary accoutrements—down to china cups and saucers. Mama always entertained in a manner befitting the descendant of Russian nobility (according to her) and the former social secretary of the Daughters of the American Revolution. In other words, when it came to entertaining, Mama never did anything half-assed, even when entertaining cops looking to nail her or her daughter for murder.

I grabbed the tray from her and set it down on the coffee table. Mama positioned herself in the center of the sofa and began her hostess-with-the-mostest ritual. "How do you take your coffee, Detective Phillips?" This was directed to the taller detective, the good cop. I made a mental note.

I also noted something else I hadn't noticed before. Phillips sported the most miniscule soul patch I'd ever seen. Or maybe he hadn't looked in the mirror when he shaved that morning.

In my book, soul patches took first place as the most dumb-ass male fashion statement ever conceived. And that includes bowties and Nehru jackets. Every time I saw a guy sporting a soul patch, I had an uncontrollable urge to grab a razor and a can of shaving cream and sneak up on him. A nearly microscopic soul patch was the most dumb-ass of all the dumb-ass soul patches to date.

"Black, ma'am," he answered. Mama handed him his coffee, then offering him a plate and napkin, said, "Please, help yourself to some cookies. My poor Lou had such a sweet tooth, and these will go stale if no one eats them."

She picked up a second cup and began to pour. "And you, Detective Marlowe?"

Wait a minute. *Phillips?* And *Marlowe?* I must have been brain dead when these guys questioned me yesterday. How else to explain forgetting such a pairing. Obviously, someone at the NYPD had a delicious sense of humor.

And let's not forget the God of Strange Coincidences. How else did I explain coming across three such weird cop pairings in the last three months? First Simmons and Garfinkle. Then Batswin and Robbins. Now Phillips and Marlowe. Either Morris County and the NYPD were in cahoots, or this was the coincidence to beat all coincidences.

"Same for me, ma'am," said Marlowe, answering Mama. Shorter cop. Bad cop. Soul patch-free cop. "Black." Mama repeated her routine for Detective Marlowe, handing him his coffee, then offering the cookies.

As she poured coffee for me and herself, I wondered if either cop got the joke. A glance at their stern faces told me these guys had slept in late the day God passed out the humor genes.

Mama turned to the detectives and asked, "Now what have you boys learned in your investigation so far?"

Instead of answering her, Marlowe studied the china cup and saucer. "Kind of frou-frou for an old bachelor, wouldn't you say, Phillips?" He turned to Mama. "More your style. You recently purchase them, Mrs. O'Keefe?"

"Goodness, no! This is Royal Albert bone china. The Duchess pattern. It belonged to Lou's grandmother on his mother's side. He treasured it. Now there's no one left in his family. I suppose the lawyers will just sell it all off." Mama heaved a huge sigh. "Such a shame, don't you think, boys?"

They both nodded. Seriously. Solemnly. Me? I felt an eye roll and a huge belly laugh coming on at the thought of Lou Beaumont sticking out his chubby pinky finger to sip daintily from a Royal Albert Duchess coffee cup.

Twenty minutes later Marlowe and Phillips had wolfed down every last cookie crumb while divulging no information in regard to their investigation into Lou Beaumont's death. They then told Mama and me we'd have to leave the apartment while they conducted their investigation. Mama finished packing up the clothes she'd picked for Lou's funeral, and we headed back to Campbell's.

———

"What did the note say?" asked Cloris when I caught her up the next morning at work. We'd ducked into the break room where she deposited a still warm loaf of chocolate-cherry bread fresh from the test kitchen.

"*A CORPSE TELLS NO TALES.*"

Cloris paused from slicing the bread. "Whose corpse? Lou's? And what sort of tales?"

I grabbed a slice and shrugged. "Beats me. The possibilities are endless. However, I'm guessing Lou knew what the note referred to, judging from the bottle of Scotch he downed."

Cloris finished slicing the bread and took a piece for herself while I poured coffee. "But he could have polished off the Scotch prior to opening his mail," she said as we sat down at the table.

"True, but it seems more likely the note led to the drinking. Mama said Lou was in a great mood when he took her home." I skipped the part about *why* Lou had been in a great mood. The thought grossed me out enough. No need to fill Cloris's head with the image of Mama and Lou dancing the naked horizontal Mambo.

"The note could have something to do with Lou's relationship with Mama or the show's new format or any number of things we're unaware of," I continued, grabbing another slice. "This is incredible! Whoever first came up with the idea of marrying chocolate and cherries should qualify for sainthood."

Cloris nodded her agreement as she gobbled up another slice.

"After all," I continued, "what do we really know about Lou Beaumont?"

Cloris closed her eyes and mulled for a moment. Or maybe she was just having a gastronomic orgasm. I know I was. "Only what you've heard from your mother and what we've heard from Sheri," she finally said. "And I wouldn't put much stock in anything Sheri said about Lou. The woman has visions of her own grandeur."

"Mama's not the most reliable source, either," I reminded her. "Which leaves us knowing very little about the man."

"Nothing else turned up at his apartment?"

I wolfed down another slice before I answered her. "The man owned a huge collection of classical CDs, treasured his grandmother's Royal Albert china, and named the American Heart Association as the beneficiary of both his will and his life insurance policy. Other than that, he's still pretty much a mystery to me. And I'm guessing to the detectives investigating his murder, as well."

"If the note refers to the new show format," said Cloris, "we're back to our same list of suspects—Ray, Monica, or Vince."

"But what if it refers in some way to Mama? What if the corpse didn't refer to Lou? Maybe the killer wanted someone else dead, not Lou."

"If that's the case, the killer might be someone we haven't even met. Certainly if he or she wanted Lou to end his relationship with your mother, the killer would've gone after her, not Lou."

I didn't even want to consider that possibility. Even with all her eccentricities and the headaches they caused me, I couldn't imagine life without Mama. "My gut tells me Lou's death is connected to the changes he made to the show."

Cloris chuckled. "Oh? Was that what the rumble I just heard meant? And here I thought it was your gut demanding the last slice of chocolate-cherry bread. I guess that means you don't want it?"

Before Cloris could lay claim to the last slice of chocolate-cherry bread, I reached behind my chair, grabbed the knife from the counter, and cut the remaining piece in half. "Guess again," I said, offering her one half as I popped the other half into my mouth.

———

Later that afternoon Mama called me at work.

"Campbell's phoned," she said.

I heard the panic in her voice. "What's wrong, Mama?"

"The coroner released poor Lou's body to them a few minutes ago. We've scheduled the funeral for tomorrow morning. Eleven o'clock."

I sensed a huge problem about to be dumped on yours truly. Almost reluctantly, I asked her, "And?"

"They said they'd be happy to contact Lou's friends, family, and coworkers for me if I e-mailed over a list."

And there was the problem. "But you don't have a list, do you? What did you tell them?"

"That I'd get right back to them. Anastasia, you have to help me. What am I going to do? We can't hold a funeral for someone as important as poor Lou and only invite a handful of people from his show."

The only person I knew who might be able to bail out Mama was the one person I knew Mama didn't want at the funeral, let alone want to speak to ever again. In Mama's eyes, Sheri was *Suspect Numero Uno.* "There is someone you could contact," I said.

"That woman." Mama spat out the words. "I was hoping you'd call her for me, dear. She's much more likely to respond in a favorable manner to you."

"Why is that?"

"Because she needs you. What would that show be without you?"

Mama always did have a very inflated sense of my importance to the magazine. And now the show. But what could I do? "I'll phone her right now. Don't worry about it."

"Thank you, dear. You know I wouldn't put you in the middle of this if there were any other way."

"I know, Mama." Actually, there had been another way. Mama could have kept her nose out of Lou's remains and left all the arrangements to his executor. Or Trimedia. But that's not Mama's way. In her eyes, she and Lou were as good as married, and that meant she was in charge of sending him off to the afterlife in the manner she had decided he'd want.

I fortified myself with another cup of coffee before dialing Sheri. What did I have to barter? How much more of my nonexistent free time would I have to hand over to the Simon—or more aptly, Simone—Legree of daytime television?

However, I needn't have worried. Sheri floored me with her response. "Don't worry yourself, Anastasia. I'd be happy to take care of it," she said after I explained the situation. "I've got everything on a database. Just give me the e-mail address, and I'll zip it right over to them."

EIGHT

TRIMEDIA HAD ISSUED A memo late the day before, stating that the *American Woman* staff would not be docked for taking the day off to attend Lou's funeral. As a matter of fact, they expected us to show up.

No, the Patron Saint of Working Stiffs hadn't performed a miracle attitude adjustment on the suits in charge. They were more concerned with a show of solidarity than losing a day's worth of work from us. To their way of thinking it was important to come across as a family in mourning for the loss of a loved one. Not to mention honoring Lou's memory by going on with the show as planned. They actually presented us with talking points in case any of us was buttonholed by local media.

Besides, they knew damn well we'd all have to bust our asses to make up the lost time. In the magazine business production schedules rule. Neither rain nor sleet nor death of a television producer would keep us from going to press and shipping on time.

Mama, on the other hand, just might hold up the funeral. I stepped out of the shower to hear her banging on my bedroom door. "Anastasia! Let me in!"

Mama barged in the moment I unlocked the lock, Catherine the Great on her heels. Ralph flew in behind both of them and took up residence on a curtain rod where he began a stare-off with the corpulent kitty.

Mama was already dressed in one of her classic Chanel suits, ebony crepe with matching satin piping and black *faux* pearl buttons, the same suit she'd worn to each of her husband's funerals, even though she hadn't made it as far as the altar this time around.

Meanwhile, I stood barefoot and dripping wet with only a towel wrapped around my torso as I waited to hear what new catastrophe had struck *Casa Pollack*. I'd bet my last nickel that even the Octomom has less chaos in her house each morning, but I no longer had any nickels left to bet.

"Really, Anastasia," said Mama, "I don't know why on earth you have to lock your bedroom door. It's not like you're living in a dormitory."

No, it's worse. I had more privacy when I shared a dorm suite with three other students. "What's so important that it couldn't wait until I was dressed, Mama?"

"Did you see what your sons are wearing?"

I hadn't even seen my sons yet this morning, let alone what they were wearing. "Why? What's wrong with the way they're dressed?"

"Jeans and T-shirts are totally inappropriate for a funeral. I'm shocked that you would allow them to dress that way for such a solemn event."

"*Now, music, sound, and sing your solemn hymn,*" squawked Ralph. "*Much Ado About Nothing.* Act Five, Scene Three."

Catherine the Great hissed her displeasure with the quoted passage, but I thought Ralph, as always, was pretty much on target.

"What makes you think the boys are going to Lou's funeral? They barely knew the man." Come to think of it, aside from that one night Lou showed up in my living room and spent most of the time cowering from Ralph, I couldn't remember a single instance when he, Alex, and Nick were together.

"Don't be ridiculous, dear. Lou was going to be their grandfather."

Look who's being ridiculous! I could play this one of two ways—say what was on my mind or keep the peace as best I could. I chose the coward's way out. "I know, Mama, but the boys can't miss school today. They're both in the middle of exams."

Actually, exams didn't start until next week, but I'd make sure the boys were aware of my lie. I knew they'd cover for me. What kid in his right mind would want to attend a stranger's funeral, even to get out of school? "I'm sure Lou would understand," I added.

Mama pouted. "I'd think it's more important to support their grandmother in her time of need. They can always make up a missed exam. Surely the school has contingencies for emergency absences like a death in the family."

Family? Lou? Maybe eventually he would have become family, but with Mama's track record? I bit my tongue and wrapped my arm around her shoulders as I escorted her toward the door. "I'll be there for you, Mama. It's more important than ever that Alex and Nick keep their grades up and don't cause any extra work for their teachers. They're going to need letters of recommendation when they apply for college scholarships."

Mama sniffed loudly. "Lou would have paid for their college educations, you know. We talked about it."

"That was very generous of him." And most likely a conversation that had only occurred in Mama's mind. However, it no longer mattered. Lou was dead, and his millions were all going to charity.

———

All the usual suspects and then some showed up for Lou Beaumont's funeral. I had feared few people would attend, and I'd have to deal with another Mama meltdown. I needn't have worried. Even though Campbell's had provided one of their larger rooms, it appeared, from the crowd milling around the chapel foyer, every seat would be taken.

I wasn't surprised to see Detectives Phillips and Marlowe observing the goings-on from two inconspicuous corners of the room. Didn't every murder mystery ever written or filmed have the investigators scoping out the mourners at the victim's funeral? Clichés had to be based on truth, otherwise they wouldn't be clichés. So the arsonist always sticks around to watch the firefighters put out the blaze, and the killer always attends the dead guy's funeral.

I scanned the room, a bit unnerved by the realization that a murderer might be lurking nearby, gloating over his handiwork. Then again, I may have been working alongside the killer from the time Trimedia indentured me to their new and improved version of morning TV.

Vince? Monica? Both had motive up the wazoo. Or was the killer someone I'd never met? The room was packed with strangers. How many of them had some reason to murder Lou Beaumont?

I eased my way around a knot of people and headed toward the room where the service would be held. The eight seats that made up the front row of the left side of the chapel had been reserved. I assumed two for Mama and me, two for Alex and Nick. Mama had probably informed Campbell's they'd be in attendance prior to me putting the kibosh on that idea.

But what about the remaining seats? According to Mama, Lou had no family. His will and insurance policy seemed to bear that out. Maybe it was just Campbell's policy to cordon off the first row. Once the service began, some of the standing-room-only crowd would surely grab up those remaining front seats.

Mama had insisted we arrive two hours early. "To make certain everything is in order, and there are no last-minute details to tend to," she said.

Given her experience with all matters funereal, I didn't question her, just played my part as dutiful daughter and chauffeur and counted the hours until I could return home, kick off my heels, and make a dent in the mountain that was my to-do list. I was so far behind that I knew I'd be pulling at least one all-nighter, if not more, before we put the current issue to bed.

Dutifully, I tamped down my feelings of resentment over the wasted hours. I was here for my mother, and that was more important than work deadlines. Or so I kept telling myself.

Campbell's had printed up programs for the funeral. As Mama flitted about prior to the start of the service, I found a few inches of unoccupied space along one wall and perused the schedule. I was soon joined by several of the *American Woman* editors.

Cloris leaned over my shoulder to see what I was reading. "*All* those guys intend to speak?"

I nodded. "From the little I'd seen of Lou, I had him pegged as a bit of a loner with few friends."

"He struck me more as the type who used his millions to buy friendship," said Jeanie.

"But notice who's missing," said Janice, looking over my other shoulder. "Wouldn't you think, no matter how they really felt about him, that Vince, Monica, and Sheri would have demanded a few minutes of mic and limelight time?"

"Definitely," agreed Cloris. "Not only are they not listed, I don't recognize any of the names that are listed except for Alfred Gruenwald."

I doubted Mama knew any of the speakers besides the CEO, either. "Perhaps when Campbell's made their notification calls, they asked people if they'd like to say a few words on Lou's behalf," I suggested.

"Well, if you ask me," said Cloris, "too many of them agreed."

"Jeez!" said Janice. "If you figure ten minutes apiece, the eulogies alone will take two hours."

"And how many of these guys will only talk for ten minutes?" asked Jeanie.

I groaned. "We'll be stuck here for most of the day."

A minute later we were all ushered into the chapel for the start of the service, and I parted from the gaggle of editors, who all grabbed seats as far to the rear as possible. Too bad I couldn't join them. As I took my seat in the front row, I noted that four women, all somewhere around Mama's age, had taken four of the remaining six seats.

Between the rabbi Campbell's provided, the requisite prayers, the music and the eulogies, the service dragged on forever. Men who were pretty much interchangeable in their ordinariness eulogized Lou with One From Column A/Two From Column B platitudes.

Each had known Lou at some point in his past, often his very distant past—the childhood friend, the army buddy, the college roommate, the guy he'd shared an apartment with after graduation, and on and on and on. I wasn't convinced any of them actually knew what had been Present Day Lou all that well, especially since most of the eulogies seemed to be more about the speakers than the deceased.

Some people just can't resist the offer of a microphone.

"We'll all miss Lou."

"Tragic loss for all of us."

"Lou was such a great guy."

Not a personal remark among them. These guys may as well have been pulled from Central Casting. Maybe they were.

After three interminable hours the service broke up, and we were all ushered into a back parlor for refreshments. The spread rivaled the cocktail hour at the most lavish of weddings I'd ever attended.

I heaped my plate. Not only was I starving, but it had been more than three months since my taste buds had enjoyed the pleasures of smoked salmon, one of my favorite foods. Given my financial situation, it would probably be my next lifetime before I'd again have such an opportunity.

Mama glanced at my plate and made a moue of displeasure. "Really, Anastasia, where are your manners? You can always go back for seconds."

"Are you kidding? It's well past lunchtime, and this crowd descended on the buffet table like vultures on carrion. They'll scarf up every last crumb within the next five minutes."

Before Mama could respond, Sheri, dressed for the occasion in a black linen muumuu, sidled up to us. One of the women, a big-boned, graying brunette who had shared the front row with Mama and me, accompanied her.

In her typical Sheri-sing-song voice she asked, "Anastasia? Flora? Have you met Rochelle Beaumont?" I swear that woman missed her calling. She would have made a perfect nursery school teacher.

"Beaumont?" I asked. "A relative of Lou's?"

"His wife," said Sheri.

I don't know whose jaw dropped faster or fell lower, mine or Mama's.

NINE

"*Ex*-wife," clarified Rochelle.

"Of course," said Mama, recovering quickly. She extended her hand to Rochelle but flashed a glare at Sheri before she continued to speak. "Flora O'Keefe. Poor Lou's fiancée. I'm delighted to meet you. Lou told me he'd been married once. A long time ago."

"Rochelle is Ex Number One," said Sheri. She didn't bother to hide her smirk as she pointed across the room to one of the other women who'd shared our row. "The blonde chatting with Monica is Adele, Ex Number Three. And over there at the buffet table? The one wearing the navy Donna Karan pantsuit?" She pointed to an over-processed redhead who had also shared our row. "That's Veronica, Ex Number Four."

"And I'm Ex Number Two," said a woman coming up to join us. The final member of our row, this one looked like the poster child for Facelifts Anonymous. She nodded to Ex Number One. "Hello, Rochelle."

Rochelle acknowledged her with a terse nod of her head. "Francine."

Francine turned her one-too-many procedures face to Mama. "You must be Lou's latest. Sheri mentioned he'd taken up with the Future Ex Number Five. Frankly, I can't see why anyone would want that cheating deadbeat. He lost his millions years ago, and that's all he ever had going for him."

"Too bad you weren't smart enough to accept a lump sum settlement," said Rochelle. "A man who cheats on his wife is sure to cheat on his girlfriend." She turned to Mama, her tone softening. "He wasn't marrying you for your money, was he, Flora?"

I'm not sure Mama heard Rochelle because she was totally focused on Sheri. If looks could kill, Sheri would already be buried under six feet of loam.

"You did this deliberately, didn't you?" Mama spat out the indictment.

Sheri placed a palm over her heart and played the innocent. "Did what? All I did—at your daughter's request, I might add—was e-mail the funeral director a copy of Lou's phone directory. How is it my fault that he wasn't honest with you?"

I grabbed Mama's arm. "I think we should say hello to Mr. Gruenwald, don't you, Mama?" With that I pulled her away before Lou's funeral ended in a knock-down, drag-out cat fight.

"Are you okay?" I whispered to her as we headed across the room.

Mama heaved a sigh. "I feel like that woman just ran me over with a bulldozer, but don't you worry, dear." She patted my hand. "Truth be told, I can't remember if I ever mentioned to Lou how many times I've been married."

"But you were widowed each time. You didn't cheat on your husbands, then divorce them. Big difference, Mama."

"True. However, every story has two sides. Maybe those women actually cheated on my poor Lou and claimed it was the other way around in order to collect alimony. What do they call that, dear? Revisionist history, isn't it?"

More like refusing to face reality. At least on Mama's part. However, I was more concerned by Rochelle's pronouncement of Lou's insolvency, especially since I'd seen financial statements that proved otherwise. Had Lou been pulling a fast one on his ex-wives all these years to avoid paying them alimony?

Or had he been pulling a fast one on Mama with doctored financials? Maybe he'd thought Mama was loaded and wanted to marry her for her money.

That made no sense. Mama had told him of my financial situation. Or so she claimed, but maybe she'd been as truthful with him as he'd been with her. In other words, maybe they'd been manipulating each other.

Then there was that Tiffany diamond the size of Cleveland. I glanced down at Mama's hand. The huge chunk of ice twinkled up at me, but was it a Tiffany twinkle or the twinkle of a very convincing fake? It certainly looked real to me, but what did I know? After all, I'm the clueless wife who thought everything was just hunky-dory in her own marriage.

What I did know was that at least one of Lou's ex-wives hadn't been receiving her alimony checks. Maybe the others weren't, either. *A CORPSE TELLS NO TALES.* The note I found may have in some way referred to a threat from one of Lou's ex-wives. I wondered if any of the ex-Mrs. Lou Beaumonts had paid a visit to the TV studio the day of Lou's murder.

Or maybe one of them had *family* connections. The thought stopped me in my tracks. It wouldn't be the first time a bitter ex-wife hired a hit man.

Mama turned to me. "What's the matter, dear? Why did you stop?"

"You look upset, Mrs. Pollack." I turned to find Detective Marlowe towering over me.

"Mama, why don't you go say hello to Mr. Gruenwald? I'll catch up with you in a minute."

"Of course, dear. Nice to see you, Detective."

Marlowe nodded to Mama. "Ma'am."

When she was out of whisper-shot, I asked, "I don't suppose you'd tell me if you found anything wonky regarding Lou's financials?"

"Sorry. Can't divulge anything regarding an ongoing investigation."

"Somehow I knew you'd say that."

"Mind telling me why you're so interested?"

"I suppose not." If he did his job properly, he probably already knew about Lou's exes. If he didn't know, he certainly should. So I reiterated what had just transpired.

"Let me get this straight," he said. "Your mother had no idea she was going to be the deceased's fifth wife?"

"None."

"Interesting."

"In what way?"

He just stared at me, close-mouthed, with not a hint of what he was thinking showing on his face. I stared back, waiting to see who blinked first. Marlowe refused to play. Instead, he turned and strode across the room toward his partner.

This guy made me long for Batswin and Robbins.

———

Mama insisted on staying at the funeral home until the last mourner had departed, which made it rush hour by the time I drove out of the parking garage. Rush hour. In Manhattan. On a Friday afternoon. The end of May. Welcome to the gridlock capital of the world. The trip from the Upper East Side to the Lincoln Tunnel queue, a distance of less than three and a half miles that would take ten minutes anywhere else in the country, took us over an hour.

The remainder of the trip wasn't much better, and it didn't help that Mama needed to make a *wee-wee* stop in Weehawken.

"Didn't you go before we left the funeral home?"

"Of course, I did, dear. But that was over an hour ago. My bladder isn't what it used to be, you know."

Oh, I knew. I prayed fervently every night to the Patron Saint of Interior Plumbing that I hadn't inherited Mama's weak bladder. Only time would tell. From what I'd observed of Mama and other female relatives, wee-wee issues didn't begin until sometime past menopause. For that reason, I also prayed my little red friend would stick around for at least another decade.

"Hold it in," I told her. "I'll pull over at the first rest area."

The Vince Lombardi Rest Area was a mere few yards beyond the Turnpike entrance. Unfortunately, it was closed due to police activity of some sort.

"I can't make it all the way home," said Mama.

Which meant we needed to detour off the Turnpike. Which meant it was past six o'clock by the time I turned onto our street—to find a black and white Westfield police cruiser parked in front of my house.

"What now?" I pulled into my driveway, turned off the Hyundai's engine, and stared at the house. Whatever awaited me inside couldn't be good news. The police never brought good news to your door, and they'd been to my home way too many times in the past few months. It was definitely someone else's turn to deal with life's crap.

I was more pissed than scared. Call it ESMP—Extra-Sensory Mom Perception—but somehow I knew my kids were okay. The eye roll Alex greeted me with when he swung open the front door confirmed that my ESMP hadn't let me down.

"Grandmother Lucille," he said. Not a question, a statement.

I could hear Lucille arguing with Harley and Fogarty. The two officers and I had more than a nodding acquaintanceship at this point, and I recognized their voices. A growling dog, a hissing cat, and a squawking parrot added to the cacophony.

"You didn't think we did anything wrong, did you?" asked Nick, standing beside his brother.

"You think I don't know who the troublemaker is in this family?"

"Just making sure," said Nick.

Forget communism. My mother-in-law had an anarchist's disregard for authority. She does what she wants, when she wants. On top of that, she expects the seas to part at her command.

This was a non-issue when Lucille first moved in with us five months ago to recuperate from the hit-and-run that nearly killed her. She could barely take a step or two at the time. Other than doctors' appointments and physical therapy sessions, she spent most of her time confined to the house. Once her mobility returned, she should have been back in her own apartment in Queens, but thanks to Karl, I was stuck with her. Permanently. And now, so was the rest of Westfield.

"What's she done this time?" asked Mama, who'd finally caught up with me and stood at my elbow.

"They're accusing her of keying a car," said Alex.

"Not just any car," added Nick. "A Z4 roadster."

Great. She couldn't pick on a twelve-year-old Hyundai. She had to key a BMW that costs almost as much as a college education.

"You can't prove a thing," Lucille shouted at Harley and Fogarty.

"We can get a search warrant for your keys to test them," said Harley.

"A fine waste of taxpayer money that would be," said Lucille.

I was about to step into the fray when someone banged on the back door. "Nick, see who that is, will you?" As he headed toward the kitchen, I entered the living room. "What's going on here?"

Harley and Fogarty turned away from Lucille and approached me. "Mrs. Pollack," they said in unison, by way of greeting.

"Seems your mother-in-law's been taking the law into her own hands," said Harley, the senior partner.

"How so?"

"She bashed her cane onto the hood of a vehicle that stopped short to avoid hitting her when she jaywalked across Central. Later, the driver came out to find his car had been keyed while it was parked in the lot behind Starbucks. He's accusing your mother-in-law."

My mother-in-law was guilty of many things, but I'd never known her to resort to vandalism. "Lucille, is this true?"

"*Yes, in truth it is, sir,*" squawked Ralph from atop the bookcase. "*Much Ado About Nothing.* Act Three, Scene Five."

"Well, there you have it," said Mama, unable to contain her gloat. "The parrot has spoken."

And this from a woman who calls Ralph a filthy bird.

"They have no proof," said Lucille. "None!" She stood defiantly, her hands fisted and resting on her hips.

Mephisto was parked between Lucille's legs, his teeth bared, a low growl emanating from his throat. Harley and Fogarty eyed him cautiously, but I could tell that was Mephisto's Catherine the Great growl. The regal empress had taken up a military stance across the top of the sofa, her claws aimed straight at Mephisto.

I grabbed the huge ball of fur from her perch and handed her to Mama. "That's not what I asked you," I said to Lucille.

"So you're taking their side? Whatever happened to *innocent until proven guilty?*"

Ralph answered her. "*Not for all this land would I be guilty of so great a sin. Richard the Third.* Act Three, Scene One."

I had a more appropriate Shakespearian quote in mind, though, one from Hamlet: *The lady doth protest too much, methinks.* The irony wasn't lost on any of us that the die-hard communist who wanted to overthrow our government used the Constitution to defend herself. Mama sputtered in indignation while Alex laughed.

I turned to glare them both into silence, then asked the officers. "You have any proof she's the culprit?"

"The driver saw her loitering in the parking lot when he returned to his car," said Fogarty. "He flagged us down and pointed her out."

"But no one actually saw her commit an act of vandalism?" This came from Zack who followed Nick into the living room. "I just got home and saw the cop car. Wanted to make sure you were all okay," he said to me, by way of explanation.

"Oh, Zachary, dear," said Mama, placing a hand on his arm, "that was so very kind of you. Wasn't it, Anastasia?"

I executed a mental eye roll, then nodded without saying anything. My mind was on Zack's question. An extremely good question. I'm not sure I would have had the balls to ask it, given I was ninety-nine percent certain of Lucille's guilt by now. My mother-in-law had a deep-seated need to get her own way. Always. Who really knew what she was capable of doing?

"We have no witnesses to the actual crime," said Harley. "However, there's something more."

And this should surprise me?

"She's constantly jaywalking," he continued. "So far she's been lucky, but one of these days—"

"New Jersey state law says cars have to stop for pedestrians," screamed the jaywalker in question. "Look it up!"

"In crosswalks!" Harley shouted back at her.

"That doesn't give them the right to mow down pedestrians outside of crosswalks!"

"Would serve her right if she got herself killed," muttered Mama, loud enough for everyone to hear.

Both officers just shook their heads. I think they were learning quickly that there's no point in reasoning with Lucille. And maybe, being the pain in the ass she'd become to them, they secretly agreed with Mama.

"She's been issued half a dozen citations over the last two months," Fogarty said.

Dumbfounded, I stared at my mother-in-law and lost what little control I had left. "What the hell is the matter with you, Lucille? Wasn't nearly getting killed once enough for you? Are you insane?"

Lucille pounded her cane on the floor, but since the carpet muffled the sound, I don't think she achieved the effect she was going for. She compensated by raising her voice to an even shriller level. Her face turned a bright shade of apoplectic purple. "How dare you speak to me like that? Those vehicles are infringing on my right to cross the street, but does anyone care about that? Of course not!"

"Has she paid the tickets?" I asked Harley.

"Not sure. Another department handles that."

"Have you?" I asked her.

"What business is it of yours?"

I took that as a *no*. "If you're hauled off to jail again, Lucille, don't expect me to bail you out. I have no money left to waste on this shit."

"I don't have to listen to any of you," she said. "I know my rights." With that she stormed down the hall, Mephisto trailing behind her. A moment later the house shook as she slammed her bedroom door. A moment after that, the lock clicked into place.

I sighed. Every time I removed and confiscated a lock from that bedroom door, the damn woman went out and bought herself another.

"Oh dear," said Mama. "Now I'll never get into my bedroom, and I so wanted to change out of these clothes and lie down for a spell. It's been such a difficult day." She directed this to Harley.

Mama had history with the older officer. Seamus O'Keefe, her last husband, was hardly cold before Mama had started flirting with Harley three months ago, but Harley didn't take the bait. Looked like he wasn't buying into her damsel in distress act this time, either. Good thing. I really didn't want my next stepfather young enough to be my older brother. Mama on the prowl was bad enough, but Mama as a cougar? I shuddered at the thought.

"Now what?" I asked both men.

"We'll keep a closer eye on her," said Fogarty. "Try to catch her in the act if she is the culprit."

"If you ask me, she's stepped up her game," added Harley. "She must be jotting down license plate numbers of cars that don't stop for her. Then if she sees one of the vehicles parked in the area at some point, she keys it. We've had a few other complaints about damaged vehicles but no witnesses to describe the perp. Could all be your mother-in-law's doing."

"She's never resorted to vandalism before to make a point, but I wasn't kidding when I said I won't bail her out."

"Maybe that's what it will take to get her to stop," said Zack.

"Somehow, I doubt it," I said. "More likely, she'll file harassment charges against the police department." Punishing me, as well as every other Westfield resident, because our taxes would surely skyrocket to pay for the town to defend its officers.

"Have you considered having her tested?" asked Fogarty as he and Harley prepared to leave. "She's crazy, you know."

"Only like a fox," I said. "She knows exactly what she's doing."

The moment I closed the door behind Harley and Fogarty, Mama, Alex, and Nick all started talking at once.

"Anastasia, how am I going to get into my room?"

"What's for dinner?"

"I'm hungry."

I turned to the one person who remained silent. "You wouldn't happen to have an axe, would you?"

"Why? You thinking of pulling a Lizzie Borden?" asked Zack.

"Tempting though it may be, I was only going to use it to chop down a door."

Mama gasped. "You can't do that! I need my privacy."

"You can't have it both ways, Mama, and I don't know what else to do at this point."

"I do," said Zack. "We take the door off its hinges the next time she comes out of the room and hang a curtain rod in its place."

"I should have thought of that," I said. "Maybe I would have if my brain weren't fried."

"Speaking of fried…" said Nick.

"I'm starving," said Alex.

TEN

Business is business, and the show must go on. That's what Naomi had said, and that's exactly what happened. Lou's death and a killer on the loose had only pushed back the production schedule by a few days. Taping began the last week in May.

When the day arrived for me to tape my first segment, the police still hadn't made an arrest. If they suspected Ray, they either didn't have enough evidence, or Ray had an alibi. I wasn't thrilled about returning to the scene of the crime with a killer still on the loose, but what alternative did I have? I couldn't afford to lose my job. Then again, my kids couldn't afford to lose their mother and sole breadwinner. My life was just one damned-if-you-do, damned-if-you-don't moment after another.

Late once again, thanks to a New Jersey Transit breakdown between Newark and Secaucus, I exited the elevator into the reception area in time to catch a uniformed officer restraining Vince while another cuffed him. Marlowe and Phillips stood nearby, Phillips with a carton in his arms, Marlowe holding a laptop. The rest of the staff huddled in groups of three and four, watching in silence as the drama unfolded.

Marlowe began to read Vince his rights. "You have the right to remain silent—"

"You can't do this!" Vince screamed, his crimson face clashing with his apricot- and aqua-striped, custom-made shirt and violet silk tie.

"If you give up the right to remain silent," continued Marlowe, "anything you say can and will be used against you in a court of law."

Vince stiffened his torso in defiance. A clump of his slicked-back Grecian Formula hair fell over his tanned-to-leather brow. "I'll sue the NYPD and every one of you for false arrest. You'll rue the day you treated Vince Alto like a common criminal!"

Marlowe ignored his outburst and continued in a modulated tone. "You have the right to speak with an attorney and to have the attorney present during questioning. If you so desire and cannot afford one, an attorney will be appointed for you without charge before the questioning begins."

The uniformed officer who had cuffed Vince grabbed him by the upper arm. The second officer took hold of his other bicep. Vince glared first at one, then the other. "You losers are in for some real trouble when my attorney gets word of how you're manhandling me."

"Do you understand your rights as I've read them to you?" asked Marlowe, his voice still showing no emotion although his eyes had narrowed and the muscles around his mouth and jaw had tightened.

Vince curled his upper lip, spitting out his reply. "What do I look like, an imbecile?"

The detective didn't flinch. "Do you waive and give up those rights?"

"Hell, no!"

Marlowe nodded to the two officers. "Okay, get him out of here."

Vince dug in his heels as the officers yanked his arms. "Not until you cover my face. I'll be damned if any paparazzi are going to get rich from snapping me in shackles."

"There are no photographers downstairs," I assured him.

Vince shifted his attention from Marlowe to me. His eyes narrowed into two dark slits, his crow's feet and furrowed brow growing more pronounced. "You wouldn't know a tabloid sleaze from a tourist."

So much for trying to help.

Monica stepped forward from behind a group of techies and tossed Vince his navy blazer. It landed on the floor several feet shy of him. Not that he could have grabbed it anyway with his hands cuffed behind his back. One of the officers scooped up the jacket and draped it over Vince's head. As they led him into the elevator, his muffled sneer echoed back toward us, "You'll get yours, bitch."

For what? Informing him he needn't worry about having his picture splashed across every tabloid in the country? Then again, maybe he hurled the threat at Monica or Sheri. Hard to tell with a jacket covering his head. Either way, it didn't look like any of us needed police protection with Vince on his way to the slammer.

"Okay, everyone back to work," said Sheri with a clap of her hands and a sing-song lilt to her voice, like a preschool teacher gathering up her class after recess. "The party's over, and we've got a show to produce."

"What happened?" I asked her as the groups of gawkers broke up and shuffled off in various directions.

She fluttered a piece of paper between her fingers and smiled in a way that brought to mind a bloated, muumuu-clad Sylvester the Cat with yellow Tweedy Bird feathers sticking out of his mouth. The black and white swirling pattern of her muumuu *du jour* only helped to enhance the image. "Monica discovered an incriminating e-mail from Vince on her computer this morning," she said. "When she showed it to me, I called the police. They arrived with a search warrant for his laptop."

"But they hauled Vince away in handcuffs."

She smirked. "He put up a stink. Wouldn't hand over his computer. So they arrested him. Serves him right."

"So he isn't under arrest for Lou's murder?"

"Obstructing a police investigation. So far. But I wouldn't be surprised if he turned out to be the killer." She handed me the paper. "Here, read for yourself. I made a copy before the police arrived. Vince hated Lou. Everyone knew that."

From the little I had observed at the studio, Vince wasn't alone in his feelings toward Lou. That didn't make him a killer, though. I read the e-mail.

From: Vince Alto [v.alto@trimedia.com]
Sent: Tuesday, May 10 10:37 AM
To: Monica Rivers
Subject: New Format

I don't know about you, sweetheart, but I'm not taking this lying down. No one screws with Vince Alto and gets away with it. Whatever it takes, I'm getting rid of these interlopers and regaining control of MY show.

I'm no cop, and I don't spend my evenings glued to the TV watching police and courtroom dramas like Mama, but even I knew this e-mail didn't amount to much in the way of evidence against Vince. "Most people dislike their bosses and bitch and moan about them," I said. "That's life in corporate America. I'm sure it's the same or worse in Morning Talk Show Land."

"People have been known to go postal over far less," said Sheri. "You never know what will push a sane person over the edge."

I wasn't buying it. Vince scored pretty high on my Sleazometer, but from what I could see, he was all bluster and bravado. Besides, he wouldn't risk ruining either his manicure or his custom-made clothing with something as messy as murder. There was something more that didn't add up. I pointed to the e-mail. "This is dated three weeks ago. Why did Monica wait so long to show it to anyone? Why didn't she tell the police about it when we were all interviewed?"

"She claims it first showed up in her mailbox this morning."

"Don't you think that's a bit odd?"

Sheri waved a pudgy hand. "Happens all the time. We've been having computer problems on and off ever since Trimedia upgraded their network months ago."

"Doesn't Trimedia monitor your e-mails?"

She hesitated. "What do you mean?"

"At *American Woman* getting caught sending personal e-mails or playing computer games can get you fired. At Trimedia Big

Brother is always lurking in cyberspace. I'm surprised Vince would risk sending an e-mail like this."

Sheri bit back a sheepish grin and darted a glance first left, then right before asking, "Can you keep a secret?"

"As long as you're not going to tell me you killed Lou."

She tapped my arm and giggled. "Of course not, silly." With a hand cupping her mouth, she spoke in a conspiratorial whisper. "One of our tech guys wrote a program to hinder Trimedia's snooping without their knowing. They see only what we want them to see."

"Really? How much do you think he'd want to share that program?" I knew quite a few people at *American Woman* who would gladly kick in their waxing money and put up with hairy legs for the next few months to foil Trimedia's spy ware.

Sheri cocked her head and offered me a rueful smile. "Sorry. He hit the lottery a month ago and gave notice the next day. Last I heard, he's island-hopping around the Caribbean in a fifty-two-foot trimaran."

I sighed. "Some people have all the luck."

———

Two hours later, Sheri hovered over us as Monica, Naomi, and I ran through a pre-taping rehearsal of Monica's guinea pig stint with mop dolls. Although we'd rehearsed some last week, no amount of rehearsing could counter Monica's uncooperative attitude and obvious disdain for anything that might cause her to chip a nail.

When Sheri took over the show, she nixed the live studio audience. At first I thought it a good idea, given Monica's and Vince's behavior. However, I'd recorded a few of the *You Heard It Here First* reruns and after watching them, had a new appreciation for Vince's and Monica's acting skills. For two people who hated each other's guts in real life, those two came across on camera like BFFs. No wonder Ray thought his wife was getting it on with her co-star. A live audience might have forced Vince and Monica to cooperate more.

However, today Monica was even less cooperative than she'd been previously. I had suggested she wear a work smock, but she refused. Hence, her midnight blue Prada, a little nothing of a raw linen sheath that I'm sure cost more than my used Hyundai, was now covered with white lint.

That's the biggest problem with mop dolls. They shed. At the height of the mop doll craze, manufacturers came up with synthetic substitutes, but no one produces those anymore. They were lousy for cleaning floors and only good for one thing—a once trendy craft that was now as popular as pet rocks.

Monica had spent the past half hour picking at the lint and paying little attention to me except to whine about the difficulty of each step I asked her to perform. Her high-pitched prattle of complaints and constant foot tapping on the stool rail sounded like she was hooked up to an intravenous drip of triple-shot espressos.

I couldn't wait to see what happened when I handed her the glue gun.

Meanwhile, Sheri had lost all patience. With both hands she slammed her clipboard onto the counter, spilling an open container of sequins and sending up a cloud of mop lint. "Damn it, Monica, we're hours behind schedule. We should have wrapped up taping this segment by now, and we haven't even started. Pay attention. A ten-year-old could make one of these dolls."

"Then find a ten-year-old!" Monica scooped up a handful of mop snippets and threw them at Sheri, but her aim was as off as her crafting skills. The scraps landed at Sheri's feet. "I'm an actress, not Suzy-Fucking-Crafter."

"I may just do that," shouted Sheri.

Monica's face lit up in a smug grin. "Be my guest. Fire me. I still get paid, and I won't have to put up with any more of this shit." She swept her arm across the counter, brushing one very sad looking, half-finished mop doll and an assortment of supplies to the floor.

"You'd like that, wouldn't you?" said Sheri. "Well, forget it, honey." She bent down, scooped up the mess and plopped everything back down in front of Monica. "If I'm stuck paying you, you're going to work for every dime of that exorbitant contract you wheedled out of Lou."

"Maybe we should take a break," suggested Naomi.

"No breaks," said Sheri. "Not until we've wrapped this segment. We're too far behind schedule."

So I took a deep breath and tried for the fifth—or was it the fiftieth?—time to show Monica, a woman whose ten digits seemed to be comprised of all thumbs, how to plait a braid.

"Maybe we could have the camera cut to a finished braid after she separates the strands into three sections," I suggested, convinced that Monica was either incapable or disinclined to master the simplest of skills. Her fidgeting fingers couldn't even count out three equal groups of mop strands.

"No." Sheri flailed her arms. "The whole point of these crafts is that *anyone* can do them." She pointed a chubby index finger at Monica. "Even someone as inept as you."

Monica stood. "I refuse to sit here and be insulted by you."

"So quit," said Sheri. "I only have to pay out your contract if I fire you or the show gets canceled."

"That's what you're hoping, isn't it?" Monica climbed back onto her stool, nearly tipping it in the process. Then, as she glowered at Sheri, she grabbed a handful of mop strands and sorted them into three unequal sections. "Guess again, Little Miss Napoleon."

Sheri's jaw dropped, but before she could respond, Vince stormed into the studio. "Heads are going to roll when I find out who planted that e-mail," he screamed, spittle flying in Monica's direction.

She dropped the mop strands, jumped off the stool, threw her hands onto her hips, and glared at him. "Are you accusing me of making the whole thing up?"

Vince laughed. "Hardly. Whoever tried to frame me has to know his way around computers. You can't find the *ON* switch without help."

"What makes you think someone tried to frame you?" asked Sheri.

Vince spun to face her, his upper lip skewed into one of his classic sneers. "Because *I* didn't send that e-mail."

"And the police are supposed to take your word against the evidence on Monica's computer?" She chuckled as she shook her head. "Not likely."

"They will when they trace back the e-mail to the perpetrator's computer and not mine."

"What if the sender used your computer?" I asked.

Vince's expression grew cocky, his speech condescending. "Impossible. My computer is password protected. Besides, I keep it locked in my desk when I'm not using it."

"Even when you go to the little boy's room?" I asked.

"Even when I go to the little boy's room," he mimicked.

"That wouldn't stop a determined hacker," said Naomi. "Those e-mails could have been sent from your computer without the perpetrator having physical access to your computer."

Both the color and cockiness drained from his face. For a split second I thought I caught a glimpse of fear in Vince's eyes, but he quickly recovered.

Monica crossed her arms over her chest. Two large patches of white lint remained on either side of her waist. Her right foot had once again begun tapping a frenzied staccato. "So the cops released you? With the fuss you put up earlier, you're lucky they didn't lock you up and throw away the key."

Vince stepped closer to her, leaving only inches between his face and hers. "You'd like that, wouldn't you, sweetheart? Think it would solve *your* problems? Don't bet on it. Maybe you paid someone to hack into my computer."

Monica took a step back and answered with nothing more than a smirk.

Vince turned to Sheri. "I'm out on bail. But you've made my lawyer's day. My legal fees over this will buy him that new Lamborghini he's been eyeing." He stomped out of the studio without another word. I guess he already knew how to plait a braid, since he didn't bother to hang around for rehearsal, much less the taping.

"Murderers usually don't get released on bail," I said, staring at the studio door swinging on its hinges. "Or it's set so high that they can't raise the money."

"The King of Drama," scoffed Sheri. "He was arrested for impeding an investigation and resisting arrest. If he hadn't put up such a fuss when the cops demanded his computer, he never would have been arrested. That'll buy his lawyer a used Chevy. Maybe."

I wondered when Sheri last hired an attorney. My legal fees from Karl's death came close to the GNP of Western Samoa. And that was with Mama's second cousin Horace Sudberry cutting me a break.

"I wonder what he's hiding," I said.

"What do you mean?" asked Sheri.

"Why would Vince put up such a fuss if he didn't have something on his computer he didn't want the cops to find?"

"Like a certain e-mail," said Monica.

"But at the time it never occurred to Vince that the e-mail could have been sent from his computer," Naomi reminded her. Monica had the memory retention of a flea.

"And he certainly doesn't strike me as a First Amendment zealot," added Naomi.

"So he did send the e-mail," said Monica. "I knew it!"

"Not necessarily," said Sheri.

"But she just said—"

"What I'm saying," I said, "is there must be something on that computer Vince didn't want the police to see."

Unfortunately, we'd probably never learn Vince's secret because sometime after midnight Sunday evening he was found in a Hell's Kitchen alley. Alongside his battered and bloody body the police found an Easter bunny mop doll sitting on a bloody brick.

ELEVEN

Only it wasn't my Easter bunny mop doll. Which I pointed out to Detective Marlowe when he and a uniformed officer arrived at my front door hours before daybreak and hauled my less-than-awake, sweats-clad tush across the Hudson River for a round of idiotic questioning.

"How do I know this isn't your doll?" asked Marlowe, pointing a mustard-stained index finger at a paraplegic, follicly challenged Easter bunny who looked like he'd indulged in one too many mugs of spiked carrot juice. Ears of two different lengths were precariously attached to a head devoid of hair. The eyes, one glued an inch higher than the other, were too large for the face. Only one arm was braided; the other hung in hacked, loose strands, hence the paraplegic affect.

I pulled my attention from the doll and studied Marlowe. A minute spec of Gulden's kissed the corner of his mouth. A matching blob had found its way onto the loosened royal blue-and-burgundy striped tie that hung from the collar of his wrinkled and stained white shirt. He wore the same suit he'd worn when arresting Vince, only on Thursday he'd worn it well. Right now it looked like he'd slept in the navy gabardine every night since Thursday. On a park bench. In the rain.

He looked the way I felt. And whose fault was that? *He'd* dragged *me* out of bed. Not to mention yanking me out of the most erotic dream I'd had in decades. I couldn't remember most of it now except that *Satisfaction* had been playing in the background, and I was finally getting some. By a hunk in tight black jeans. Only he had discarded the jeans. In a heap. On my kitchen floor.

"Mrs. Pollack? I asked you a question."

Yikes! Was I desperate or what? I'm being questioned about a murder, and I'm fantasizing about sex with my tenant. I shook the image and the cobwebs from my brain.

Marlowe repeated his question. Before answering, I yawned, then drained the cup of sludge he'd poured me. My eye caught the clock mounted on the wall opposite the door—4:45 in the morning. Morning? As far as I was concerned, anything earlier than 6:30 fell into the realm of middle of the night. However, considering the circumstances and wanting to avoid a forced vacation in the slammer, I swallowed my Inner Bitch and reined in the acid remark straining to leap from my lips.

Offering Marlowe a bitch-free smile, I said, "Detective, if I produced such shoddy workmanship, I'd be out of a job. Whoever crafted that doll is either trying to frame me or send you on a wild goose chase."

He scrubbed his chin and flashed a grin, exposing a set of coffee-stained, less-than-pearly whites. "Yeah, we sort of figured that one out on our own."

"So I'm not a suspect?"

"Everyone's a suspect until we find our killer."

"I have no motive."

Marlowe cocked his head, narrowed his gaze, and frowned. "By your own admission you were forced to take on work you weren't getting paid for. To some that's motivation enough to kill."

"Not for me. Besides, if I did kill Lou and Vince—which I didn't—do you think I'd be stupid enough to leave such obvious clues leading right back to me?"

"Probably not, but maybe you left them for just that reason. And maybe you deliberately crafted a doll that would look like someone else made it."

"Detective, you need to catch a few z's. You're not making any sense." I pointed an accusing finger at the mop doll. "You just said you knew I didn't make that piece of crap."

"Doesn't matter. I still needed to question you about the doll."

I slapped my palms on the table and leaned forward. My Inner Bitch burst free with a menacing growl. "You couldn't have waited until morning?"

He hauled his rumpled body out of the metal chair, strode to the coffee pot at the far corner of the room, and poured himself another cup of sludge. "Refill? Sounds like you could use one."

"No thanks." I pitched my empty Styrofoam cup at an overflowing waste basket. It fell three feet short. Even I, the Caffeine Queen of Westfield, didn't have the cast-iron stomach for more than one cup of the acidic mud the NYPD passed off as coffee.

Marlowe returned the pot to the burner, scooped up my cup and deposited it in the can before settling back into the seat opposite me. "Time is of the essence in a murder investigation. We don't have the luxury of working nine-to-five. Clues disappear; leads dry up."

The man looked beyond haggard. Stubble covered his face. Mud splattered his rumpled shirt. Or maybe it was blood. I shuddered and softened my tone. "Am I free to leave?" By the time I arrived back in Westfield, I'd have just enough time to shower, dress, and make it to the office without accumulating another demerit from the Human Resources Attendance Nazi. If I were lucky. Not that luck had deigned to grace my path in several months.

He shook his head. "I've got two related cases. Two dolls. We know you made the first one. I was hoping you'd have some idea as to who constructed this one. Might give us the lead we need."

The Easter Bunny Mop Doll from Hell sat at the far end of the battered wood table. I held out my hand. "May I?"

He stretched one beefy arm down the length of the table, retrieved the doll, and handed it to me.

I inspected Bugs from all angles, turning him upside-down and nearly inside-out, but a closer examination revealed nothing in the way of a clue. "You weren't able to find anything?"

"Like?"

I scowled at him. "I don't know. You're the cop. Fingerprints. A stray hair. The *CSI* thing."

He rose and paced the small space between the table and door. One hand combed through his salt and pepper crew cut; the other jingled the change in his pants pocket. "Yeah, forensics did their *thing*. Came up with nothing. That's why I thought maybe you could help."

I sighed as I set Bugs back on the table. "Sorry."

Marlowe returned to the table and dropped back into his chair. "Were you looking for anything special?"

"No, but thanks to Monica's lack of cooperation, we went through several mop dolls during rehearsals. We weren't making bunnies, but this could have been one of the early rejects that wound up in the trash. The killer may have taken it and added the ears. Only I don't see anything that would tell us one way or the other whether this is one of the rehearsal dolls."

Marlowe picked up on the lack of cooperation comment. "Want to explain that?"

I filled him in on the back-stabbing soap opera antics of *Morning Makeovers* and ended by saying, "Didn't anyone mention this when you questioned us after Lou's death?"

He nodded. "Just wanted to hear your take."

His bleary-eyed stare held mine for a moment as if waiting for me to pull some important tidbit out of the dark recesses of my brain, but I had nothing more to add. "You've heard it. *Now* can I *please* go home?"

Marlowe nodded. "I'll have a uniformed drive you back to Westfield."

Had I been more awake, I might have asked him what he found on Vince's computer, but I didn't think of that until I was standing under a stream of steamy water an hour later. Not that he would have satisfied my curiosity. From my experience of a few months back, cops ask the questions and expect you to cough up the answers. It doesn't work the other way around.

BUNNY MOP DOLL

Turn a basic mop doll into a bunny with these simple additions.

Materials (in addition to materials used for Basic Mop Doll): one white and one pink felt square (9½" x 12"), fusible web, two 1½" white pompoms, one 1" pink pompom, two 12mm pink oval wiggle eyes, water-soluble fabric marker, iron and ironing board; six straight pins.

Directions: Cut the white felt in half to 6" x 9½". Following manufacturer's directions for the fusible web, fuse the pieces together. Cut two pieces, each 6" x 2¼". Mark the centers of the sides, top, and bottom with the water-soluble fabric marker. For each ear, at the bottom edge measure out from either side of the center ⅝". Draw a curved line from the center side markings to the ⅝" markings. Then draw a curved line from the center side markings to the top center, rounding the point where the two lines meet. Cut out both ears. Remove the pen markings with a spritz of water.

Following the manufacturer's directions, apply fusible web to the pink felt. Using the white ears as a pattern, cut two pink inner ears. Trim the inner ears ¼" around the sides and top edges. Fuse a pink inner ear to each white ear.

Apply a drop of glue to the bottom center of each ear. Fold the ears in half to form a dart. Allow the glue to dry. (Hint: hold the ears together with a spring type clothespin while the glue dries.)

Before applying 3" lengths of the mop strands to the doll head, glue the ears in place on either side of the head. For additional security, dip straight pins in glue and pin through the felt into the head at bottom edges of the ears. Apply mop doll hair as directed in Basic Mop Doll directions, omitting the pigtails.

Glue a pink pompom to the center of the face for the bunny's nose. Glue white pompoms horizontally centered under the pink pompom to form a muzzle. Glue the eyes in place.

After the murder and mayhem of the past few weeks at the television studio, the normal insanity of magazine publishing and my own cubicle of an office came as a welcome relief that Monday morning.

"Done with your taping?" asked Cloris, popping in from her own cubicle across the hall.

I collapsed into my chair. "We finished Friday. One fifteen minute segment wound up taking more than a day to shoot. I don't envy the segment editor."

"Let me guess. Monica?"

I nodded. "The woman acts incapable of mastering the most basic of skills. Emphasis on *acts*." I mentioned my epiphany regarding the reruns I'd watched. "I'll bet if she'd been cast in the title role of *The Life of Martha Stewart*, we'd all marvel at her crafting skills."

"I don't see how Sheri's going to pull this off," said Cloris.

"I know. Seems to me she'd be better off firing Monica, even if Trimedia has to pay out her contract. Unless Sheri's aiming to create *The Gong Show* of morning television."

Cloris crossed the hall and offered me a chocolate chip muffin. Cloris never comes empty-handed, and for that fact alone she's earned her place in Heaven. "Let me know what you think of this," she said. "It's a reader's recipe I'm thinking of featuring in the next issue."

I inhaled half the muffin in one bite. "Hmm," I said over the mouthful. I closed my eyes and savored the fudgy cake. My stomach growled as it received the first offering in over twelve hours. NYPD sludge didn't count.

"No time for breakfast this morning?" she asked, eyeing my hastily assembled, mismatched outfit and my in-need-of-a-good-washing, limp hair.

"Or much of anything else." My weekends consisted of forty-eight hours of nonstop parenting, errands, and chores. When Mama offered to take care of the laundry, I gladly accepted. When would I learn? Flora Sudberry Periwinkle Ramirez Scoffield Goldberg O'Keefe might have the best of intentions, but intentions don't wash, dry, and fold. This morning I discovered a mountain of dirty laundry in the basement and my clean wardrobe reduced to a pair of olive drab Dockers and a slate blue, scooped-neck T-shirt with a bleach spot that drew attention to my left boob.

"Good thing you're not the Fashion Editor," said Cloris, pointing to the amorphous-shaped white dribble.

I grabbed my smock off a hook and stuffed my arms into the sleeves, buttoning the front up to my chin.

"So I guess you didn't catch the morning news," she said.

"About Vince Alto? Firsthand from Detective Marlowe about five hours ago."

Cloris nearly choked on a bite of her muffin. "Dish!"

So I dished. When I finished catching her up, she said, "I'll bet it was Monica's husband."

"That's what I thought at first, given that he accused Monica of having affairs with both Lou and Vince."

"And he was at the studio early on the day Lou was killed," said Cloris, licking flecks of chocolate from her fingers. "Maybe he really didn't leave after dropping Monica off."

"According to Detective Marlowe, Ray has an alibi."

"Alibis can be bought."

Something else occurred to me. "I wonder . . ."

"What?"

"Maybe everything is an act with Monica. What if she and Ray are secretly working together to sabotage the show? And have been even before the revamp."

"That would mean Ray's accusations—"

"Were all part of an elaborate scheme to get the show cancelled and rid Monica of Vince. She and Ray collect the balance of her contract, and she's free to star in her own show without competition from her former partner."

"You think another network would hire Monica? She's a has-been."

"With delusions of her own grandeur. It doesn't matter whether I think she'd get another show, only that she believes she would."

"So how do you prove this theory, Sherlock?"

I grinned at her. "Up to a little spying, Watson?"

Since Cloris was scheduled to tape her segment the next day, we decided that I'd tag along. Afterward, we'd tail Monica to see what we could learn.

I spent the rest of the day catching up on the three issues that were in various stages of production. Half the editorial staff were either at the studio or out on photo shoots. The rest were holed up in their cubicles, also playing catch-up, so aside from an occasional chat with Cloris and a break for lunch, I worked free of interruption.

By four-thirty I'd accomplished more than I'd expected, considering I was operating on less than four hours of sleep. And a good thing, too, since work came to a halt the moment Tessa arrived back at the office.

"I'm going to kill that bitch!" she screamed.

Cloris and I both ran out into the corridor at the same time.

"Who?" asked Cloris

"What happened?" I asked.

"Sheri-Fucking-Rabbstein. Who the hell does that muumuu-clad whale think she is, telling me how to do *my* job?"

TWELVE

Cloris grabbed Tessa by one arm, I grabbed her by the other, and we steered her into the break room. I kicked the door shut with my heel. "From the top," I said.

"And don't leave out any details," added Cloris.

Tessa flailed her arms as she paced back and forth in the tiny space between the mini-fridge and the seating area. "That woman is certifiable. She's got this asinine idea that she can be the next Donna Karan with a line of ready-to-wear muumuus."

"And you didn't know this until today?" I asked. "What about the presentation books she handed out at our first meeting? They outlined the content of each segment."

"Didn't you bother reading it?" asked Cloris.

"I read it," said Tessa. "However, now that she's in charge, she's made a few changes. She no longer wants a wardrobe make-over for the show. She wants exposure for her Frankenstein creations. Turns out she designed and sewed all those tents she wears. She wants the fashion segment of the show to feature Sheri Originals *and* she expects me to showcase them in the magazine. Not that she's got any buyers lined up. She hasn't even contacted anyone yet."

"So where's she going to sell them?" I asked. "On the Internet?"

"Hell, no." Tessa snorted. "She expects buyers from Saks, Bergdorf, Bloomie's—you name it—to line up at her door once the first fashion segment airs."

"And who's going to buy these tents?" asked Cloris. "Besides descendants of Queen Liliuokalani."

"Or senior citizens touring Waikiki Beach," I added.

"Oh, she's got that all figured out," said Tessa. "Claims she's done market research." She made quote marks in the air with her fingers. "'Muumuus aren't just for the fashion-challenged, full-figured woman. Muumuus are for everyone. They maximize comfort and minimize figure flaws.' She's got an entire ad campaign mapped out and is convinced that once American women embrace the muumuu—her muumuus, mind you—they'll never go back to T-shirts and jeans."

"What did you do?" I asked.

Tessa dropped into one of the mismatched molded plastic chairs. "I told her to kiss my ass. There's no way I'm going to let that woman make a laughingstock out of me."

"So you didn't tape your segment?" I asked.

"No way." She folded her arms across her surgically enhanced chest. "And I'm not going to."

"You'll lose your job," said Cloris.

"Unless she loses hers first," said Tessa, a sly smirk flirting at the edges of her mouth.

"There's something she's not telling us," I said to Cloris. Tessa's smirk grew wider. Her predecessor had slept her way into the position of Fashion Editor. Had Tessa done likewise? I stabbed an index finger in the air, inches from her too-perfectly-pert-to-be-real nose. "You know someone on the Trimedia board, don't you? That's how you got your job. And you're planning to pull a few strings to get Sheri axed, aren't you?"

She brushed my hand away. "My connections may have opened a few doors for me, but my talents landed me this job."

Cloris raised both eyebrows. "What sort of talents?"

Tessa gasped. "Nothing like that! My Uncle Chessie sits on the Trimedia board."

"Uncle Chessie?" asked Cloris. I could see the wheels spinning. "As in Chester Longstreth? Of Longstreth Pharmaceuticals? The man who owns half the state?"

Tessa nodded. "My grandmother's brother on my mother's side. But Uncle Chessie only owns half of Warren and Sussex Counties, not the entire state."

"We'll take up a collection for the poor man," said Cloris under her breath.

Ignoring Cloris, I peppered Tessa with questions. "And you've put in a call to him? What's he going to do?"

Tessa's chin notched up an inch. "Of course I called him. Wouldn't you? I told you I wasn't going to sit still for this crap. Working the show without extra compensation is bad enough, but that woman's a certifiable lunatic. Someone has to stop her."

"So what did dear old Uncle Chessie say?" asked Cloris.

Tessa lost her smirk and began to worry the lipstick from her bottom lip. "I haven't exactly spoken to him yet."

"Why not?" I asked.

"He's been on safari in Kenya for the last month. I've e-mailed him several times, but I haven't heard from him. He must be out of satellite range."

Or he had no intention of getting involved. Especially if the other board members were solidly behind Sheri and her vision for the show and its marriage to the magazine. "So you got into a cat fight with Sheri, stormed off the set before taping your segment, and can't get in touch with your uncle. Now what?" I asked.

Tessa stood and headed for the door. "I'll think of something."

"She'll be gone by morning," said Cloris after the click-clack of Tessa's Manolos on the terrazzo floor faded into the general office hubbub of ringing phones and whirring computer printers.

I couldn't disagree. "I'll bet Sheri placed a call to the board the moment Tessa stormed out of the studio."

Cloris sighed. "Wish I'd been there."

"Why?"

"Must have been some cat fight. A real battle of the prima donnas."

"Not me, thank you. I have enough of that on a daily basis with Mama and Lucille."

———

The next morning I took the train into the city instead of driving to the office, and met up with Cloris at Penn Station. I grabbed two of her four tote bags and together we hopped on the subway to the studio.

Twenty minutes later the usual suspects were gathered around the set's kitchen island where Cloris attempted to instruct Monica in the fine art of separating yolk from white. Not surprisingly, Monica handled eggs as well as she handled mop strands. An hour later Cloris was down to her last three eggs from her original four dozen.

"That's it," she said. "The recipe calls for three eggs, and I'm not running out to buy any more." She quickly snatched and separated two of the remaining eggs into two glass bowls. Then she grabbed both the last egg and Monica's hands.

"Hey, camera guy," she called out, "this is going to be the one and only take for the eggs, so put down the donut and roll the tape or press the magic record button or whatever it is you guys do."

Sheri stormed across the set. "What the hell do you think you're doing?"

"Making sure the city doesn't run out of eggs."

"Screw the city. I'll send someone out to buy more eggs. Monica has to separate them."

"Says who?" asked Cloris, still holding fast to Monica's hands.

"Little Miss Napoleon here," said Monica, indicating Sheri with a tilt of her head. "In case you hadn't heard, she's running the universe now. It's her way or the highway."

Sheri had turned an unflattering shade of purple that perfectly matched her muumuu *du jour*, several flowing yards of plum and indigo vertical stripes. I suppose she thought the stripes were slimming. Hardly. She looked like a giant eggplant with short, stubby arms and legs.

Naomi stepped between Cloris and Sheri. "Cloris is right. Let her do it her way. Some of us have other jobs to get to. We can't stand around here all day."

"I'm the producer," screamed Sheri.

"And I outrank you on both the corporate management chart and in seniority," said Naomi, her voice remaining calm. "You have a problem with that, *Ms. Rabbstein*, file a complaint with Human Resources."

Sheri and Naomi stared each other down for what seemed like forever, Sheri about to explode, Naomi maintaining her dignified and elegant but determined persona.

Of course, Sheri flinched first. "Fine, we'll do it your way. For now." Then she spun on her heels and marched off the set.

"I'd clap but my hands are occupied," said Monica.

Naomi turned back to her. "Let's just get this over with, shall we?"

"Fine by me," said Monica, "but I'm out of here at noon whether we finish or not."

Cloris and I exchanged a quick glance. If Monica left the set at noon, so would we.

"Ready?" asked the cameraman.

"As we'll ever be," said Cloris.

While the cameraman recorded them, Cloris instructed Monica, at the same time manipulating Monica's hands. The egg cracked in half perfectly. Cloris continued her puppet master technique, separating the final egg.

Still holding the empty shells in Monica's outstretched hands, she smiled into the camera. "See? Easy peasy, as one of my cooking colleagues likes to say."

"Cut!"

The remainder of the taping went relatively smoothly, mostly because Sheri didn't return to the set. Cloris treated Monica like a spoiled, petulant three-year-old as they proceeded to whip up the ingredients for apple zucchini sponge cake muffins. Between Naomi, Cloris, and the director, they worked out a system whereby Monica seemed to be mastering each step, but in reality, did very little. Without Madame Napoleon dictating orders, we finished up well before noon. I helped Cloris clean up her equipment while Monica headed for her dressing room.

"We can share a cab back to Penn Station," said Naomi.

"I'm staying in the city," said Cloris. "I scheduled an interview with the owner of Rice to Riches."

Naomi turned to me. "Anastasia?"

"Can't. I need to pick up some supplies first."

Naomi nodded. She started to head out, then turned back. "Why were you at the studio today?" she asked me.

"Uhm ... Cloris needed help carting all her stuff." *Lame, Anastasia.* You'd think being the mother of two teenage boys I'd be able to come up with a better excuse than that! After all, I'd heard every excuse in the proverbial book from the time Alex and Nick could string together two sentences.

"I see." Naomi eyed us both. "Whatever the two of you are planning, don't call me to post your bail."

"Are you sure about this?" asked Cloris after Naomi left the studio.

"All we're going to do is follow her. Surreptitiously, of course," I added. I found it hard to believe Monica was as inept as she'd like to make us believe. Whether it was connected to the vandalism and murders? Who knew? Maybe we'd get lucky with a little Sher-locking.

Putting my own New York spin on a tired cliché, I continued, "Something definitely stinks in Staten Island, and it's got Monica's name written all over it."

"As long as we don't wind up on Staten Island," said Cloris.

"Hey, it's Monica," I assured her. "Do you really think she'd be caught dead on Staten Island?"

"Point taken, Sherlock."

We headed for the elevator. My plan required we make it down to the lobby and plant ourselves in an inconspicuous spot before Monica headed out. We should have plenty of time. Monica always took forever in her dressing room. Once she left the building, we'd follow at a discreet distance.

As the elevator descended, something occurred to me. Since we were the only people occupying the car, I said. "Did you notice no one mentioned a word about the not-so-dearly departed Vince Alto?"

"Maybe they're all talked out from yesterday."

"Maybe. I just expected at least a bit of snark from Monica."

"Or Sheri," Cloris added. "Neither one of them seemed to like the guy."

"He did come across as the personification of slime. Still, no one deserves that fate."

Cloris thought for a moment. "I don't know about that. I can think of a few brains that could use a good bashing."

Good thing I knew her sense of humor. Besides, if Cloris wanted to kill someone, she'd just clog his arteries with cholesterol.

Once the elevator arrived, we headed for the lobby entrance of Duane Reade where we positioned ourselves to observe without being observed. One thing you can always count on in New York— either a Starbucks or a Duane Reade on every corner, equally handy for caffeine hits and pantyhose rips. I never thought I'd wind up using one for surveillance, though.

After ten minutes of trying to look inconspicuous and not like shoplifters, we spied Monica step from the elevator and head for the street. Cloris and I slipped out of Duane Reade and followed her. What we hadn't planned for was the town car with driver waiting at the curb. As soon as Monica slipped into the back seat, the car pulled out into traffic.

THIRTEEN

"Now what?" asked Cloris.

I jumped off the curb, flagged down an oncoming cab, and yanked open the door before the driver even came to a complete stop. "Hurry. Get in," I said, pushing Cloris in front of me. She scooted across the seat. I dove in behind her. "Follow that town car!" I yelled at the turbaned driver.

He turned and stared at me through the Plexiglas partition. "You are kidding me, missus?"

"Do I look like I'm kidding? Go. Now. Before we lose them!"

"I will follow, but I do not break New York state driving laws," he said.

Leave it to me to wind up with the one law-abiding cabbie in Manhattan. I glanced at the name on his license, then glanced at Monica's town car, already at the next block. "Look, Rajat, I'm not asking you to break any laws, but I do need to know where that town car goes. It's very important. A matter of life and death." I did a quick mental inventory of my wallet before adding, "I'll make it worth your while."

Rajat flashed me a huge and very white-toothed grin from his rearview mirror as he pulled away from the curb.

Just as the light at our corner changed to red.

A block ahead of us Monica's town car raced through a yellow light.

"We may as well get out," said Cloris. "We'll never catch them now."

"Not to worry, missus," said Rajat. "I will find the destination for your car and deliver you there directly." He picked up his cell phone and placed a call, breaking one of those very same New York State driving laws. Shortly, he began speaking in rapid-fire Urdu. Not that I would know Urdu from Swahili, but I was assuming someone named Rajat Patel spoke Urdu and not Swahili.

"For all we know," whispered Cloris, "he's placing a take-out order for Tandoori chicken."

"And taking us for a *ride*," I whispered back, but I was willing to give Mr. Rajat Patel a few minutes benefit of doubt. I leaned forward and strained to locate Monica's town car while keeping tabs on the ticking meter.

Make that a *very* few minutes.

Three blocks later I rapped on the partition. "You've lost him. Pull over."

Rajat shook his head. "No, no, missus. I will bring you to the destination of the town car. You are not to worry, please."

Easy for him to say. He wasn't the one with only twelve dollars in his wallet. What was I thinking when I told him I'd make it worth his while? The meter already read over seven and spun higher with every passing second. "I'm running out of money, Rajat."

"Do not worry, missus. We accept credit cards. VISA. Master-Card. American Express. Discover."

Too bad mine were all maxed out, thanks to my dead louse of a husband.

"We will arrive momentarily at your desired destination," added Rajat. Several blocks and several dollars later he turned the corner and pulled up behind a parked Yellow Cab. The driver of the other taxi walked over to our cab and began speaking with Rajat.

"There's no town car here," I said.

Rajat pointed to a brownstone across the street. "The passenger from the town car you wished to follow is inside that building."

"How the heck do you know that?" asked Cloris.

Rajat rolled down the back window on Cloris's side. "May I present my cousin Bashir, missus. He was in a taxi cab in front of us and followed your town car for you."

Bashir stuck his hand through the open window. Palm up. "Please to pay me twenty dollars, missus."

Twenty dollars for Bashir. Eleven plus a *worthwhile* tip for Rajat. No matter what the meter said, he'd never settle for less than the twenty demanded by his cousin. And me with twelve dollars in my wallet. It was a good thing Cloris had come along for the ride. I showed her the ten and two ones.

"You owe me," she said, whipping out her wallet.

"You bump all others to the bottom of the list." And it was a very long list, thanks to Karl Pollack, the aforementioned Dead Louse of a Spouse.

———

Rajat had driven us to the middle of a residential block between Second and Third Avenues in the Kips Bay section of Manhattan. "We'll have to position ourselves outside at one end of the block or the other," I said. "We'll never see her if we duck into one of the shops on Second or Third."

"It could be hours before she reappears," said Cloris. "And what are the chances of her spying us spying on her when she does? If she's even in there."

There was that to consider. We had no way of knowing whether or not two Indian cabbies were now laughing their asses off at our expense. Monica could be in Gramercy Park for all we knew. "Let's give it an hour or so," I suggested.

"The things I do for friendship," grumbled Cloris. She reached into the one tote bag she'd brought with her and withdrew a plastic container filled with some of the apple zucchini sponge cake muffins from the taping. She popped the lid. "Lunch is on me. I rescued a few before the crew scarfed them all down. You want to head to Second or Third to set up surveillance?"

"Second. We can take turns dashing into Starbucks if we need a potty break. I'm not sure what's on Third."

Cloris dropped the remaining muffins back into the shopping bag, and we headed east. Several yards from where Rajat dropped us off, we passed a dark blue Taurus with two men sitting in the front seat. I had the odd sense that they were watching us, but it was hard to tell, given their aviator shades. I don't think Cloris noticed, and I didn't want to spook her, so I kept walking and didn't say anything.

After what I'd been through the past few months, I've developed a heightened sense of paranoia when it comes to anything out of the ordinary, but how unusual is it for a couple of guys to be waiting in a car for someone? Not unusual at all. I shrugged off my newly acquired phobia, took another bite out of my muffin, and continued walking.

For the next hour Cloris and I kept tabs on the brownstone from up the street. Several times a town car pulled up and deposited someone who entered the residence. From our vantage point it was hard to tell much about them other than three appeared to be well-dressed men and one was a rather elegant-looking woman, the kind of people who looked right at home shopping at Barney's or dining at Nobu.

"Time is standing still," said Cloris as she glanced at her watch for what seemed like the hundredth time. "I can't believe we've only been here a little more than an hour. How much longer do you want to wait?"

"Let's give it another ten minutes or so," I suggested. "Maybe it's a meeting of Has-beens Anonymous. If so, they should all be leaving soon."

Cloris agreed, and we split the last remaining muffin. However, before we each took our final bite, a town car pulled up in front of the building. Less than a minute later, one of the men who had arrived shortly after us walked out the front door, stepped into the waiting car and drove off. A second town car pulled up to the curb shortly after the first departed. Five minutes later, Monica exited the brownstone and entered the waiting car.

The dark blue Taurus pulled out and followed Monica's town car down the street.

"Well, that was a huge waste of time," said Cloris.

"Maybe not." I mentioned the guys in the dark blue Taurus.

"You think they're following Monica?"

"Sure looks that way. Don't you think it's pretty coincidental that they were parked on the street when we arrived, sat there for over an hour, then left as soon as Monica left?"

Cloris mulled this over for a minute. "Maybe the police aren't buying Ray's alibis after all."

"And they're watching Monica for the same reason we followed her."

"So what do you think she was doing in that brownstone for over an hour?"

I shrugged. "For all we know, that's her agent's office."

"Do agents hire town cars to pick up and deliver their clients?" Cloris didn't wait for me to answer, not that I would know one way or another, but neither would she. "Maybe if the clients are Brad Pitt and Angelina Jolie," she continued, "but Monica? I don't think so."

"Does seem rather unlikely. Maybe it's one of those exclusive day spas, and she set up an emergency appointment to have a chipped nail repaired."

"I suppose we could walk up and ring the bell. See exactly what kind of business goes on there."

"Suppose you don't."

Cloris and I spun around to find a very annoyed looking Detective Marlowe glaring at us.

"This can't be coincidence," I said. "How did you know we were here."

"I think you're smart enough to figure that out, Mrs. Pollack."

"The guys in the Taurus called you?"

"Bingo. Now get lost and leave the police work to the professionals. I don't need Cagney and Lacey wannabes fucking up two major police investigations."

Cagney and Lacey? Marlowe was older than I thought. That show went off the air when I was still a teen. However, something else he said triggered my curious gene. "*Two* major investigations? You mean there's more than murder going on here?"

Marlowe flushed an unflattering shade of red. Apparently, he'd accidently spilled some beans from his jar of closely guarded police secrets. "Get the hell out of here before I lock you both up for impeding an investigation," he said behind gritted teeth.

When given the choice between lock-up or a swift departure, there really is no choice. Cloris and I didn't even bother with a *yes, sir* response. We spun around and race-walked as fast as we could down the block toward Third Ave.

But all the way home I wondered what else was going on.

———

Since I saw little point in driving to the magazine after arriving home shortly before the start of rush hour, I figured I might as well not even bother. After the last few days, I deserved a moment or three to myself. The boys weren't home from baseball practice yet. I had no idea where Mama or Lucille were and didn't care. Ralph was in his cage, Catherine the Great was sunning herself in the living room bay window, and Mephisto was snoring on Lucille's bed. If I were lucky, I'd have just enough time to put my feet up on the back porch and sip a glass of wine before chaos once again reigned at *Casa Pollack*.

Too bad I didn't have any Merlot. Or Shiraz. Or Pinot Noir. I thought about searching through Lucille's drawers and under her bed. Chances were good she had another bottle or two stashed somewhere, but I didn't want to run the risk of waking Devil Dog. No way was I giving up precious *me* time to march up and down the sidewalk, pooper-scooper in hand, while that picky canine searched out the perfect place to make his doggie deposit.

So after tossing in a load of wash, I microwaved a cup of coffee left over from breakfast. I was about to take my second sip when Zack's silver Porsche Boxster rolled down the driveway.

He waved as he killed the engine and jumped out. Returning the wave, I watched—no, I stared like a star-struck teeny-bopper at a Justin Bieber concert—as he retrieved his overnight bag and camera case from the trunk. Where is the justice? No man, especially one in his mid-forties, has the right to look that damn good in a pair of jeans.

"Coffee?" I called, hoping I sounded more neighborly than desperate for adult male conversation.

"Thanks, but after a trip from Hell, I need something much stronger. Got any bourbon?"

"Sorry. Not even a bottle of outdated light beer."

"Then the drinks are on me." Bags in hand, he bounded up the stairs to his apartment.

A minute later he returned with two ice-filled glasses and a bottle of Maker's Mark. As he poured, I questioned him about his trip. "Flight problems?"

"People problems." We both took a sip before he continued. "Security breach in Chicago. TSA shut down the terminal for three hours while they searched for the guy. Then they first had to re-screen everyone."

I took another sip, trying to remember the last time I'd had hard liquor. I couldn't. Which could just mean that the first sip had already started working on me. I'm such a cheap date. "Life in the new millennium." I said.

"Sucks, doesn't it?"

I shrugged. "Life in general sucks, in case you haven't noticed."

Zack eyed me over the rim of his glass. "More of the same or something new?"

I caught him up on events since I'd last spoken with him, forgetting until halfway through that he'd warned me to leave the detecting to the detectives. Too late now. I plowed ahead as Zack's features grew tighter and tighter. "With Vince out of the picture, Monica and Ray are the likeliest suspects. Monica's hiding something. I'm sure of it. Especially after Marlowe showed up at our stakeout."

I took another sip of bourbon, held my breath, and forced myself to make eye contact with Zack. Why did I feel like I'd just been caught cutting class?

He didn't speak for the longest time, just shook his head and looked at me with those Paul Newman blue eyes of his. "I may regret this," he finally said.

"Regret what?"

"I have connections."

"Good guy connections or bad guy connections?"

His eyebrows shot up.

"Hey, this is New Jersey. You never know."

"Good guy connections. In New York. I'll see what I can find out if—"

I knew what was coming. "If I promise to keep my nose out of police business?"

"Think of your kids, Anastasia. They've already lost their father. Now their mother is sticking her nose into a killer's business. You're untrained and unarmed. Do you really want your mother and mother-in-law raising those boys?"

"Seemed like a good idea at the time," I mumbled. Then clarified, "The detecting, not Mama and Lucille raising Nick and Alex." However, I really had no defense. I'd acted irresponsibly and downright dangerously. Not to mention stupidly.

"I never used to be like this," I said. "Ask anyone. It's all Karl's fault."

"Karl?"

"AKA Dead Louse of a Spouse?"

"Right. Karl. He's dead. How's this his fault?"

"I never would have been forced to start acting like Jessica Fletcher if he hadn't screwed his bookie, not to mention me and our kids."

"That was three months ago, and the bookie's behind bars."

I shrugged. "Once you unleash the sleuthing genie, she digs in her heels."

"Then I suggest you find a way to shove her back into her bottle and cork it good and tight before you find yourself in a situation you can't craft your way out of."

"Point taken," I conceded.

FOURTEEN

KARL USED TO CALL me a cheap date because more than one cocktail or glass of wine usually puts me to sleep. Several hours earlier I had polished off enough of Zack's Maker's Mark to give Rip Van Winkle a run for his money. I should have been out cold, yet at one in the morning I was still wide awake. My brain refused to shut down, hammering me with questions when I should have been deep in Slumberville.

I decided that rather than toss and turn and stare at the alarm clock for the next five and a half hours, I might as well get up and get some work done. Since I'd pay for my lack of sleep tomorrow—correction, later today, given the hour—I might at least have something to show for pulling an all-nighter other than a rumpled bed.

I donned my robe and slippers and padded down to the basement. Naomi wanted crafts projects for the magazine that tied into the television show but didn't duplicate the crafts presented on the show. String dolls seemed a logical off-shoot of mop dolls.

Because the show schedule and the magazine production schedule weren't in synch yet, along with everything else we editors were juggling, we also had to scramble to revise magazine issues already in various stages of production. Luckily, *American Woman* featured a Christmas All Year Round column where I showcased a Christmas craft project in each issue. This made it relatively easy for me to swap out the ornament scheduled for the September issue with an angel string doll ornament.

As I mindlessly assembled the materials and tools I'd need from my cache of supplies, my mind focused on questions that had nothing to do with dolls of any sort: Had Lou been a multimillionaire, a con artist, or just a cheap son-of-a-bitch looking to screw his ex-wives out of their alimony? Who sent Lou that cryptic note, and what did it mean? What was on Vince's computer that he'd rather go to jail than hand over? Who did Monica visit in that Kips Bay brownstone, and did it have anything to do with the murders? Why were the cops following her? What was the other investigation Marlowe let slip? I couldn't make sense out of any of it. The only thing I was certain about was that a killer was still on the loose. A killer who might have his or her sights set on the *American Woman* editors. Or Mama.

ANGEL STRING DOLL ORNAMENT

Materials: 24 yds. white/silver crochet cotton, small amount of white crochet cotton, 18mm painted wood head bead, ½ yd. each ⅛" wide red and green satin ribbon, three miniature red silk poinsettias, 12" silver chenille stem, 5" x 5" piece of cardboard, tacky glue or glue gun, scissors.

Directions: Cut three 10" pieces of white/silver crochet cotton and set aside. For the body, wrap white/silver crochet cotton around the cardboard 70 times. Tie at one end with one of the 10" pieces of crochet cotton. Cut through all the lengths of crochet cotton at the opposite end.

Thread the loose ends from the body tie through the bead head. Apply a dab of glue to the bottom of the bead head to secure the head to the body. Tie the ends into a knot at the top of the head. Tie another knot close to the cut ends to form a hanging loop.

For the arms, wrap white/silver crochet cotton around the cardboard 12 times. Cut open at one end. Cut the second piece of 10" crochet cotton in half. Use one half to tie off one end of the arm ½" from the cut edge. Braid the lengths for 5" from the tied edge. Tie off the braid with the second 5" piece of crochet cotton. Trim the arm ends ½" from the tie.

Place the braid centered in the middle of the body. Using the remaining 10" piece of crochet cotton, tie the body under the arms.

For hair, cut 1" lengths of white crochet cotton. Fold in half. Glue the cut ends to the top of the bead head for looped bangs. For the remainder of the hair, cut 3" lengths of white crochet cotton. Glue in the same manner around the sides and back of the head, working in even rows from the neck up to the crown.

Fold the chenille stem into a sideways figure 8. Bend the loops up slightly. Tie the chenille stem to the center back of the angel with a piece of white/silver crochet cotton. Secure in place with a dab of glue.

Make a small bow from the green ribbon. Glue under the bead head at neck. Make a small bow from the red ribbon. Glue to the top of the head.

Twist the poinsettias into a bouquet. Glue the arms around the bouquet. Tie the remaining ribbon together into a bow with long streamers. Glue the bow under the flowers.

I crafted a dozen angel string dolls in three different color combinations, using white/silver crochet cotton and a silver chenille stem for four, red/white/green variegated crochet cotton and a red metallic chenille stem for a second group of four, and white/gold crochet cotton with a gold chenille stem for the remaining four. My fingers worked from rote while my mind dwelled on murder. Several hours later I was still wide awake, my angels finished but my head no closer to puzzling out who had killed Lou and Vince or why.

I padded back to my bedroom, took a shower, and dressed for work. The clock read 4:38. I sat down at my computer, typed up the directions for the string dolls, and transferred them onto a jump drive. I checked the clock again. 5:10.

Still wide awake, I headed for the kitchen, dragged out the crock pot, and prepared a slow cook meal for dinner. 5:43. I grabbed eggs from the fridge and whipped up one of Cloris's quiche recipes for breakfast.

6:12. Quiche in oven. Coffee made. Dinner cooking. Murder still unsolved.

"Yo, Mom! Wake up!"

My eyelids sprang open. I lifted my head to find myself staring at a perplexed looking Alex. In the kitchen. Totally disoriented, I tried to find my bearings, but an incessant *beep, beep, beep* kept me from focusing on the here and now.

"You want that out of the oven?" he asked. "It smells like it's done."

"What?" I yawned, filling my lungs and brain with much needed oxygen. Slowly, very slowly, both last night and my senses came back to me. Especially my sense of smell. I turned toward the stove. The clock read 6:52.

The quiche!

I jumped up, donned a pair of oven mitts, and pulled the slightly scorched quiche from the oven. "Breakfast's ready," I said.

"You okay, Mom?"

"Sure. I couldn't sleep last night. Guess it finally caught up with me."

Did it ever! Middle-aged moms definitely shouldn't fall asleep at the kitchen table. Face planted on a bamboo placemat. I gingerly touched my embossed cheek. My shoulder screamed four letter words at me. Every other body part chimed in with a rousing chorus of profanity.

Alex was giving me one of those *Who are you and what have you done with my mother?* looks.

I chose to ignore him. "Tell your brother breakfast is ready."

"Nick! Breakfast!" he shouted.

"I could have done that." Actually, maybe not. Right now forming words in my brain, then moving them from my vocal chords and past my lips, was taking Herculean effort. Raising my voice to shouting level? Way too much work.

Alex set a glass of orange juice on the table for me. I gulped down the rush of sugary vitamin C.

"Coffee?" he asked.

I held out my arm. "Intravenously." How the hell was I going to get to work, let alone get through the day?

Three cups of coffee and a huge helping of protein-rich quiche later, I headed back to my bedroom, stripped, and stepped into an icy cold shower. If that didn't wake me up, nothing would.

Twenty minutes later I sent up a prayer to the Goddess of Over-Stressed Single Parents as I slid behind the wheel of my Hyundai. Thankfully, she heard me because I managed to arrive at work on time and in one piece, albeit with still wet hair.

"You look like drowned shit," said Cloris as I passed her in the hall.

"Would you believe that's a compliment, given the way I feel?"

She pulled me into the break room and poured me a cup of coffee. "Something happen last night?"

"Actually, it was a very productive night." In between yawns and gulps of coffee, I caught her up on my insomniac exploits.

My cell rang as I was finishing my Tale of the Sleepless Night. I checked the display. Zack. "Hi, Zack."

"Can you talk?"

"Sure."

"I mean in private."

"I'm in the break room with Cloris. What's up?"

"Find someplace where you won't be overheard by anyone, then call me back." He disconnected. I pushed *End Call.*

"That was short," said Cloris. "Everything okay?"

"I'm not sure. Zack wants me to call him back where no one can overhear me."

"Sounds very cloak and dagger. Are you sure he's not really a spy? Maybe the photography gig is his cover."

I suppose anything was possible. The man did jet all around the world, sometimes at a moment's notice. And he did mention having *connections.* How many freelance photo-journalists who worked for *National Geographic* and the World Wildlife Federation had the sort of connections that gave them access to NYPD murder investigations?

The one place I was guaranteed not to run into anyone else was my Models Room. Really more of a windowless walk-in closet, the Models Room housed finished craft projects and photo props from past, current, and future *American Woman* issues, along with new product samples sent by manufacturers. Cloris receives champagne truffles; Nicole, the latest products from Bobbi Brown and Chanel; Tessa, all sorts of designer swag. Me? I get pompoms and embroidery floss.

Freebie envy aside, though, entering my Models Room used to fill me with both a sense of accomplishment and bring out the little kid in me. It now filled me with a sense of dread—ever since three months ago when Ricardo stepped out of that room and pulled a gun on me.

I walked down the hall and took a deep breath before reaching for the knob. Once inside, overhead light on, door closed and latched behind me, I returned Zack's call.

"Are you sure no one can overhear you?" he asked.

"I'm positive." But all the same I kept my voice just above a whisper. "Why all the secrecy?"

"First, you have to promise you won't breathe a word of what I'm about to tell you to anyone."

"You're creeping me out, Zack."

"Promise?"

"I promise. You want me to cross my heart or something? Spit on my palm? Swear on my father's grave?"

"Not necessary. I believe you're a woman of your word."

"Thanks for the vote of confidence. Now, spill."

"Let me ask you something," he said. "Who told you Vince Alto was dead?"

"Marlowe. He said Vince was found in an alley, his head bashed in with a brick. It was also in the papers and on the news."

"That he was found in an alley with his head bashed in?"

"That's what I just said." I knew I wasn't operating on all cylinders this morning, but I was awake enough to realize this conversation was going around in a great big non-productive circle. "What's going on, Zack?"

"Vince Alto isn't dead."

Huh? "Okay, run that by me once more because I could swear you just said Vince isn't dead."

"That's what I said. He's in a coma. Apparently, the cops want everyone to believe he's dead."

"How can they keep something like that a secret? Whether on purpose or accidentally, someone at the hospital is bound to let it slip."

"He's in the prison hospital at Rikers."

"Vince is in jail? Why? He can't be a suspect in Lou's murder if the killer tried to kill him, too."

"The cops found tons of kiddie porn on his computer. Really sick stuff."

So that's why Vince put up such a stink when Marlowe subpoenaed his laptop. I wasn't surprised. Vince came across as the slimiest of slime bags. The man made my skin crawl. Now I knew why. Still, the entire sequence of events all seemed too orchestrated. "I think someone set Vince up," I said.

"You think someone planted the kiddie porn on his computer? Not according to my source. The computer forensics show a damning trail pointing directly to Vince."

"Oh, I'm sure the kiddie porn is his. I think someone else knew about his sick predilection and sent that bogus e-mail from him to Monica."

"Knowing the cops would subpoena his laptop."

"And that *someone* has to be the killer. What better way to misdirect the murder investigation away from yourself than set someone else up for the crime?"

"I'm sure the police are considering that angle," said Zack.

"According to your source? Just who is your source, Zack? Wait. Don't tell me. Let me guess. You can't reveal your source, right?"

"Something like that."

"Cloris thinks you're CIA and the photo-journalism gig is your cover."

"Cloris has a vivid imagination."

"Are you?"

"Am I what?"

"CIA or something."

Zack laughed. "We're all *something*, Anastasia. Listen, I've gotta go. I'll see you later."

With that he disconnected, having neither admitted nor denied the supposition. Maybe Cloris's imagination wasn't all that vivid after all.

That made me wonder. If Zack really did lead a double life, was having him live above my garage a good thing or a bad thing? Did it place my family in danger, or provide us with an added amount of safety and security?

I thought about how Zack had come to my aid, helping me secure my home, installing surveillance equipment, after the Ricardo incident. However, Zack's tale of being captured in Guatemala also came to mind. Maybe documenting native tribal costumes for *National Geographic* had merely been his cover. Maybe he hadn't *accidently* stumbled upon that pot farm but had been sent specifically to hunt down villages that had switched from growing corn to growing something far more lucrative.

If Guatemalan drug lords were anything like Mexican drug lords, were we all in danger thanks to my too-sexy-for-his-own-good tenant? After all, a significant number of Guatemalan immigrants lived in New Jersey. Any number of them could be part of that Guatemalan drug pipeline.

For all I knew, Zack had a price on his head. That meant none of us was safe. I didn't care what sort of security clearance the government required for Zack to divulge his true occupation. He'd damn well better come clean to me. I had my kids and Mama to think of, as Zack so often reminded me.

————

As soon as I returned home that night, I jotted a note and taped it to Zack's door. *Need to see you ASAP. A.* Then I waited. And waited. And waited. By ten o'clock I could no longer keep my eyes open. I opened the back door and stepped out onto the porch. No lights on in Zack's apartment. No silver Porsche Boxster parked in the driveway.

I returned to the kitchen and called his cell.

This is Zachary Barnes. If I'm not answering, I'm probably on a plane to somewhere or already there and out of satellite range. Leave a message, and I'll return your call as soon as possible, which could be anywhere from a few minutes to a few months.

Great. I hung up without leaving a message.

FIFTEEN

For the next two days I obsessed about Guatemalan hit squads, even though I so didn't need another obsession taking over my life. Obsessing about my lack of money, mountain of debt, looming college tuition, and whether or not Lou's killer had his sights set on Mama or me should have been enough obsession for any one person. Whoever doled out obsessions needed to start picking on someone else. The last thing I needed was worrying about some machete-wielding maniac out to revenge his brother/cousin/uncle/warlord back in the hills of Guatemala, while the cause of that obsession was out gallivanting who-knew-where doing who-knew-what.

By the time Zack arrived home late Friday afternoon, I'd obsessed myself into a frenzy of unprecedented histrionic proportion. Lack of sleep—due to said obsessing—and a case of PMS to end all PMS had contributed to my Crazy Lady transformation which I unleashed on an unsuspecting Zachary Barnes the moment he pulled into the driveway and parked his car.

"You and I need to talk," I screamed, not caring whether the neighbors heard me. Hell, people clear across town probably heard me.

"I want answers, and I don't care what sort of government clearance I need. You're not putting my kids in danger. I won't allow it." I shook with rage. Tears rushed down my cheeks. "You tell me the truth, Zack. You tell me now. Or you can pack up and clear out this minute."

I don't know what I expected after that tirade, but it certainly wasn't what happened next. Zack closed the gap between us in one long stride and wrapped me in his arms.

"I'll tell you whatever you want to know. Just take a deep breath and calm down. No one is going to hurt you or the boys. I promise."

I gulped air and tried to stop crying, but the damn dam had burst, and the tears wouldn't let up. Deep in the back of my mind I realized I was in the throes of a full-fledged panic attack, but rational Anastasia had fled the scene, leaving a bundle of raw emotion in her place.

Yet in another recess of my emotion-soaked brain it suddenly occurred to me that having Zack's arms wrapped around me felt incredibly wonderful. My PMS-rampaging hormones began to mellow. One by one they sighed in contentment. Even though my tears continued to flow, they now spilled forth for an entirely different reason.

Zack's reaction to my meltdown gobsmacked me with the reality of my life. I was lonely. I was hurt. I was damn angry. And it was all Karl's fault. Even the Guatemalan hit squad.

Without Karl's deceit, I would have had no need to rent out the apartment over the garage. I'd still be using it for my studio. I never would have met Zack, and I wouldn't now be worrying about Guatemalan hit squads coming after me and my family. Even in death Karl had found a way to continue screwing me.

While my mind was placing blame on Karl, Zack led me upstairs, unlocked his door, and sat me down on his sofa. My anger at Karl settled my sobs, although the tears continued to fall silently, splashing onto my lap. I swiped at my eyes, trying to stem the tide, but I had little success.

This was the first time I'd allowed myself to cry since Dead Louse of a Spouse had died. From time to time I'd well up, especially in the first few weeks as my life devolved from American Dream to Teeming Landfill of Shit, but anger had kept the tears at bay. No longer.

"Here. Drink this," said Zack.

He held a glass of something dark and rich looking and most likely alcoholic in front of me. I reached for it. "Will it help?"

He shrugged. "Can't hurt. Drink up."

I did as I was told, taking a tentative sip at first. Cognac. Zack held an open bottle of Remy Martin in his other hand. My tears abated; my anger returned. "You live above a garage but drink cognac that costs more than my weekly supermarket bill? Who the hell are you?"

"Ah, we're back to that." Zack poured himself a glass of the cognac and sat down beside me.

I gulped down the remainder in my glass, letting the burn reinforce my anger. Slamming the glass onto the coffee table, I twisted to face him. "Damn right. You owe me some answers."

He refilled my glass. "Sip. Don't gulp."

Damn him. "I'll gulp if I want." I picked up the glass and polished the cognac off in one chug. The jolt skyrocketed straight to my head. Damn. Why was I acting so peevish?

Zack shook his head. "Maybe we should talk before you get too drunk to hear anything."

That jolt had reinforced my peevishness. I picked up the bottle and poured more into my glass. "Maybe I need to get drunk. It will help me forget."

Zack grabbed both my glass and the bottle. "That's not going to solve anything."

I grabbed the glass back. "Says who?"

"Forget what?"

"Huh?"

"See, you're already having trouble following. What are you trying to forget?"

"Oh, that." I waved away my confusion with another long swallow. "Everything. Karl. Bills. Guatemalan hit squads—"

"Guatemalan hit squads?"

"Don't play dumb with me, Zack. I figured it all out. Cloris was right. You are CIA or something. You didn't go down to Guatemala to shoot a spread about inda ... inde ... indig—." Oh hell. I couldn't even get the word out. At least, the cognac was working.

"Indigenous?" he offered.

"Right. That. Whatever. Native costumes. That was only your cover. You went to flush out pot farms and disrupt a drug pipeline. And now they're probably after you, and that puts me and my kids and Mama in harm's way.

"And what about that voicemail of yours? Who goes off where they can't be reached for months at a time? No photo-journalist I've ever known. Only spies and Special Forces and Navy SEALS. You lied to me. You men are all alike. Karl. Lou. You. All liars."

"Really? How many photo-journalists have you known?" he asked. "Not to mention Special Forces and Navy SEALS."

"None. But that's besides the point. No one is out of communication these days unless they choose to be. Even the astronauts up in the International Space Station make and receive calls."

With that last bit of information my steam ran out. I started crying again, all the more so because Zack hadn't denied anything I said. Through my tears, I watched him get up and walk into the bathroom. He returned shortly and placed a wet washcloth on the back of my neck.

"You've been keeping a hell of a lot bottled up for the past three months," he said. "Cry as much as you need to. Then we'll talk." He strode across the room and opened the door.

"Where are you going?"

"To let Alex and Nick know where you are. Have they had dinner yet?"

I shook my head. "I'm a lousy mother."

"You're a great mother, just scared and overwhelmed. Had you planned anything?"

"Chicken. In the fridge. Needs to go on the grill."

"I'll take care of it."

I gulped back a huge sob. "Why are you being so nice to me?"

"Somebody has to." With that he was out the door.

———

I woke to a full bladder and the sound of chirping birds. I had no memory of how I got into bed. No memory of anything beyond Zack leaving to cook dinner for my kids. Zack! Talk about recall remorse. One minute I'm blubbering all over the man; the next minute I'm screaming at him like a half-cocked banshee. Pathetic! Maybe if I kept my eyes closed, I'd never have to face him again.

Unfortunately, my bladder had a different agenda. I tossed off the quilt and rolled over—right into an upholstered barrier. My eyes sprang open. This wasn't my bed. This wasn't even my house.

"Good morning," said an all too familiar voice. "Coffee will be ready shortly."

"What time is it?" I asked, stretching the kinks out of my body. Forty-two-year-old women should not spend the night on a couch. I ached in places I didn't even know could have aches.

"Nearly six."

"What? I slept twelve hours?"

"I don't think—"

"Hold that thought." I raced to the bathroom, hoping I made it before my bladder gave out.

When I returned, Zack continued, "As I was saying, I don't think a ten on the Richter scale would have woken you. Around eleven I removed your shoes, tossed a blanket over you, and went to bed."

He handed me a cup of coffee, and I polished off half before speaking. "I can't remember the last time I slept twelve hours. Hell, I can't remember the last time I slept for five uninterrupted hours."

I noted Zack had already dressed for the day and that a packed duffle stood by the door. "Another trip?"

"I haven't had time to unpack."

185

"Where were you the last few days."

"D.C."

"D.C.? As in home of Spies R Us?"

"As in headquarters of *National Geographic*," he said. "I'm not a spy, and there are no Guatemalan hit squads after me. Where did you ever get that idea?"

I tried to explain the convoluted path to my hysteria, but my explanation sounded irrational and lame, even to me. Still, was the idea really that farfetched? Finally, I just said, "How do I know you're telling me the truth? It's not like I can call the government and ask if they have a spy named Zachary Barnes on their payroll."

"I guess you're just going to have to trust me."

"I trusted Karl. Look where that got me."

"Point taken, but I'm not Karl."

"Point taken. Will you at least tell me how you found out about Vince?"

"If I do, you're going to owe me big time."

"I already owe you. Who is it?"

"My ex-wife."

"How—?"

"She's with the Manhattan D.A.'s office, and she could get into a hell of a lot of trouble if word got out that she discussed an ongoing investigation with me. That's why I got all cloak and dagger with you and why you can't breathe a word of what I told you to anyone. Okay?"

I nodded. "So you're really not a spy? The photo-journalism isn't a cover?"

Zack pointed to the bookcases across the room. "Feel free to check out my work from my first published spread over twenty years ago to the latest issue of *National Geographic*.

"I'm really a photo-journalist, Anastasia. I've never wanted to do anything else. I've never been a spy, and I have no plans to change my career now or ever." He paused while this sank in. "Are we cool?"

"We're cool. Can you forgive me for being such an irrational idiot?"

"Already forgotten." He flashed one of his sexy Zack smiles, and I couldn't help but wonder what the hell was wrong with his ex-wife that she let such a great guy get away.

When I rented the apartment to Zack, I had expected a tenant I'd rarely see, given his work schedule. I never anticipated the man would insinuate himself into my life the way he had in such a short time.

"The least I can do is make you breakfast," I said, needing to put some space between us. "Give me a few minutes to shower. I'll leave the back door open for you."

With that I ducked out of his apartment. My hormones had started raging again the moment the man smiled at me, and this time PMS had nothing to do with it. The shower I planned for myself wouldn't be including any water from the hot water faucet.

SIXTEEN

AFTER MY LIBIDO-SQUELCHING COLD shower, I threw on a pair of jeans and a faded *Defy Gravity* T-shirt from back before my life had ended up in the crapper and I used to enjoy attending a Broadway show at least once a month. Sadly, theater-going had gone the way of every other luxury. Broadway? Hell, I couldn't even afford a ticket to a third-rate community theater production.

With that sober thought, I headed to the kitchen to whip up an enormous stack of pancakes. Everyone else was still asleep, but I knew they'd be clamoring for breakfast soon. Alex and Nick had a baseball game today, and I'd promised Mama I'd take her to the Tiffany's up at Short Hills Mall.

Mama needed to get Cleveland appraised for the insurance company since I hadn't been able to find a receipt anywhere in Lou's desk. Either he was one of those guys who never saved receipts, or he'd left it in his desk at work. Frankly, I'd rather pay for the appraisal out of my own pauper's pocket than explain to Sheri why I needed to rifle through Lou's office.

Of course, after meeting Lou's ex-wives at his funeral, I also had my doubts as to whether Lou had actually purchased the ring at Tiffany's, even if I had seen his latest stock statement. Something definitely wasn't Kosher on that front. His ex-wives claimed the guy was broke and hadn't paid alimony in ages, but his investments portfolio stated otherwise.

Either way, the possibility existed that the only genuine Tiffany owned by Mama was that signature robin's egg blue box. I only hoped for her sake that Cleveland was indeed the real deal, even if a second-rate diamond, and not *faux*.

Zack walked in just as I cracked the last egg into the flour and our resident Shakespearian scholar squawked his daily wake-up greeting. "*I am so hungry, that if I might have a lease of my life for a thousand years I could stay no longer. Henry the Sixth, Part Two*. Act Four, Scene Ten."

"Hell hath no fury like a food-deprived parrot," I said, turning on the mixer and handing Zack a spatula. "Would you mind while I feed the ruler of the roost?"

Zack grabbed the spatula and stood over the mixer while I filled a water bottle and scooped bird seed into a clean bowl. I had learned shortly after Ralph came to live with us that when the bird wanted his breakfast, *now* wasn't soon enough. Ralph had no patience for waiting while I collected his empties, cleaned the containers, and refilled them. He expected me, his servant, to arrive with sustenance in hand.

When I returned to the kitchen, Zack was dropping the first ladle of batter onto the hot griddle. "Hey, I thought I was making you breakfast."

I took over pancake duty while he poured us each a cup of coffee and began to set the table. One by one the rest of the household woke up and wandered into the kitchen.

Lucille arrived first, Mephisto in tow. "You again," she said to Zack as she sat down and waited to be waited on. Then she turned to me. "Some example you're setting for my grandsons the way you dishonor your husband's memory."

"Good morning to you, too, Lucille," I said, slapping a plate of pancakes in front of her.

She grunted. I didn't fool myself into believing the grunt represented a thank you, but I took the high road anyway. One of us had to act like an adult. I pasted on a smile and said, "You're welcome."

She ignored me, choosing instead to tear off a corner of pancake and feed it to Devil Dog.

"Maybe you should stop being so accommodating," suggested Zack. He grabbed Lucille's plate out from in front of her. "Good morning, Lucille."

"How dare you! Give me back my plate!"

"Good morning, Lucille," he repeated.

Ralph swooped into the kitchen at that moment and took up residence on top of the refrigerator. "*Have I thought long to see this morning's face, and doth it give me such a sight as this?*" he squawked. "*Romeo and Juliet.* Act Four, Scene Five."

Lucille shot Ralph one of her evil-eyed glares and sent a second one Zack's way.

"Right on, Ralph," I mumbled to myself, trying to keep from laughing out loud. I don't know how he did it, but Ralph never failed to amaze me with his situation-appropriate quotes.

Zack ignored Ralph (how, I'll never know) and kept his voice calm. "Good morning, Lucille."

I suppose she finally decided winning the battle of wills wasn't worth the spoils of cold pancakes. "G'morning," she muttered through clenched teeth.

Zack returned her plate and turned to me. "See? All she needs is a bit of training."

"Great. I'll add it to my to-do list."

"Stop talking about me behind my back," said the chore in question.

Alex and Nick arrived next. "Morning, Mom," they said in unison. They sandwiched me between them and each gave me a peck on the cheek.

"Have an enjoyable night?" asked Nick in a sing-song voice. "You're looking very sat—"

"Get your minds out of the gutter!" I snapped at them.

"We're not little kids," said Nick.

"You don't have to pretend for our sake," added Alex. "We're totally cool with you and Zack hooking up."

"We did not hook up!" I turned to the hunk in question. He had a bemused expression plastered across his face. "Would you please set my sons straight? They're obviously not going to believe a word I say."

"Nothing happened, guys. Your mother fell asleep on my sofa and slept for twelve hours. I think you owe her an apology."

"Likely story," muttered Lucille.

Nick shrugged. "Sure. If that's the way you want to play this. Sorry, mom."

"Yeah, sorry," said Alex.

Neither of them could hide their smirks, and Alex gave Zack one of those guy shoulder punches as he headed for his seat at the kitchen table. I slammed a plate of pancakes in front of him. "We're not *playing* anything. Eat your breakfast."

"Playing what?" asked Mama as she entered the kitchen.

"Mom spent the night at Zack's," said Nick.

"Well, it's about time!" said Mama. "I was beginning to wonder what was the matter with the two of you."

I didn't know whether to laugh or cry. I turned to Zack for support, but all he did was shrug.

From the top of the refrigerator Ralph added his two cents, "*The lady doth protest too much, methinks. Hamlet.* Act Three, Scene Two."

"Traitor," I said.

Having wolfed down her pancakes, Lucille hoisted herself out of her chair and shuffled out of the kitchen. God forbid she bother to place her dirty dishes in the sink.

"That does it," said Mama. "I'm petitioning the Pope. You deserve sainthood, dear."

"We're not Catholic," I reminded her. "Besides, I'm still very much alive and planning to stay that way for quite some time to come."

"I certainly hope so," said Mama, totally ignoring the part about us not being Catholic. "Although if anyone could drive someone into an early grave, it's that pinko battle axe."

———

An hour later, Zack had departed for his apartment, and the boys and Mama were dressed for the day, Mama in one of her classic Chanel summer suits—apricot with white piping—and the boys in their baseball uniforms. I remained in *Defy Gravity* and my jeans since I was merely the chauffeur.

After dropping Alex and Nick at the ball field, Mama and I headed up to Short Hills. I hadn't been to the Short Hills Mall since Batswin and Robbins coerced me into a sting operation meant to nab Ricardo. The sting failed big time. That day my life got a whole lot worse before it got any better. Not that my life was anything near a bed of roses at the moment, but at least Ricardo continued to reside in barred and razor-wired accommodations provided by the federal government.

Aside from reminding me of Ricardo, the Short Hills Mall dredged up memories of a life no longer mine. Not that I shopped often at the upscale stores that comprised the mall, but I had shopped there once in awhile. I've since gone from an occasional splurge at Bloomingdale's to being a regular at Wal-Mart.

As I pulled into the parking garage, I wondered if after Mama's visit to Tiffany's, I'd be adding another line item to my *Reasons For Not Shopping At Short Hills Mall* list. I kept my reservations to myself, though. If needed, I'd be there to support and comfort Mama, but I wasn't about to fill her head with anxiety over my suspicions concerning Cleveland when I might be wrong.

After all, Mama knew more about diamonds than I did, and as far as she was concerned Cleveland was the real deal. Karl had never given me a diamond engagement ring. He thought we should use the money he'd spend on a ring for a down payment on a house.

Practical me agreed. Now I wish I hadn't been so practical. If I had my own mini-Cleveland, I could hock it and pay off a lot of Karl-induced debt.

I parked the car, and Mama and I headed for Tiffany's. "I'll wait for you over there," I said, pointing to the chairs and tables set out in front of the Nordstrom coffee bar. Did I dare splurge and treat myself to a four-dollar latte?

"I'm sure I won't be long, dear."

Mama headed into Tiffany's, and I headed for the coffee bar. Hell, four dollars wouldn't mean the difference between solvency and bankruptcy. I'd lived like a monk for three months. After all I'd been through—and was still going through—didn't I deserve a four-dollar indulgence? After all, it's not like I was walking into Georgette Klinger for a spa day.

I purchased a caramel latte and sat down at one of the wrought iron ice cream tables to enjoy my decadent purchase. I hadn't taken more than three sips when Mama came storming out of Tiffany's.

Damn. I'd really hoped I was wrong about Cleveland, but the expression on Mama's face told me otherwise. She yanked out the chair opposite me and sat down. Instead of being on the verge of tears, anger colored her a frightening shade of red that clashed with her apricot suit. Her lips tightly clenched, her hands balled into fists, she didn't say a word. I waited for her to gain control.

After about a minute, she took a deep breath, and the muscles in her face relaxed enough for her to speak. "That man!" She yanked Cleveland off her finger and slammed it onto the table. "And to think I believed him. 'Don't worry about anything, Flora.

I'll take care of you, Flora. You're my delicate flower, Flora.' Bullshit. All of it. Thank God I didn't marry him."

I picked Cleveland up and studied the ring. It certainly sparkled like a real diamond. If fakes could look as real as real, what made diamonds so damned expensive in the first place? "What did Tiffany's say, Mama?"

"That Lou certainly didn't buy my ring from them because they'd never sell a ring of such poor quality."

"So it's still a diamond? Not a fake?"

Mama snorted a loud *harrumph*. "A seriously *flawed* diamond. I looked at the stone through a jeweler's loupe. My diamond is full of inclusions. The gemologist said stones like this are only sold at discount stores. Discount stores! The man bought me a Wal-Mart diamond and stuck it in a Tiffany box! If someone hadn't already killed the cheap weasel, I'd do it myself."

"I'm sorry, Mama."

"Don't be," she said. "It's Karma. What I get for almost marrying a man I didn't love."

"You had the best of intentions."

"Of course, I did, dear. And I guess it all worked out in the end. Had I married him, I'd have been stuck with him."

Given Mama's track record, I seriously doubted that, but if Lou—and I noticed she no longer called him *poor Lou*—had lied to Mama about his net worth and really didn't have much money, what would have happened had he lost his job? The last thing I needed in my life was another mooching relative. I guess *poor Lou* really had been *poor* Lou.

That didn't explain his stock statement, though. I saw the figures. All eight of them lined up to the left of the decimal point alongside the words *Total Assets*. If Lou had that kind of money, why had he bought Mama a bargain basement diamond?

Mama picked up the ring and with a loud sigh, placed it back on her finger. "The jeweler said with all the inclusions, it's probably not worth more than a few thousand dollars. At least that will make a small dent in your bills, dear."

"Mama, the ring is yours. You don't have to sell it to help me get out of debt."

"I don't want the ring. It's a reminder that I nearly married a con artist. One of those in the family was more than enough. Whatever I get for it is yours. Consider it rent for the many times you put me up."

Although I hadn't thought of Karl as a con artist, I suppose that's exactly what he'd been. After all, he'd certainly conned me into a false sense of security.

I leaned over and kissed the top of Mama's head. "You're welcome to camp out at *Casa Pollack* any time you want. Don't ever think you've been a burden to me."

"Unlike someone else?"

Now it was my turn to sigh. "I'm afraid I'm stuck with her."

"Why?"

"Really, Mama, I can't throw her out into the street."

"That's only because you're too nice."

"That's me. Anastasia the Nice." And because I was so nice, I offered Mama the rest of my caramel latte. Somehow I'd lost my taste for it.

———

On the way home we got caught in a huge traffic jam as we approached downtown Westfield. I couldn't tell how far the backup went because of the twists and turns of our route, but the road we sat on resembled a parking lot. Nothing was moving, and I had no place to turn off to detour around the mess.

"Must be an accident," I said, turning off the engine to conserve gas.

"A bad one from the looks of things," said Mama.

Every so often the traffic inched along in fits and starts. I'd turn the ignition key, inch up a car length or two, then shut down the engine to wait for the next creep-along session. We eventually made enough progress that I could see traffic being diverted left onto Broad Street. Normally that intersection is a no left turn. Whatever was going on, it must be blocking the T-intersection of Central and Broad, the main intersection in the heart of the downtown district.

Mama began to squirm, and I knew that could only mean one thing. I shouldn't have been so generous with my latte. Mama's bladder waits for no man—even traffic cops.

We were about a dozen cars back from Broad Street when Mama jumped out of the Hyundai. "The nearest restroom will be at Starbucks," I said, knowing where she was headed without having to be told. "I'll meet you at the back entrance."

She nodded, setting off at a brisk pace. I hoped she made it the short distance without suffering a public embarrassment. As I continued to wait in traffic, I once again recited my prayer to the Internal Plumbing Gods, hoping I'd inherited my bladder from another family member and not from Mama.

Mama returned before I'd made it through the detour around whatever was happening. She settled back into the car and said, "I figured you'd still be here when you weren't waiting in the back parking lot. It's not an accident."

"So what's causing the tie-up?"

"I think you're going to have to see this for yourself, dear. I don't want to spoil the impact."

Mama had that Sylvester the Cat look about her, the one he always got after stuffing Tweedy Bird into his mouth. An uneasy feeling settled in the pit of my stomach. "What's that supposed to mean?"

"You'll see."

As we finally neared the intersection, I saw Officer Harley directing traffic. He started to wave the one panel truck and three SUVs ahead of me to turn left, then abruptly put up his hand, stopping the flow. He then pointed to me and signaled me to drive around the truck and SUVs. I hoped none of those vehicles contained people I knew because as I passed them, I sensed some very sharp daggers directed at me.

I drove up alongside Harley. "What's up?"

"You'd better park your car, Mrs. Pollack." He pointed toward Elmer Street. "Pull up behind that squad car."

I knew not to worry that something had happened to Alex or Nick because no way would Mama sport such a satisfied look on her face. Her grandchildren meant the world to her. When I passed the truck and SUVs, I had glanced in my rearview mirror, trying to see what was going on, but because the panel truck and first SUV had started to make their left turn before Harley stopped them, they blocked my view of the intersection at Central and Broad.

I parked as directed, noting the presence of news vans from ABC, CBS, NBC, and Fox all parked farther down the street. Mama and I jumped out of the car and hustled back to where Harley continued to direct traffic. However, as soon as I reached the curb, I had a clear view of the blocked intersection and no need for any explanation from Harley or anyone else.

My mother-in-law had staged a walker-in!

SEVENTEEN

BLOCKING THE TWO CROSSWALKS at Central and Broad stood all thirteen members of the Daughters of the October Revolution, six per crosswalk. Large red helium balloons that stated *Pedestrians Have the Right of Way!* in bright yellow lettering were tied to each of their walkers. Lucille and her comrades in crime must have been planning this little civil disobedience ever since Harley and Fogarty accused her of keying that BMW.

Lucille stood in the middle of the street. She leaned on her own walker, which she hadn't used in months, while a reporter from ABC interviewed her. The other network reporters and camera crews stood off to the side, no doubt awaiting their turns.

"Why don't you haul them away and lock them up?" I asked Harley. "Don't they need a permit to congregate or something?"

"The mayor and police chief don't want the negative publicity. Can you imagine how the networks would skewer us if we cuffed a bunch of semi-invalid old ladies and tossed them into lock-up?"

Personally, I thought a night in lock-up might shock some sense into Lucille, but I saw the mayor's and police chief's point. Westfield was one of those New Jersey towns prized by Hollywood film companies for location shoots, and I was all in favor of Hollywood filling the town coffers to keep my taxes down. We certainly didn't want to create a situation that gave the film companies an excuse to move to Chatham or Upper Montclair.

"How long have they been here?" I asked.

"Couple of hours. Eventually they'll get tired and leave. At least, that's what the mayor and chief hope."

"Have they made any demands?"

"None that I know. They just took up positions and blocked traffic. Haven't said a word except for your mother-in-law talking to the cameras. Wonder who called them?"

"I've got a pretty good idea," said Mama.

I couldn't disagree. I turned back to Harley. "Anything you want me to do?"

"Nah. Just thought you'd want to know what's going on. You can leave any time you want."

After we returned to the car, Mama asked, "What do you plan to do about her?"

I thought for a minute before answering. How I responded to Lucille's protest might negatively impact an already precarious relationship. "Nothing," I finally said. "I'm going to pretend not to know anything about it. And so should you, Mama. Lucille acts too much like a tantrum-prone toddler. Let's deny her a stage."

"What about all the TV cameras? This will be all over the six o'clock news."

I braked for a stop sign and turned to her. "Really, Mama, when was the last time I had a chance to watch the evening news?"

———

I might not have time for the news media, but as it turned out, the news media had plenty of time for me. We arrived home to find additional reporters and camera crews camped in front of the house. They didn't even give me time to get out of the car before shoving microphones at me.

"Mrs. Pollack, what do you think of your mother-in-law's protest?"

"No comment."

"Is it true she was the victim of a hit and run?"

No, actually she was the victim of an unsuccessful *hit*, but even Lucille didn't know the truth about the accident that resulted in her coming to live with us, not that I was inclined to spill the beans to the obnoxious Barbie doll reporter currently invading my personal space. "No comment."

"Mrs. Pollack, would you like to make a statement for the press?"

I turned to the reporter who'd asked that question. "Yes, I would." They all clamored closer, their mics held in outstretched arms to capture my words.

I paused for dramatic effect, then spoke, "You're all trespassing on private property. Leave or I'll call the police." With that I took hold of Mama's arm and pushed our way through the fourth estate gaggle and into my house, slamming the door behind me.

"So much for pretending we don't know anything," said Mama.

"We can still refuse to engage her in conversation about it," I said. "Don't bait her."

"Me?" Mama walked across the living room to where Catherine the Great was sunning herself in the bay window. She picked up the corpulent kitty and kissed the top of her head. "Really, Anastasia, I'd never stoop to that commie pinko's level."

Really, indeed. But I kept my mouth shut as I executed a huge mental eye roll.

Lucille's shenanigans were the least of my worries, though. Staging protests came second nature to my mother-in-law. Rumor had it, she went into labor with Karl in the middle of a sit-in, protesting the country's involvement in Vietnam. She'd refused to leave, even after her water broke. Karl was born under the arch in Washington Square. Literally.

Her personality aside, part of me admired Lucille's dedication, passion, and courage when it came to standing up for what she believed in. I saw nothing wrong with protesting something that mattered. Our country was founded on such principles. However, her latest cause made me suspect she'd developed a Moses complex, expecting traffic to stop for her the moment she stepped into the street the way Moses had stepped off the shoreline and parted the Red Sea. That kind of behavior was not only nuts, it would eventually get her killed.

Unfortunately, once Lucille made up her mind about something, nothing would sway her from her cause. Not a baby who decided to arrive at an inconvenient moment and certainly not our local police department. Lucille had taken on the NYPD. To her the WPD was no more a nuisance than a gnat to a gorilla. I don't know why I'd thought a night in lock-up might bring her to her senses. Knowing Lucille, she'd look forward to lock-up, all publicity being good publicity. Who else would have called the press to both the center of town *and* my home?

Lucille would always march to the beat of her own Kremlin Marching Band. Somehow we'd deal. Right now, though, I was more concerned with protecting the rest of my family from whomever killed Lou and attempted to kill Vince. I had no idea whether or not Lou and Vince were the killer's only targets or if more killings were planned. Not knowing the killer's motive made protecting us nearly impossible. How do you protect yourself and your loved ones from an unknown, mysterious assailant?

The more I pondered my dilemma, the more my thoughts kept zeroing back to Lou's finances. I thought that if I could solve that mystery, I'd be well on my way to figuring out the identity of the killer.

Of course, Zack would say to leave all this to the detectives investigating the case, but how could I? When your family is in danger, you don't sit back and wait for help to arrive. You do whatever it takes to protect them from that danger.

I wondered if I'd overlooked some essential clue at Lou's apartment, perhaps a clue that even Phillips and Marlowe had also missed. Mama still had Lou's keys. I could run into the city, give the apartment a thorough search, and arrive home in time to cook dinner.

"Why do you need Lou's keys?" asked Mama.

I told her my plan.

"I'll go with you. Two can search faster than one."

I really didn't want Mama playing sidekick, but she'd made up her mind, and getting Flora Sudberry Periwinkle Ramirez Scoffield

Goldberg O'Keefe to change her mind was as impossible as getting Lucille to accept someone else's opinion. On anything.

―――――

An hour later, thanks to reporters blocking my driveway, the ever-present Lincoln Tunnel backup, and cross-town gridlock, we stood in the outer lobby of Lou's building. Mama pulled a key ring from her purse and proceeded to unlock the door that led from the lobby to the first floor hallway and staircase.

"What are all those other keys?" I asked, noticing for the first time that the key ring held more than just the key to the foyer lock and the three deadbolts on Lou's apartment door.

Mama shrugged. "I have no idea. Lou just handed me an extra set of keys. He pointed out the ones I'd need to get into the apartment but never told me about the others. I suppose some are his office keys."

Which meant I could also search Lou's office today. Forget dinner. I'd scramble up a batch of eggs for all of us when we got home. I wasn't about to pass up the chance to do a bit of Sherlocking without fear of discovery by Sheri or anyone else connected with the show.

Mama and I climbed up the two flights to the third floor. "Good." I sighed in relief as we stood in front of Lou's apartment door. "No crime scene tape."

I wasn't sure what I would have done had I found the yellow and black DO NOT CROSS warning crisscrossed over the entrance. Lucille might not mind an occasional night in lock-up for the cause, but I wasn't about to learn first hand whether I did or not.

"Why would there be crime scene tape, dear? Lou was killed at the studio, not in his apartment. This isn't a crime scene."

I suppose Mama had learned that from watching *Law & Order*. Still, I wasn't convinced and was relieved to discover I didn't have to contemplate breaking the law to solve a murder.

I didn't know what I hoped to find, especially since I had no idea what to look for. Besides, Phillips and Marlowe had already searched the apartment. Was it likely two NYPD detectives would overlook or dismiss, a piece of crucial evidence? I had to do *something*, though, and right now the only *something* I could think to do was search through Lou's belongings.

The apartment was much the way we'd left it three and a half weeks ago. The empty bottle of Glenlivet still stood on the coffee table, the mail still scattered around the table and couch. I walked over to Lou's desk and opened the file drawer to find the folders containing Lou's will, insurance policy, and brokerage statement all still in place. I guess Phillips and Marlowe hadn't found anything amiss with them either.

I pulled the brokerage statement from its folder and studied it. Last time I'd focused on nothing other than the bottom line—all those numbers to the left of the decimal point. This time I started at the top. "Oh. My. God."

"What is it, dear?" Mama stood behind me, looking over my shoulder.

I pointed to the name of Lou's brokerage firm. Bernard L. Madoff Investment Securities LLC. How had I missed that? "I suppose now we know what happened to all of Lou's money."

Like many other New Yorkers, Lou Beaumont had invested his life's savings with the man responsible for pulling off the largest Ponzi scheme in history. I checked the date on the statement. November 30, 2008. Less than two weeks before Madoff's arrest. I suppose Lou had held onto this last statement all these years as a reminder of the fortune he thought he owned.

This explained why Lou wasn't paying the alimony he owed his ex-wives and why he'd bought Mama a cheap diamond. Had he not died, I wonder how long he would have tried to string Mama along with false promises. Or maybe the man had lived in total denial, unable to accept the fact that his fortune wasn't worth the paper this last statement was printed on. We'd never know.

———

"To the studio?" Mama asked as we exited Lou's building.

"Home," I replied.

"I thought you wanted to search through Lou's office?"

"Not anymore. We've unraveled the mystery of his finances. What would be the point of searching through his office?"

Mama gave me one of those looks that translates into did-I-really-raise-such-a-dense-daughter? "To discover who killed him, of course."

"Don't you think that if there were some major clue concerning Lou's killer lurking within his desk drawers, the police would have discovered it by now?"

"Like they discovered he'd been swindled by Bernie Madoff?"

"I'm sure they already know. I'm the one who didn't look closely enough at that brokerage statement the first time we were here. Besides, it doesn't seem likely that Lou was killed over his finances."

"What about those money-grubbing ex-wives of his?"

"First of all, only one of Lou's ex-wives complained about money. Rochelle said she took a lump sum when she and Lou divorced, and we never talked to any of the other wives besides Francine."

"She certainly seemed bitter enough to kill."

"But it was old news, Mama. Why would she wait years after the fact?"

"Maybe she wasn't desperate enough until now. She did look like she needed some corrective plastic surgery."

"I think Francine's problem is that she's had one too many plastic surgeries. The woman has a face only the late Michael Jackson could have loved. Anyway, if she'd killed Lou, she would have been arrested by now."

"How can you be so sure?"

"For one thing, she didn't strike me as someone with enough gray matter to plot a murder and get away with it. More importantly, the building has surveillance cameras at all the entrances. If Francine had showed up at the studio that day, she would have been caught on camera."

Mama finally conceded. "I suppose you're right, dear. Might as well go home and see what kind of trouble the commie pinko has gotten herself into since we left. Do you think she's still blocking traffic? Or maybe the police finally hauled her off to jail."

Mama relished that idea a little too much. I understood she and Lucille would never get along, but the discord they created in my home only added to the stress in my life. Each took too much pleasure in egging the other on.

Part of me wished Mama and Lou had married and ridden off into the sunset for whatever time they would have had together—with or without Lou's millions. There would have been a lot less bickering at *Casa Pollack*.

————

We arrived back in Westfield to find the news vans gone from the street but my house overrun with Daughters of the October Revolution.

EIGHTEEN

THE DAUGHTERS OF THE October Revolution, none of whom had been alive during the actual October Revolution of 1917, had taken over my living room, dining room, and kitchen. Some of the women assembled picket signs; others pecked away on laptops; still others yakked on cell phones while stuffing envelopes.

Thirteen folded walkers cluttered the foyer. Like my mother-in-law, none of Lucille's cohorts needed the aid of a walker. I knew that from my previous encounters with the Daughters of the October Revolution. They all managed to navigate fine on their own or with the use of canes.

"Look at that," said Mama, waving her arm in the direction of the commie klatch. "They don't need walkers. They just used them as sympathy props. Talk about manipulating the press!"

I realized that when we saw them blocking the intersection, but I hadn't bothered to mention it to Mama at the time. She already had enough ammo in her verbal arsenal to fire at Lucille. I didn't need to hand her more.

I stepped into the middle of the living room. "What's going on here?" I asked.

A woman I recognized from previous encounters with the Daughters of the October Revolution glanced up from her computer. If Touchstone ever decided to do a remake of *The Golden Girls*, they could cast Harriet Kleinhample as Sophia. The woman was a dead ringer for Estelle Getty, right down to her diminutive stature and oversized attitude. She'd only have to act herself to clinch the role.

"We're organizing our campaign," she said. "You have any more 24-lb. bright white stock? Recycled, of course. We're almost out. I only found half a ream downstairs."

"You helped yourself to my office supplies?"

"For the cause. Lucille said you wouldn't mind."

I took a better look at the items scattered around the dining room table. All mine. My paper. My stapler. My glue gun. My markers. Right down to my computer printer plugged into Harriet's laptop and spewing forth page after page of full-color, high-quality printed flyers that were quickly drinking up my last color ink cartridge.

I pressed the cancel button on the printer, then the OFF switch.

"Hey! I was still printing."

"Not anymore." I pulled the plug, wrapped the cord around my hand and hoisted the printer into my arms. The thing weighed a ton. How in the world had gnome-sized Harriet Kleinhample dragged it into the dining room?

"Wait until Lucille hears about this!"

"Why wait? Where is the rabble-rouser?"

Harriet shouted at the top of her lungs, "Lucille!"

By this time all the other Daughters of the October Revolution had stopped their typing, stapling, yakking, and stuffing to glare at me with one collective Lucille-type glare. They must practice that look at their weekly meetings.

We waited, me hugging the printer to my chest, the Daughters continuing to shoot me with their *en masse* evil eye.

"Anyone see Lucille?" asked Harriet.

The eleven other women looked questioningly at each other, all shaking their heads.

"She's probably in the bedroom, taking a nap," suggested Mama, "while her minions do all the work. Want me to go wake her?"

"I'll do it," I said. "You'd enjoy yourself too much." Not trusting Harriet, I placed the printer back on the dining room table but kept the cord as I headed toward the bedroom. Mama followed me.

We'd only gotten halfway across the living room when we heard the toilet flush. I stopped and waited for Lucille to reappear.

"Your daughter-in-law refuses to let us use the printer," said Harriet, the moment Lucille rounded the hallway into the living room.

Lucille immediately got up into my face and started yelling at me at the top of her lungs, her face and neck turning a mottled maroon. "We have important work to do, and you're not going to stop us."

I kept my voice at a normal level, refusing to stoop to her tantrum level. "I'm not stopping you from doing your *important work*. I'm simply reclaiming my possessions. Take up a collection, and do your *important work* on your own dime. I can't afford your nonsense."

Purple quickly replaced the maroon of Lucille's neck and face. "Nonsense? How dare you! Our work is far more important than yours!"

"My work keeps a roof over your head and food in your belly, Lucille. Don't forget that. You're welcome to leave at any time if you don't like the living conditions here." I grabbed the printer off the table and started for my bedroom.

"Give me that!" Lucille grabbed for the printer and tried to tug it out of my arms. "You have no right! Lives are at stake here, and all you care about is yourself. You're selfish, Anastasia. You always have been. My son never should have married you. You were never good enough for Karl."

"You stupid communist cow," shouted Mama, tugging at Lucille's arm. "Let go. If it weren't for the kindness of my daughter, you'd be living out of a cardboard box."

"I've had about enough of you," said Lucille. She lurched from Mama's grasp and pushed her aside. Luckily, Mama landed on the sofa. Unluckily, Lucille advanced, her cane raised.

"Don't you dare," cried Mama.

My mother-in-law raised her arm higher.

"Lucille!" I screamed. "Stop!"

Lucille lowered the cane and turned to me. She stared as if she didn't recognize me, her features sagging more than ever. "Rye showering?" she asked, sounding like a confused child. Then she collapsed in a heap on the carpet.

Suddenly I remembered a news segment I'd heard on the way to work recently. F.A.S.T.—face, arms, speech, time. "Call 911," I told Mama as I kneeled down beside my mother-in-law and checked for a pulse. Before passing out, Lucille had exhibited two of the three signs of a stroke. Time was now of the essence.

"What's the matter with her?" asked Mama.

"I think she's had a stroke."

"This is your fault," said Harriet. The others nodded in agreement as they hovered over their Fearless Leader.

"It always is," I muttered under my breath.

———

I followed the ambulance in my car. With Harriet at the wheel (Lord knew how she reached the pedals!), the Daughters of the October Revolution, all crammed into a rusted-out circa 1960s Volkswagen minibus, followed behind me.

Mama offered to stay home to prepare dinner for the boys. I wasn't sure who'd fare better that night, me eating hospital cafeteria food or Alex and Nick eating Mama's cooking. Such idle thoughts danced around in my head as I headed toward the hospital. I didn't want to think about the more serious issue at hand— what I'd do if Lucille survived but became permanently incapacitated. The Scarlett O'Hara in me decided to deal with that crisis another day.

A contingent of hospital staff and an emergency room doctor met the ambulance. Within seconds they rushed Lucille off for tests. The Daughters of the October Revolution camped out in the waiting area while I chose a corner of the corridor, away from incriminating glares.

No matter their accusations, I knew I wasn't to blame for Lucille's stroke. Lucille had high blood pressure and a stroke-inducing personality. Most likely, she'd been on the verge of stroking out for years.

Besides, I'd tried to get along with her from the day I first met her, but my mother-in-law wasn't interested in my friendship. She viewed me as the woman who'd stolen away her doting son. I'd tell her the truth about that son, but like everything else, she'd only accuse me of lying. Or worse yet, blame me for Saint Karl's fall from grace.

Damned if I did, damned if I didn't, I steered clear of Lucille as much as possible until the day I'd been forced to take her into my home for what was supposed to be a short recuperative period. Thanks to Karl's lack of control with Lady Not-So-Lucky, short had morphed into forever.

At least I didn't have to worry about her hospital bill. Thanks to her many years editing *The Worker's Herald*, the weekly newspaper of the American Communist Party, Lucille received a meager pension but lifetime health benefits. I found that kind of ironic, given she didn't believe in insurance. When her apartment, along with all her worldly possessions and her life savings, went up in flames, she was left with nothing. Not even the clothes on her back. The emergency room had cut those off her body in the aftermath of the jaywalking episode that had brought her to live with us. To this day I have no idea how she had managed to find 1970's style polyester pantsuits to replace the ones lost in the fire.

I also didn't understand how a woman who'd come so close to death after stepping out between parked cars on Queens Boulevard six months ago would continue to jaywalk. Stubborn was one thing; repeatedly placing herself in physical danger was something else. Maybe Fogarty was right when he said Lucille was crazy. Maybe I did need to have her evaluated, no matter how much she'd object.

Three hours after we'd first arrived, Dr. Pavlochek, the doctor who'd ordered Lucille's initial tests, returned with the results. The Daughters of the October Revolution had posted a look-out at the entrance to the waiting area. As soon as the doctor approached me, the look-out signaled to the others. Dr. Pavlochek and I were quickly surrounded by a dozen yammering and demanding biddies, each peppering the doctor with non-stop questions.

He frowned at them, his bushy salt and pepper eyebrows joining together above the bridge of his nose. "Ladies, I'm afraid privacy laws forbid me from speaking to anyone not listed on the patient's medical disclosure form."

"Lucille wouldn't mind," said one of them. "She wanted us listed." The rest nodded in agreement.

"As a matter of fact," said Harriet, "Lucille trusts us more than she trusts *that one*." Harriet indicated me with a tilt of her head and a sneer.

The doctor consulted his clipboard for a few seconds. I knew he wouldn't find any names listed on Lucille's HIPAA privacy form other than mine and Karl's. I'd insisted on that much when Lucille first came to live with us after her hit and run accident. If we were going to be responsible for her recovery, we had to have access to her medical information. Lucille balked at first, but Karl saw the sense of my argument. Besides, neither of us had relished doing battle with any of the other Daughters of the October Revolution, the names previously listed by Lucille.

Eventually, Dr. Pavlochek gave up on his clipboard perusal and said to me, "Let's continue this discussion in my office." He turned to the commie gaggle and added, "The rest of you will have to wait here."

Like their Fearless Leader, the Daughters of the October Revolution didn't take kindly to authoritarian figures. No one told them what to do. Not traffic cops. Not doctors. The only authority they held in esteem was their own. Ignoring the doctor's orders, they followed after us. Dr. Pavlochek thwarted them when he ushered me into a small, windowless office and closed the door on their collective faces.

"Your mother-in-law has some very loyal friends," he said, taking a seat at a desk and indicating I should sit in the chair pulled up alongside the desk.

"Loyal," I repeated. "That's one word for it." Others came to mind, but I refrained from uttering them. Instead, I changed the subject. "So what happened to Lucille? Did she have a stroke? As I told the EMT at the scene, right before she lost consciousness, she appeared confused and slurred her words."

"A very minor stroke. It's a good thing you were there and recognized the signs. Because she received immediate attention, she should recover without any problems. However, the MRI showed something more problematic."

"More than a stroke?"

"Mrs. Pollack, your mother-in-law has a brain tumor."

NINETEEN

Not only did Lucille have a brain tumor, but according to Dr. Pavlochek, she'd probably had it for some time. "We won't know for sure until we operate, but my initial assessment is that it's benign. Of course, we can't operate until she's stable."

"Could this brain tumor be responsible for irrational behavior?"

"Due to its location, definitely. Has your mother-in-law exhibited unusual behavior lately?"

I gave him a quick run-down of Lucille's "normal" personality and the changes I'd noticed over the last few months, including her new campaign on behalf of jaywalkers' rights.

"Lucille has always been defined by her causes," I said. "She lives to protest, but protesting the rights of jaywalkers to jaywalk? That's a bit much even for someone as doggedly stubborn as she is. Not to mention totally irrational."

"As people age, certain traits become more pronounced," said Dr. Pavlochek. "A stubborn person might become even more stubborn, for example, but it's quite possible you'll see some improvement in her demeanor after the surgery. Certainly what you've described aren't the actions of a person with a full grasp of reality and could be the result of the tumor."

One could only hope.

Lucille was in the ICU, which had limited visiting hours of only twenty minutes at a time and only for immediate family. As the Daughters of the October Revolution argued with the charge nurse, I slipped into my mother-in-law's room.

She was hooked up to a myriad of monitoring devices and looked anything but her feisty crusader self. Aside from a lack of cuts and bruises, she appeared much the way she had after the hit and run—very old and extremely frail.

I picked up the hand not connected to the IV and whispered her name. "Lucille?"

No response. Either she was sleeping or chose to ignore me. Not seeing much point in sticking around, I placed her hand gently back on the bed and headed home.

———

By the time I arrived home, Mama and the boys had finished dinner, as evidenced by the sink full of dirty dishes, some brown gooey stuff spilled over the stove, and one very sticky kitchen floor. I should have handed Mama twenty dollars and told her to order in pizzas, but it's hard to blow a twenty at Papa John's when a stack of unpaid bills clutters my desk.

I marched through the house, noting jaywalker rights junk still strewn throughout my dining room and living room. Lucille's tumor explained her devotion to such an irrational cause, but what about the rest of the Daughters of the October Revolution? Surely, they weren't all suffering from tumor-induced delusions or dementia. Those women were like lemmings, following their Fearless Leader over any cliff, all for *the cause*, no matter how ludicrous the cause.

I found the boys and Mama camped out in the den, a Mets game on the TV, Ralph perched on Alex's shoulder, and Catherine the Great curled up on the sofa between Mama and Nick.

"I hope you have plans to clean up the kitchen once the game is over," I said in as evenly modulated a tone as possible, which given my mood, was pretty much a feat of Everest-climbing proportions.

"Sure, Mom," said Nick.

"No, *problemo*," said Alex. "What's up with Grandmother Lucille?"

"Have you had dinner, dear?" asked Mama. "There's leftover meatloaf in the fridge."

That explained the brown gooey stuff—congealed gravy—and sticky floor. In the Periwinkle household of my childhood, Mama's meatloaf was legendary, and I don't mean that in a good way. Even the thought of Mama's meatloaf still sent my tummy into nightmare mode. I was always amazed that Nick and Alex could stomach the stuff, but teenage boys often ate anything not nailed down.

"I grabbed a sandwich at the hospital," I said, crossing my fingers behind my back. I'd sneak into the kitchen after Mama went to bed and pour myself a bowl of Raisin Bran.

"Did the pinko have a stroke?" asked Mama.

I filled them in on the details. "Bottom line, she'll be hospitalized for some period of time. Once she's stabilized, they'll operate on the tumor. At this point I'm not sure what will happen after she's discharged from the hospital. Probably a rehab and convalescent center before she comes home."

"What about Mephisto?" asked Nick.

"What about him?"

"Does he have to stay here while she's gone?"

"Well, he certainly can't stay in the hospital with her, and I don't have the money to board him."

"Which means you and I are stuck with caring for him, little bro," said Alex.

"Think of it as a challenge," I told them. "If you can learn to manage Mephisto, you can do anything. Remember, that which doesn't kill you, makes you stronger."

"So those are our two choices?" asked Nick. "Death or Mephisto?"

"You got it. Now, did anyone bother to walk and feed the devil dog in question since you've been home?"

"Don't look at me," said Mama. "I won't get near that beast."

"I'll do it," said Alex. He hoisted himself up from where he lay sprawled on the floor and handed Ralph over to me. "Pause the game, Nick, and if I'm not back in ten minutes, call out the army."

"*My lord, there's an army gathered together in Smithfield,*" squawked Ralph. "*Henry the Sixth, Part Two.* Act Four, Scene Six."

"Forget the army," I told Alex. "Remember the pooper-scooper." I turned to Nick. "While your brother walks the dog, you can start on the dishes."

He began to protest, but I guess he saw something in my expression that told him I'd reached my limit. Without another word, he headed for the kitchen.

"Well, it will certainly be a lot more pleasant around here with that commie gone," said Mama. "Almost like a vacation."

"Maybe we need to cut Lucille some slack, Mama."

"Why? She certainly doesn't deserve any."

"Maybe she does. The doctor said the tumor has probably been growing for some time and could be the reason behind her irrational behavior."

"I don't buy it. Do I need to remind you that your mother-in-law has been a selfish, belligerent thorn in your side for more than eighteen years? Surely that tumor hasn't been growing nearly two decades."

She had a point.

"Besides," she continued. "I don't remember Karl having many kind words for his mother when he was alive. You were the one who constantly tried to make peace with her, not him, no matter how much she claims he was such a doting son before you came along."

Another good point. "Still, maybe she'll be just a bit nicer and less belligerent once the tumor is removed. That's not too much to hope for, is it?"

"Hope all you want, dear. Just don't be disappointed when you wind up with exactly the same Lucille you had yesterday."

———

That night I had trouble falling asleep. Too many thoughts skipped around in my brain like the air-blown numbered balls of a lottery machine. Along with my usual worries about finances, I worried about Lucille.

What if something went wrong during her surgery and she wound up incapacitated? Did her lifetime health care contain yearly caps of any sort?

How would I cope if she wound up disabled but not disabled enough for the insurance to allow for nursing home care? As frail as she looked in her hospital bed, Lucille was still way too big for me to manage moving her in and out of a wheelchair or bed. Would the insurance cover in-home health care? How much and for how long?

I tried to stop dwelling on the what-ifs of Lucille's situation, but when I blocked them from my mind, up popped Lou's unsolved murder and the questions still unanswered about who killed him and why.

A CORPSE TELLS NO TALES.

The discarded note I found at Lou's apartment held the key to his killer's identity. I was certain of it. If I could figure out what the note meant, I should be able to figure out who killed him. Except the police probably thought the same thing, yet they still hadn't made an arrest.

Lou had been dead three and a half weeks. Somewhere I remembered hearing that if a murder isn't solved within the first forty-eight hours, it usually remains unsolved. But someone had also tried to kill Vince. A killer was on the loose, and no one knew if he had any more of us in his sights.

A CORPSE TELLS NO TALES.

Lou knew something the killer wanted kept quiet. Was it in connection with the show or somehow tied to Vince's child pornography charges? Or maybe neither.

What was Monica involved in that had the police so interested? Maybe Lou discovered something she wanted kept quiet at any cost. Although I couldn't see Monica plunging a knitting needle into Lou's heart. She might break a nail. However, Monica did strike me as someone who would pay for a killer's services.

The fact remained, something illegal was going on at that brownstone. Why else would the police have it under surveillance? Monica was somehow connected to whatever that something was. Was she desperate enough to resort to murder to keep her secret?

Questions, questions, and more questions but no answers. Even though I'd solved the puzzle of Lou's finances, maybe I still needed to search his office.

————

The next morning I rose early, showered, and dressed in a pair of old jeans, black T-shirt, and running shoes while Mama and the boys slept. As soon as I heard Mama shuffle into the hall bathroom and close the door, I stealth-walked into her room and lifted Lou's keys from her purse. I'd ground Nick or Alex for life if either of them ever pulled a stunt like that on me, but if I told Mama I needed the keys, she'd have insisted on tagging along. The last thing I needed this morning was Mama as my sidekick.

I left a note on the kitchen table, explaining I was off running some errands—only a teeny white lie—and hopped into my Hyundai.

Unless something huge is going on in the city, Sunday mornings are usually the one day of the week you can zip in without hitting any traffic. And that's exactly what I did, arriving in less than thirty minutes and even finding on-street parking. I considered both good omens.

"Working today?" asked Hector when I pushed through the front door and flashed my ID at the security desk.

"You, too, I see."

"Not by choice. The weekend day guard caught a bug, and I drew the short straw. How about you?"

I'd come prepared. Pointing to the large canvas bag dangling from my shoulder, I said, "Still playing catch-up. Seems our killer has chosen my crafts projects as his calling card. They keep getting impounded as evidence."

"So I've heard."

Hmm … I wondered what else Hector had heard. Maybe he could shed some light on why Phillips and Marlowe hadn't made an arrest yet. "I guess the cops found nothing suspicious on the security tapes, huh?"

"Couldn't say."

"Why's that?"

"I pulled the tape for them but never saw what was on it. Just handed it over as instructed."

"What about when Sheri—Ms. Rabbstein—came down to check the tapes after the vandalism?"

"Huh? What vandalism?"

I'd forgotten Trimedia refused to file a police report, but I would have thought Lou had at least notified building security. Apparently not, although I found it hard to believe word hadn't trickled down through the union grapevine. Since I'd already spilled some of the beans, I dumped the rest.

"When was this?" Hector asked after I filled him in on the trashing of the studio set.

"We discovered the vandalism the day before Mr. Beaumont was killed. It must have occurred the previous Friday night after everyone left the studio, or sometime during that weekend."

Hector scratched his head. "Don't remember Ms. Rabbstein ever coming down to look at any security tapes," he said. "Not that day or any other day. Could've been while I was on my lunch break, though. One of the other security guards probably handled it."

"I guess so." I paused for a moment, then added, "Any chance I could have a look? Maybe she missed something. I'd really like to nail the bugger responsible for making me do all this extra work."

Hector shrugged his enormous shoulders. "Don't see why not. Give me a minute to pull them up." He fiddled with some equipment behind the desk. "Now that's damned odd," he said.

I darted around the counter to look at the screen. "Find something?"

"Static. Must be a bug in the system."

"You're saying there's nothing at all on the recording? Which day?"

"I started with that Friday. I'm fast-forwarding through the entire day. Doesn't look like we got anything."

"What about Saturday and Sunday?"

Hector tapped a few keys on his console, and I watched as he zoomed through two days of static.

"Try Monday, the day we discovered the vandalism."

More tapping. "Damn."

More static.

"Definitely a bug in the system." He picked up the phone. "I'd better notify the service company."

Disappointed, I headed for the elevators. Maybe I'd have better luck upstairs. Then a thought occurred to me. I turned back to the desk. "Hector, just out of curiosity, check the tapes for the Thursday before the vandalism and the day after the murder."

He hung up the phone mid-dial and pressed a few more keys on his console. I stood behind him, looking over his shoulder. "Worked Thursday," he said. He pounded a few more keys. "And the following Wednesday."

"And it's definitely working now," I said, pointing to the real-time screen.

"It was working those other days, too. I would've noticed if a screen went down."

"I don't think the system has a bug," I said. "I think it was deliberately hacked. Probably by the killer."

"Must've been after the cops took a look. They didn't question me about any problems."

I didn't believe that for a minute. I was certain the reason the cops hadn't yet made an arrest was because they, too, had seen nothing but static when they viewed the security tape, and for whatever reason, they were keeping that information to themselves.

I left Hector to make his phone call and headed for the elevators.

When I arrived upstairs, I discovered a change since my last trip to the studio. Sheri's name now replaced Lou's on his door. Not only had she been handed his title but his office. I wondered if she also received his salary. Not that I begrudged her a raise, but Trimedia had every excuse in the book for not giving me or my fellow editors more money, and we were the ones doing twice the work we'd done only a few short weeks ago.

I unlocked the door and stepped inside, although I hardly expected to find anything. This was Sheri's office now, as evidenced by the fresh coat of lavender paint on the walls, a color no guy would ever use to decorate a room, let alone a producer's office.

I looked around anyway, pulling open the top desk drawer, only to find all things Sheri—a box of Tampax, a bottle of Midol, a bag of M&Ms—and no evidence that Lou had once occupied the place. So much for ferreting out the author of that note. Still, as long as I was there, I decided to snoop—er, sleuth—further, rifling through the contents of all the desk drawers, scanning the shelves, nosing through the closet.

I found nothing more than typical business files and office supplies in the drawers and Sheri's misshapen black cardigan, speckled with mop doll fuzz, hanging in the closet. Aside from the sweater, the only other personal item in the room was a framed photo of Sheri with another woman.

I picked up the photo and studied it. The two resembled each other somewhat, down to their roly-poly bodies and dark hair, the other woman's streaked with gray. An older sister or cousin, maybe? They stood with their arms around each other, both wearing muumuus, a sandy beach and ocean waves in the background.

I placed the photo back on Sheri's desk. I had hoped to find something searching through Lou's stuff, not Sheri's. Guilt forced me to exit the office and lock up.

On the off chance that the contents of Lou's office weren't already in a Dumpster, I decided to check out Sheri's old office, the storage closet, and anywhere else I thought someone might stash a few cartons of unwanted odds and ends. I found nothing.

So much for my brilliant idea. I might as well head home to tackle the laundry. I started for the elevator, but paused as I approached Monica's dressing room. I held Lou's key ring in my hand, a key ring with dozens of keys. I wondered if one of them opened the door in front of me. Only one way to find out.

I systematically made my way through the collection of keys. On the fourteenth key, the tumblers clicked into place. I turned the knob, pushed open the door, and stepped back in time several centuries.

Only the mini-kitchen, complete with sink, fridge, and microwave, kept the room from resembling a period piece out of a classic Hollywood movie. Floor to ceiling mirrors covered the walls. I looked up. Ceiling, too. Holy vanity! Everywhere Monica turned, she'd see herself. Over and over again. Ad infinitum. As I was now seeing myself. Only I didn't quite fit in with my worn jeans and old T-shirt. This room called for silk negligees and feather boas.

A crystal chandelier hung from a gilt medallion in the center of the mirrored ceiling. Crystal sconces dotted the mirrored walls. An enormous dressing table stood against one wall, a pink velvet lounging couch, piled high with satin floral print pillows, sat against a perpendicular wall. A hand-painted silk dressing screen, complementing the print of the throw pillows, blocked off the corner between the dressing table and couch.

I poked my head through one interior doorway to find a mirrored bathroom, complete with Jacuzzi tub and gold fixtures, down to the toilet flusher and bidet faucets. A bidet! Jeez! The woman must channel Madame Pompadour in this crib.

A second door led into a walk-in closet filled with racks of dresses and shelves of shoeboxes. Right then and there I decided to hire the guy who negotiated Monica's last contract. The woman had perks up the wazoo.

That thought reminded me of the conversation the day of the vandalism, when Sheri blew a gasket over Vince's and Monica's contracts. She'd called their dressing rooms a recreation of Versailles. Now I understood why. Lou had said there were *extenuating circumstances* and that the negotiations were *rather complex.*

Did Vince and Monica have some dirt on their producer? Lou had refused to go into details, as if he were ashamed or embarrassed. Or maybe scared? Yet another mystery that would remain unsolved unless Vince and/or Monica fessed up, which appeared highly unlikely. What would they have to gain at this point?

Yet another reason to cross both Vince and Monica off the suspects list. Both profited by Lou's continued good health and had nothing to gain by his death.

I had no qualms about snooping through Monica's things. Something was up with her, something that involved police surveillance, and I was curious to learn what was going on with that. So I started nosing around, poking through drawers and cabinets.

Finding nothing of interest in the dressing room, I headed for the closet. The woman had enough shoes to satisfy the most avid foot fetishist. Manolo Blahnik. Ferragamo. Christian Louboutin. Henry Beguelin. Jimmy Choo. Every imaginable designer label on one box after another. A freaking wall of overpriced stilettos. I could put my kids through college on what Monica spent on footwear. And it wasn't even her money. This was her studio wardrobe. Trimedia had paid for it all.

As every teenage girl knows, shoeboxes make for ideal hiding places. A small step stool stood in the middle of the walk-in closet. I pulled it over, climbed up, and reached for the highest box, one with a Bottega Veneta label. But when I lifted the lid, I didn't find a pair of Bottega Veneta shoes. Instead, I found Monica's secret.

TWENTY

"MONICA'S A JUNKIE?" CLORIS screamed the question so loud she almost didn't need a phone for me to hear her.

"Can you think of any other reason someone would hide a lighter, a metal spoon, and a syringe in a Bottega Veneta shoebox?"

"*Boat* what?"

"Never mind. It's not important." Cloris could rattle off the names of every five-star chef in the country, but when it came to anything outside the cooking world, she was clueless. I may never be able to afford any of their high-end leather goods, but I certainly knew the name Bottega Veneta. A girl can drool, can't she?

"That certainly explains the constant fidgeting and lack of co-ordination," she said.

"Not to mention the extended periods of time closeted away in her dressing room."

"No wonder she couldn't crack an egg."

"Or plait a braid."

"I wonder how that brownstone fits in. Think she's also dealing?"

"Could be why the cops have the house under surveillance. Maybe that's the distribution hub."

"If Monica is caught up in a drug sting, Sheri will have cause to terminate her contract without paying out the balance. Maybe Monica killed Lou because he found her shooting up."

"She'd certainly have motive, but I just can't see Monica stabbing Lou with a knitting needle, can you?

"Besides, Lou was killed in the storage area. Monica wouldn't shoot up someplace where anyone might walk in on her when she has the privacy of her own dressing room."

The other end of the phone went silent while Cloris chewed on those thoughts. And something else. "What are you eating?"

"Chocolate-covered pretzels."

"I hate you."

"No you don't. You just hate my metabolism."

"True."

"Getting back to Monica, I have to agree with you. She would have either been high or jonesing for a hit. Either way, she's too much of a klutz. If she went after Lou, I see her lunging for him and tripping over her own feet. Or his. And falling flat on her face."

"I can't disagree."

"Could have been Ray. Was he at the studio that day?"

"I don't know."

"The police would. From the security tapes."

"Not necessarily." I caught Cloris up on what Hector and I discovered about the tapes. "I think someone tampered with them to cover up both the vandalism and the murder."

"Don't you think it's odd that Sheri never said anything about the tapes? Wasn't she supposed to check on them after the vandalism?"

"Yeah. And I intend to ask her about that. You'd think she'd have a vested interest in finding the culprit who tried to destroy her show."

"Might be better to leave all the questioning to Detectives Phillips and Marlowe."

"You sound like Zack."

"Maybe you should listen to him," suggested Cloris. "I get a weird vibe around that woman."

"Now you're sounding like Mama."

"Seriously, Sheri strikes me as someone you don't want for an enemy. Start questioning her integrity, and you'll wind up on her Shit List."

"Sheri seems to like me, even with my Mama baggage. I'll figure out a way to drop the topic into conversation without sounding accusatory. Just curious."

"Watch your back. Curiosity killed the cat."

"Ah, but satisfaction brought her back."

———

Since I was scheduled to shoot another craft segment the following day, I didn't have to wait long to have a conversation with Sheri. You can't shoot when one of your stars is supposedly dead, and the other never shows up at the studio.

———

"She hasn't bothered to call in, and she's not answering either her cell phone or her home phone," said Sheri when we'd waited over an hour for Monica to make an appearance.

Naomi slammed her palms onto the island countertop. "This is getting ridiculous. My editors and I have work to do back at the office. We're on deadline. We can't afford to hang out here constantly waiting on that *prima donna* to make her grand entrance."

"Even when she is here, she might as well not be," I said, and added, "given her lack of cooperation." I wondered if Monica had OD'd, but obviously couldn't voice that concern without giving away my snooping of yesterday. Instead, I asked, "Have you tried calling her husband?"

"I'll be right back," said Sheri, then added louder, "Take five, everyone!" Which was rather ridiculous, being that everyone had been milling around for over an hour already. However, unlike me, the rest of them were getting paid to do nothing.

Sheri waddled off, presumably to her office to call Ray Rivers. Her pink, green, and white *faux* Pucci print muumuu flapped in the breeze created as she pushed through the studio doors.

"That woman is setting herself up as the laughingstock of morning TV," said Naomi, *sotto voce* to avoid being heard by any of the studio crew.

"I feel sorry for her," I said. "She's totally out of touch with reality."

"Look at the upside, though. This show is going to tank within days of its debut. Then we can all go back to our normal work schedules."

"I hope you're right. I'm not sure how much longer any of us can keep up this pace."

"Tell me about it. At least the rest of you are only here for your individual segment shoots. I'm stuck here for all of them."

"Two full-time jobs for the pay of one?"

"Exactly."

That cleared up one mystery. Right from the editorial director's mouth. Naomi definitely hadn't cut a deal with Trimedia at her editors' expense.

Sheri pushed through the studio doors less than five minutes later. "She seems awfully pleased with herself," said Naomi.

I studied Sheri as she approached us. No mistaking the grin on her face or the glint in her eyes.

"I have good news and better news," she said.

"Oh?" Naomi raised an eyebrow.

"Naomi, I'm pleased to announce that you're now the sole host of *Morning Makeovers*."

I looked at Naomi. I didn't need to be a mind reader to know congratulations were definitely not in order. "What happened to Monica?" I asked.

"Monica violated the morals clause in her contract," said Sheri. "She's out of here. Permanently."

"How?" asked Naomi. She sounded as if she just might consider doing whatever Monica had done in order to be rid of Sheri and the burden of *Morning Makeovers*.

"Monica was arrested in a sting operation yesterday afternoon."

"Drugs?" I asked.

Sheri focused on me. "How do you know that?"

"I don't. Just a wild guess."

"Not so wild," said Naomi. "She often acts like she's high on something."

236

"Well, maybe she was and maybe she wasn't," said Sheri, "but that's not what got her busted. Are you ready for this?" She paused for effect.

"Out with it already," said Naomi.

"Monica had a side job." Sheri giggled. "As a—call girl."

So that's what was going on at that brownstone! Those were vice cops staking out the place, not homicide detectives connected to Lou's murder and the attempt on Vince's life.

"How did you find out about this?" I asked Sheri.

"Ray told me. He's livid. You weren't off base with your wild guess. Turns out Monica has a heroin habit to support, and this was the only way she could pay for it without Ray suspecting something since he controls her finances."

"But he did suspect something," I said. "According to Lou, Ray was always accusing Monica of having affairs."

Sheri shrugged. "Not my problem. I'm just happy to be rid of both her and Vince. I'll have to work up a new production schedule. We're going to have to reshoot everything now that they're not part of the show." She clapped her hands together and bounced on her toes, unable to contain her giddiness. "Wonderful, isn't it?"

Neither Naomi nor I shared her enthusiasm. "Reshoot everything?" asked Naomi.

"Of course," said Sheri. "We can't start off our new show featuring a pedophile and a prostitute."

I hadn't forgotten about the security tapes and now saw my opportunity to jump in with a question. "What about the vandalism that first day? Did you find one of them sneaking back into the building when you checked out the tapes? You never mentioned anything."

This caught Sheri off guard. "The tapes? Oh. Uhm … they were inconclusive. Lots of people entered the building between Friday night and Monday morning, but I didn't see anyone connected with the show."

Which could only mean that whoever hacked into the system and destroyed the recordings did so after Sheri viewed the tapes that Monday morning. Either that or Sheri was lying to me, but what would be her motive?

"So whoever trashed the set could still be out there," I said. "And might also have murdered Lou."

"And Vince," added Naomi.

Or at least attempted to murder Vince. Neither of them knew that Vince was still alive.

"I wouldn't worry about it," said Sheri. "It's obvious Monica is the killer. Lou must have discovered her drug habit, and she killed him to shut him up. As for Vince, you know there was no love lost between the two of them. Maybe he also discovered the drugs and attempted to blackmail her."

"You've missed your calling," said Naomi.

Sheri shot her a quizzical look. "What do you mean?"

"You should be working for the police."

Or writing fiction. No way was Monica capable of killing either Lou or Vince. Not in her constant drug-induced state. "I'm sure the detectives will be exploring those angles," I said. "Meanwhile, we should all still be diligent just in case your theory doesn't pan out."

"Right," agreed Naomi. "We could still have a killer lurking around here."

"Doubtful," said Sheri. "We haven't had any further problems."

"That could just be because he's gotten what he wanted," said Naomi.

"At least for the time being," I added.

"What a bunch of Negative Nellies!" said Sheri. She clapped her hands together and called out, "Back to work, everyone. We've got a show to tape."

———

After the taping, which occurred with few retakes and in less than an hour, thanks to Monica's absence, I headed for the office. Not only did I need to put in a few hours of editorial work on the current issue, but I was bursting with the news of Monica's arrest. As soon as I arrived, I gathered everyone into the break room. While I downed a late lunch of coffee and a slice of raspberry chocolate chip cheesecake, compliments of Cloris, I spilled the news.

"Do we know for sure that Sheri's right about Monica?" asked Janice.

"She got her info straight from Ray," I said around a mouthful of cheesecake. No wonder I never lost weight. Between Cloris's temptations and my erratic schedule and total lack of willpower, the battle of the bulge had a forgone conclusion.

"I didn't see anything in the morning paper," said Sheila. "Anyone catch anything on one of the morning news shows?"

"Nothing on *GMA*," said Nicole.

"Or *Today*," added Jeanie.

"Maybe the story didn't break yet," I said.

"We should check the Internet," suggested Janice.

Trimedia maintained a zero tolerance when it came to surfing the 'net. Anything not connected with doing one's job was grounds for immediate dismissal. Since a daily newspaper, Internet hookup, and a cell-phone data plan were all early victims of my forced pauperdom, I found myself constantly out of the loop when it came to newsworthy events the last few months.

However, in a cost-cutting move, Trimedia hadn't yet replaced the position of assistant fashion editor. The cubicle, once home to Erica Milano, had remained vacant ever since Marlys Vandenburg's murder this past winter. Feeling guilty over nearly getting me killed, Erica had generously provided me with her password before going into the Witness Protection program. I, in turn, had shared the password with my fellow editors.

We all trooped over to the empty cubicle to Google Monica. The others hovered around me as I typed in Erica's password, then input Monica's name into the search engine.

"Bingo!" I said, clicking on the first link to pop up, the *New York Times* homepage. "Breaking news. Actress arrested in Manhattan escort sting."

"I don't get it," said Tessa. "Why would any guy pay to fuck someone that old? Monica's what? Thirty-nine? Forty?"

"Now you've done it," Nicole whispered to her.

"You hold her down," said Jeanie to Cloris, "while I bitch slap the clueless twit."

"Get in line," said Sheila. "Age should have some advantage. She's mine first."

Tessa looked at all of us as if we'd lost our proverbial marbles. "What did I do?"

"Forget it," I told my fellow editors. "She's not worth the assault charge." Besides, given *American Woman*'s track record with fashion editors, we'd be waving bye-bye to Tessa soon enough.

"I'm glad we finally have definitive proof that Naomi didn't throw us under a bus," said Janice, changing the subject.

"Unless she's lying," said Tessa.

"If Naomi is lying, she's one hell of an actress," I said. "I believe her."

"So what?" said Tessa. "We're still stuck with working for the Muumuu Queen of Morning TV. What difference does it make that Monica and Vince are gone? That only impacts Naomi. The show still goes on for all of us."

"She has a point," said Cloris.

"Naomi thinks the show will be cancelled quickly," I told them.

"Good for Naomi," said Tessa. "Meanwhile, we're all still working as slave labor until that happens. It's the middle of June. The show doesn't debut until Labor Day. Even if it tanks after the first week or two, we've all got to put up with this shit for another three months."

"Another good point," muttered Cloris.

"Maybe you should make more of an effort to contact your Uncle Chessie," I told Tessa.

That got me speared by an evil eye. Apparently, Uncle Chessie wasn't interested in bailing out his niece. Or any of her fellow editors.

———

On my way home that evening, I stopped at the hospital to check in on Lucille. She turned to face the door as it swooshed open from my push.

"Oh, it's only you."

Typical Lucille. All piss and vinegar with never a kind word for anyone other than her fellow Daughters of the October Revolution. "Sorry to disappoint you."

"They won't let any of my sisters visit."

"That's because only immediate family members are allowed in the ICU."

"I told them they were my sisters."

"You lied."

"Hardly."

"Would you rather I leave?"

She turned to face the window. "Suit yourself."

I pulled up a chair alongside the bed and sat down. I hope someone upstairs is keeping score because I'm sure I've filled my lifetime patience quota and should now qualify for living sainthood. "Did the doctors explain what happened to you?"

She grunted. "A minor stroke. You need to change the way you cook."

"Your stroke is my fault?"

"Of course it's your fault! I never had high blood pressure and high cholesterol before I came to live with you. Get me out of here. Now. If I get flesh-eating bacteria, I'll know who to thank for that, as well."

Count to a thousand, Anastasia.

Scratch that. A thousand wouldn't cut it. I'd better count to a million. I took a deep breath, bit down on my tongue, and willed myself to stay calm. "You can't leave, Lucille."

"Why the hell not?" She pounded her fists on the bed, then rattled the side rails. "I know my rights. You can't keep me here against my will. No one can."

Actually, I could, and I had the papers to prove it. "You have a brain tumor, Lucille. You need an operation."

"That's ridiculous! There's nothing wrong with my brain. I'd know. I'm perfectly sane."

Yes, and crusading for the rights of jaywalkers definitely comes from the workings of a rational mind. "No one said you were insane. Did the neurosurgeon speak with you today?"

"How should I know? There's a constant parade of snot-nosed white coats in and out of here. Half of them don't even speak English. All poking and prodding and none of them over the age of twelve. What kind of hospital is this you stuck me in?"

Again, my fault.

"They allow children to practice medicine here. Did you know that? I'll bet you did. You're letting them use me as a guinea pig, aren't you? Well, I'll have none of it. I demand to see birth certificates and medical licenses before I allow another one of them near me.

"And you get out! I don't want to look at you. You're trying to kill me. I know it."

With that she started to stab the call button and yelled, "Nurse! Nurse! Where the hell is everyone? Nurse! Get your ass in here now. Who the hell do you think pays your salary?"

Having been dismissed, I left the room.

"Don't let it get to you," said the duty nurse. "It's the tumor talking."

Or in Lucille's case, screaming. "You heard her?"

"Are you kidding? They can hear her in Newark."

TWENTY-ONE

ON MY WAY HOME my phone rang as I crept along with rush hour traffic. I didn't answer. Having once missed a head-on collision by mere inches, thanks to the other driver talking on his cell instead of paying attention to the road, I take the state law against phone usage while driving quite seriously.

As soon as safely possible, I pulled off the road and checked my missed calls. Mama. I didn't bother to call her back. Within seconds, the phone rang a second time. I checked the display, then powered the phone off before I pulled back into traffic.

Some people have a very odd concept of what constitutes an emergency. Mama was one of them. I'm sure her call had to do with the breaking story that most certainly had headlined the six o'clock news. Mama would have to wait another twenty minutes for her gossip fix regarding Monica's arrest.

Sure enough, the moment I pulled into the driveway, Mama rushed out the front door and was upon me before I even turned off the engine. "Anastasia, why didn't you answer your phone? Did you hear the news? Monica Rivers is in jail."

Nothing like a grand bombardment before I even entered the house. I pulled my key from the ignition and exited the car. "I know, Mama."

"What? And you didn't call me? Really, dear, you can't leave me out of the loop like this. I have a vested interest in *Morning Makeovers*. After all, the show was my idea."

In *The History of the World as Told by Flora Sudberry Periwinkle Ramirez Scoffield Goldberg O'Keefe*, the annals will record *Morning Makeovers* as Mama's idea. She'd see to it, and the truth be damned.

"Not to mention I was nearly poor Lou's wife," she added, ending her statement with a dramatic sniff accompanied by a misting of her eyes.

I noted Lou's formerly ever-present adjective had returned, although given recent discoveries, *poor* Lou would have been a more accurate appellation than *poor Lou*.

Mama took another sniff and a deep breath before continuing. "The evening news gave very few details. Tell me everything you know. Don't leave out anything."

"You probably know as much or more than I do, Mama."

"Nonsense. You were there."

"At the arrest scene? Of course, not."

"No dear, at the studio. Did Monica kill poor Lou because he found out about her extra-curricular activities? Surely the detectives filled you all in."

"Only on *Law & Order* and in mystery novels, Mama. Denouements rarely occur in real life."

Mama grabbed my arm. Her eyes grew wide with excitement. "You're going to be on *Law & Order*? How long have you been keeping this secret? *SVU* or *Criminal Intent*? I do love that Jeff Goldblum. Do you think they'd allow me on the set when you shoot your scenes?"

"Focus, Mama. No *Law & Order*. And no detectives showing up at the studio to fill us in on Monica's arrest."

"But you just said—"

"I was only trying to make a point. Real life is different from fiction."

Mama glared at me. "And you think I don't know that? Since when do you make fun of your mother, Anastasia? I brought you up better than that."

My stomach rumbled. I suppose now wouldn't be the best time to ask if she'd prepared dinner. Instead, I kissed her cheek. "Yes, Mama, you did, and I'm sorry."

Although no doubt Anastasia Pollack costarring with Jeff Goldblum would also one day become a chapter in *The History of the World As Told by Flora Sudberry Periwinkle Ramirez Scoffield Goldberg O'Keefe*. If only! I could sure use a *Law & Order* costar's paycheck.

"Oh, by the way," said Mama as we entered the house, "*that woman* called for you."

That woman could only mean one woman. "Sheri?"

"That's what I just said, didn't I?"

"Did she leave a message?"

"She wants you to meet her somewhere for a location shoot tomorrow."

"What location shoot? I wrapped up taping my latest segment this morning."

"How should I know? We're certainly not—what is it the kids call it nowadays? BFFs? Anyway, I didn't speak with her. Alex answered the phone and took the message. He said she told him it was part of the revised schedule, be there at eight, and don't be late. He wrote the address down on the pad by the kitchen phone. And she said you'd probably do better taking the subway, that there's next to no parking in the area."

I went into the kitchen and grabbed the note off the pad. The Bronx? The woman expected me to be in the Bronx by eight in the morning? I'd have to set my alarm for the crack of dawn.

As I'd expected, Mama had done nothing in the way of dinner preparation. Given Mama's abilities in the kitchen—or more accurately, lack of them—perhaps that wasn't such a bad thing. However, it would be nice to come home occasionally and not find everyone waiting around for me to fill their empty, growling bellies.

Admittedly, I enjoyed those evenings when I arrived home to find Zack in my kitchen. Along with all his other admirable qualities, the man was a damned good cook. Too bad he wasn't standing in my kitchen right now.

"Where are the boys?" I asked Mama. "I don't suppose anyone bothered to walk Mephisto?"

"The boys are out running an errand with Zack, and you know I won't go near that demon."

"What kind of errand?" I asked as I headed for the mud room to grab Devil Dog's leash.

Mama shrugged. "Just an errand of some sort."

"What aren't you telling me?"

"Nothing, dear. Why do you always believe I have ulterior motives?"

With that, Ralph made his presence know for the first time since we entered the kitchen. From his perch on the refrigerator he squawked, "*Had he the motive and the cue for passion that I have? Hamlet, Prince of Denmark*. Act Two, Scene Two."

Ralph spread his wings, then preened, awaiting applause for his outstanding performance. Mama graced him with a screwing up of her face and a muttered "filthy bird" under her breath. Then to me, "You didn't answer me, dear."

"I should think it's obvious, Mama. Because you usually do have ulterior motives. Alex and Nick—and you—need to leave Zack alone. I rely on his rent money and don't want him running off because you're all trying to create some sort of romantic set-up."

Mama gave me one of those I-know-something-you-don't-know smiles of hers. "I hardly think you need worry about that, dear."

"Oh?"

"Really, Anastasia, you can be so dense sometimes. Haven't you noticed the way that man looks at you? And don't think I haven't noticed the way you look at him when you think no one is watching you."

"Mama, stop playing matchmaker. I'm recently widowed, remember?"

"Under the circumstances, I think you have every right to jump back into the dating pool. Sooner rather than later. There's a lot of competition out there, dear, in case you hadn't noticed, and you've got a very eligible and interested bachelor practically living under your roof."

"He's living over my garage, not under my roof."

"Same difference."

"This conversation is over. I need to start dinner."

"No need. Dinner should arrive momentarily."

———

"You really have to stop doing this," I told Zack later that evening as we cleaned up from a Chinese take-out feast.

"Doing what?"

"Allowing my mother and kids to manipulate you."

"Is that what you think is going on?"

"Isn't it pretty obvious?"

Zack placed a plate in the dishwasher, then turned to face me. "I'm a big boy, Anastasia. I don't do anything I don't want to do. Haven't in a long time."

"But—"

"I spend most of my life alone. It's an occupational hazard. I enjoy spending time with you and your family, but if you think I shouldn't—"

"I didn't say that. I just don't want my sons taking advantage of you."

"And you?" He smiled, a mischievous smile with a glint in both eyes. "What about you?"

I stared at him, unsure how to respond. Was Mama right? Did Zack have feelings for me beyond casual friendship? I knew what the man stirred in me, and I'd tried my damnedest to stomp out those feelings.

Hell, drop-dead gorgeous and successful, Zack Barnes was a dream catch. He could have anyone he wanted. Why on earth would he be interested in a middle-aged widow with a spreading bottom, debt up the wazoo, and two teenage sons? Not to mention Mama, Lucille, and a motley menagerie. Any sane man would break the world's sprint record fleeing the scene.

But Zack wasn't any man, as I found out, when a moment later—before I'd figured out how to answer him—he cupped my face in his hands, dipped his head, and kissed me. The man kissed me like I'd never been kissed in my life. *Sorry Karl. Had I known there were men who kissed like Zack, I never would have married you.*

And look how much better off I'd be right now. Damn. I'd been cheated in more ways than one. Not only by Karl but by every other guy I'd ever dated.

All these thoughts tumbled through my brain and more, while in the background I could swear I heard Alex, Nick, and Mama high-fiving each other. I didn't care. I was too busy kissing Zack back. And having the time of my life doing so.

All good things must come to an end, though, and eventually both Zack and I needed to come up for air. I dreaded the awkwardness that I anticipated, the moments after the kiss. What to say? I hadn't experienced a first kiss in a very long time and never one that made every other kiss—first or not—pale by comparison.

But Zack didn't let awkwardness ensue. "I'm glad that's over with," he said.

Then we both laughed.

And kissed again.

"Mama is going to be impossible to live with from now on," I told him a few minutes later after we traded the kitchen for the greater privacy of the back porch.

"Cheer up," he said. "With her track record, she'll be on to Husband Number Six in no time."

"Which will leave me with Lucille." A less than happy thought. I'd rather have ten conniving Mamas living under my roof than one curmudgeon of a mother-in-law. Unfortunately, I was stuck with Lucille. Till death do us part.

I caught Zack up on my hospital visit before turning the conversation to Monica's arrest. "But I guess you knew about that investigation, too? From your ex-wife?"

In the fading light he answered with an enigmatic smile. Nothing more.

"As I suspected. Keeping any other secrets from me?"

He made an exaggerated show of pondering the question for a moment before answering, "No, I think that's about it."

"Good to know."

"Do you have any idea how Monica's arrest will impact the show? Vince certainly won't be coming back and now Monica."

I told him what Naomi thought and how Sheri was already revamping the program, including dragging me to the Bronx early tomorrow morning. "I sure hope Naomi is right about a quick cancellation. This crazy schedule has to end. Fifteen minutes once a week has morphed into two full-time jobs without the benefits of a second pay check. Trimedia is either going to have zombies for editors or a strike on their hands. None of us can keep up this pace much longer."

I punctuated my words with a yawn before nestling into Zack's chest and promptly falling asleep.

———

I woke up the next morning in my own bed. Alone. Someone had removed my shoes but not my clothes, tossed a quilt over me, and set my alarm for five thirty. Zack. Mama would have said to hell with Sheri and let me sleep.

After showering and dressing—or more accurately, redressing—I left the house before anyone else woke up and hiked the three blocks to the train station. If I lived to see retirement—a rather speculative *if*, given my financial situation—I planned to celebrate by catching up on all those missed Z's. At my present rate of sleeplessness, I figured that would place me in contention to overtake Rip Van Winkle's record.

The address Alex had scribbled down wasn't far from the Castle Hill Avenue station on the 6 line. According to Google maps, somewhere around thirty-five miles as the crow flies. More like forever and a day via public transportation.

Other than the occasional trip to the Bronx Zoo when Alex and Nick were little, I'd never set foot in the Bronx. Then again, I'd rarely set foot in any of the outer boroughs except for taking the subway to Queens for Mets games, and I hadn't done that since before the demise of Shea Stadium and the erection of the new Citi Field.

For the most part, Staten Island, Queens, Brooklyn, and the Bronx were as foreign to me as Kalamazoo, Michigan, or Kracker Station, Mississippi. I had no idea how long it would take to arrive at my destination and hoped the two hours I'd allotted for the commute would be sufficient, given that once in Manhattan, I'd first need to take three subway lines, then walk several blocks.

Two hours and fifteen minutes after leaving my house, I arrived at the Castle Hill Avenue station, already late, dripping sweat from an exceptionally hot June morning, and still blocks from my destination. I glanced around to get my bearings. The area resembled Chicago more than New York, due to the train switching from underground to elevated tracks once we crossed the Harlem River from Manhattan into the Bronx.

One-story retail shops lined the main thoroughfare—a nail salon, thrift shop, real estate office, bank, hardware store, bodega, and several take-out restaurants featuring Mexican, Indian, and Chinese menus—most with signage declaring *Habla Español* or advertising *Halal* foods. An odd neighborhood for a *Morning Makeovers* photo shoot. What was Sheri thinking?

Maybe Alex wrote down the address wrong? I pulled out my phone to call Sheri and realized when I flipped it open that I should have charged it last night. I guess I had other things on my mind. Like a kiss that had not only rocked my world but turned it upside-down, inside-out, and sideways.

Talk about a seismic shift! Talk about anything. Zack and I definitely had lots more talking to do. Right now I could barely think straight about what had happened last night. Besides, I needed to concentrate on my present situation and leave my future love life for the future.

Sheri had insisted on giving all the editors her cell phone number as well as her direct office line. At the time I thought it a bit of overkill, not to mention controlling, since she wanted our cell numbers as well, but now I was glad to have hers.

I brought up the number, hit send, and waited while the phone rang. And rang. And rang. After five rings the call went to voice-mail.

"You've reached Sheri Rabbstein, producer of *Morning Make-overs*. Sorry I can't take your call, but I'm sure you know how it is. Busy, busy, busy." This was punctuated with a Sheri giggle. "Leave a message, but don't forget to wait for the beep." Yet another giggle, then, "Ba-bye."

Great. I waited for the beep. "Sheri, it's Anastasia. Just wanted to double-check the address for the location shoot. Not sure I'm in the right place. Call me as soon as you get this message."

I hung up and speed-dialed Cloris.

"Cloris McWerther here. I'm either on another call or pulling something from the oven. Either way, I promise I'll return your call as soon as I can. Don't forget to wait for the beep."

Beep!

"Hey, I'm up in the Bronx for a location shoot, but I may have the wrong address, given what the area looks like. Sheri's not pick-ing up her phone, and my battery's got one foot in the grave. I'm heading over to the address I have. Can you track someone down at *Morning Makeovers* and get back to me if I'm in the wrong place? Thanks." I gave her the address Alex had written down, then hung up.

As I headed away from the main drag, the neighborhood changed from retail to residential. Pre-war two- and three-story apartment buildings, duplexes, and small single homes lined the street. Suddenly, the location made sense. We must be shooting at

Sheri's apartment. She wanted to showcase the various crafts I'd designed in a home setting. I just never pictured Sheri *Rabbstein* living way up here in such an ethnically diverse area. She had to be the token Jew of the neighborhood.

I checked the address once more and made my way down the street to a one-story white clapboard house reminiscent of the bungalows that once lined much of the Jersey shore. Except for needing a fresh coat of paint, the home looked well-maintained, with neatly trimmed hedges lining the walkway and impatiens blooming from Williamsburg blue painted window boxes. Matching shutters and a navy blue front door added to the welcoming ambience.

A *For Sale* sign hung from a post sticking out of the postage stamp-sized front yard. Now that Sheri had inherited Lou's position, I supposed she'd also inherited his salary and had plans to move into Manhattan. Or at least to one of the classier neighborhoods of the Bronx. I certainly couldn't blame her. She really was way out in the boonies here, and although the neighborhood didn't give off a ghetto vibe, neither did it strike me as the safest of places for a single woman living alone.

I made my way down the path that bisected the front yard and rang the bell. The door flew open a few seconds later, but not by Sheri.

"I'm sorry," I said. "I think I may have the wrong house. I'm looking for Sheri Rabbstein."

"Right house," said the woman standing in front of me. She stepped aside and waved me in. "Anastasia, right? I'm Maxine. Sheri's off picking up the camera crew and all their gear. Their van broke down a few miles from here. Rather than having them wait for a tow and screw up the schedule, she ran off to rescue them."

Maxine looked vaguely familiar, and I searched my brain, trying to place her. When I took note of her dress, a green and brown palm tree print muumuu, it hit me. This was the woman from the picture in Sheri's office. The one who looked like an older version of Sheri. A sister or cousin. However, afraid of making assumptions, I went with a more generic association. "Are you Sheri's roommate?"

"In a manner of speaking. How about a glass of ice tea? I just made a fresh batch."

"Thanks. I'd love some."

"Have a seat. I'll be right back."

Maxine toddled off to the kitchen. I sat down on the sofa in the small but neat living room furnished in country-style Ikea and decorated with crafts-fair kitsch.

Maxine returned a minute later with two tall glasses of ice tea and handed me one. I gladly accepted and began to drink. That's the last thing I remembered until I woke up to find myself bound, gagged, and tied to a chair.

TWENTY-TWO

"I SUPPOSE WE'VE GOT to get rid of her."

"Of course we do. Why else did we lure her here?"

I was having some sort of weird dream about Sheri and Maxine. I couldn't move, having twisted myself up in the blankets, but I didn't have the strength to untwist. My limbs refused to budge. My eyelids wouldn't open. Throbbing and spinning, my head slumped on my left shoulder, producing a painful neck cramp, but I had no energy to either lift my head or shift position.

Then, slowly, as I focused on the voices around me, I realized this was no dream.

"What have we done, Max? This has gotten so out of control. We've murdered people. We're not killers. We're good people. It wasn't supposed to be like this. All I wanted was for you and me to work together on our dream show."

"I know, sweetie, but there's no turning back now. We'll dump her in the river after it gets dark. We can drive upstate and find some out-of-way place along the Hudson. Weight her down so the body never surfaces. I saw some barbells around here that we can use. No one will be able to trace her disappearance back to us."

Body? Were they talking about me? I forced myself not to panic, to keep still and concentrate on the voices.

"I know the others had it coming to them," said Sheri, "even if I never meant to kill Lou, but I actually liked Anastasia."

"And look where it got you. Don't blame yourself. This is her own fault for snooping around. Good thing you set up those hidden spy cameras, or we might be in deep shit. God bless your tech skills is all I can say. No telling what she would have figured out if we hadn't caught her snooping around your office."

"You're right. She's been asking too many questions from the very beginning. I should have known she'd cause trouble for us."

Stay calm, Anastasia! Let them think you're still unconscious from whatever Maxine used to spike the ice tea. I forced myself to breath slowly and not move a muscle, not that I could. As my brain continued to unfog, I realized I wasn't tangled up in blankets but tied to a chair. Not with rope, though. Duct tape. My chest was bound to a hard chair back, my arms pinned behind me, each of my legs secured to a leg of the chair from my ankles up to just below my knees. More tape secured my thighs to the hard seat. Someone had made damn sure I wasn't going anywhere. A final strip taped my mouth closed.

I forced myself to remain as still as possible and listened, hoping to learn more. Not that it would do me any good. I was at a severe disadvantage. At least the last time I'd found myself tied up, I'd had the use of my cell phone and an X-acto knife to save the day. And my butt. This time, nothing. If I didn't figure out some way to escape, I was going to be fish food.

How soon, I had no idea. I had no way of telling how long I'd been unconscious. Moisture crept behind my closed lids, and I fought back the sob collecting in my throat. If I let them know I was awake, they might kill me right now.

"You're sure there's no way to trace the call back to you?" asked Sheri.

"Absolutely not. I used a disposable cell phone and called when you told me she wouldn't be home. Only, the mother didn't answer. One of her kids did."

"Even better," said Sheri. "With my alibi of being at the studio early this morning and you sending her to a vacant house, no one can connect me to her disappearance. Too bad with all the bad publicity, Trimedia will probably cancel the show before it even debuts."

"I'm not worried. Screw Trimedia. We don't owe them a damn thing. You'll get enough publicity out of this that we'll have our pick of networks and for a lot more money. From here on *we* dictate the terms."

"Damn straight."

"Come on, let's head upstairs and see what there is to eat in this dump. I'm hungry, and we've got hours before it will get dark enough to move her safely."

"Maybe we should dump her in the van now and get out of here. We can leave her locked up in it until dark."

"Too risky in daylight."

"But what if someone shows up to look at the property while we're still here?"

"Relax, sweetie. You worry too much. No one is going to show this house today."

"How can you be certain?"

"Because I made sure of it. If anyone calls the office to set up an appointment, they'll be told the house is undergoing termite extermination."

"And the owners?"

"House hunting in Georgia. Trust me. We're safe."

"That's why I love you, Max. You think of everything."

"Of course I do. Now, can we get some lunch?"

Sheri giggled. "Unless you'd like dessert first?"

"I could be persuaded."

I heard them start up a flight of creaky steps, then stop.

"Wait," said Sheri. "She's not going to wake up anytime soon, is she?"

"And what if she does?"

Sheri giggled again. "You're right. I worry too much."

They continued to lumber their way up the creaky stairs. I heard the flick of a switch. What little light had permeated my blindfold disappeared. A door slammed.

I couldn't hold back the tears any longer. I was going to die a horrible death, and no one would know what happened to me. No one would ever find my body. I'd leave my sons orphans.

I should have listened to Mama. She pegged Sheri from the very beginning, but I refused to listen to her. Now I'd never have the opportunity to tell her she was right and that I was sorry for not believing her.

Stop sniveling and think, Anastasia!

I couldn't let Sheri and Maxine get away with murder. I had too much to live for. My kids. Mama. And now Zack. Damn, now that I'd discovered what I'd been missing all these years, I wanted

261

more. A man who kissed like Zack probably excelled in other areas I wouldn't mind exploring. Maybe there really were men out there whose lovemaking skills—or lack of them—didn't necessitate faking orgasms. Damn it! I wanted the chance to find out for myself.

I saw no viable escape, though. Even if I had my trusty X-acto knife in my pocket, I couldn't reach it. No cell phone, either, assuming the battery hadn't already died. My purse was most likely still on the living room couch.

The dank mustiness told me I was probably in a basement. As the fog continued to lift from my brain, I saw fuzzy, indistinct shadows through the fabric blindfolding my eyes.

Investigating further by scooting the chair toward those shadows wasn't an option, not with the way my legs were bound to the chair. My feet dangled above the floor. If I tried to rock the chair to move it, I'd tip it over. The noise would surely bring Sheri and Maxine running, and that would most likely shorten my already short life expectancy.

Think!

What would Stephanie Plum do?

Sadly, nothing. She wouldn't have to. Ranger would rescue her in the nick of time. Stephanie had to survive for the next book in the franchise. Kill off Stephanie and Janet Evanovich killed off her cash cow. Sadly, I was no one's cash cow. Quite the opposite. Besides, I wasn't playing a character in a mystery series. This was scary real, and in the scary real world, there was never a sexy man in black around when you needed one.

Once more my eyes filled with tears. I couldn't even blame my latest predicament on Dead Louse of a Spouse. Had Karl still been alive, I'd still be about to die. However, I wouldn't be leaving my kids orphans, just motherless. For that I did blame Karl. Everything always came around to being Karl's fault, one way or another these last few months. Why should this be an exception?

Above me, bed springs bounced as Sheri and Maxine enjoyed a little Sapphic afternoon delight, totally unconcerned about the murder they planned to commit hours from now. I, on the other hand, once accidently ran over a squirrel and was more upset by that mangy critter's death than those two were concerning my impending demise. And I hate squirrels!

Funny how the mind works. I had hours at the most to live and what was I thinking about? Squirrels. What might Sigmund Freud say about that?

The banging upstairs—both figuratively and literally—grew louder. Those two sure knew how to have a rollicking good time, at my expense and on someone else's bed. I wondered if they'd bother to clean up after themselves.

And why did I care?

Because maybe they'd leave behind some DNA that just might lead the police to their capture and eventually to my remains. And because if I thought about what really mattered to me, I'd spend the last hours of my life driving myself nutso. Far better to think of a dead squirrel and hair follicles left by two lesbians having sex in a stranger's bed.

Damn, those two were going at it like sex addicts at an all-you-can-fuck orgy. What could they possibly be doing up there to create so much banging and thumping?

And now screaming? Both of them at once. At the top of their lungs.

Then I heard shouting, but not from Sheri and Maxine. Footsteps pounded above me. The door banged open. Someone hit the light switch.

"She's down here."

Through the blindfold I made out a hulking figure bounding down the creaky staircase and heading toward me. He pulled down my blindfold. I squinted. He wasn't Stephanie Plum's Ranger, but he was wearing a black suit, and I'd never been so happy to see anyone as I was to see Detective Marlowe at that moment.

"She's alive," he yelled. Marlowe grabbed onto a corner of the duct tape securing my mouth. He yanked, and I screamed. "Sorry," he said. "Should've warned you it would hurt like hell."

I flexed my jaw. "Are you kidding? Pain never felt so good. Those two were planning to dump me in the Hudson in a few hours."

Marlowe pulled out a knife and began working on the tape that bound my hands. "How did you know to come here?" I asked as he cut away the layers.

"You can thank your friend Cloris. She put two and two together and got suspicious when they didn't add up. Good thing you gave her this address."

"Yeah, I thought at first this was Sheri's house. It isn't."

"We know."

"What else do you know?"

He paused from his slicing and turned to face me. "Time for that later. Let's get you out of here first and checked out by the docs."

I nodded. "She drugged me with something."

"They usually do."

"They? How many cases have you had like this?"

"Too many."

All I could think was, thank God for experienced detectives. And thank God for Cloris. Marlowe finished ripping the tape from my legs (I wouldn't need a wax job any time soon) and helped me stand. My legs refused to comply.

"Let's sit you back down before you fall flat on your face. I'll call for a bus."

"Bus?"

"What we call an ambulance."

Mama probably would have known that from all her *Law & Order* viewing. Maybe I needed to watch television, especially police dramas, given that Mama also pegged Sheri as Lou's killer from Day One.

"I heard Sheri admit to killing Lou," I told Marlowe. "And I think the two of them had something to do with Vince." I didn't mention that I knew Vince was still alive. No need wading in those shark-infested waters with Marlowe.

"We'll get them to talk."

Had he told me this at any point in the past, I wouldn't have believed him, but the man had just rescued me from certain death. If he said he could capture every member of Al Qaeda, blindfolded and with one hand tied behind his back, I'd believe him.

———

Two EMTs arrived, checked my vitals, then lifted me onto a gurney and carried me upstairs. As they wheeled me through the house to the front door, I saw no sign of either Sheri or Maxine, but I did spy my purse with its contents spilled across the living room coffee table.

"That's mine," I said, pointing.

A uniformed officer standing nearby called to Marlowe, "Okay if the vic takes her purse?"

Marlowe lumbered in, made a quick check of my wallet, keys, phone, and lip gloss, then scooped the contents back inside my purse and handed it to one of the EMTs. They pushed me outside, into a waiting ambulance, and whisked me away, sirens blaring. I never saw Sheri or Maxine.

Once at the hospital, a team of medical personnel poured over me, poking and prodding, taking blood for tests. "I wasn't raped," I said when a nurse asked permission to do a rape kit.

"We don't know what the perps may have done to you while you were unconscious."

That creeped me out enough to give permission for any test they wanted to perform. With my legs splayed and my eyes closed, I took a deep breath and let her poke my privates.

"Was I?"

"No indication." She offered her hand and helped me sit up. "The police will need your clothes for evidence. I'll bring you some scrubs to wear."

I itched where the duct tape had contacted my skin. The area had turned red.

"Do you have a latex allergy?" asked the nurse.

"Not that I know of."

"Sometimes people develop latex allergies after repeated exposure. The duct tape may have triggered one in you. I'll bring you an antihistamine and some salve."

Great. Scratch the idea of using duct tape as a cheap alternative to waxing. My arms and legs started to grow redder before my eyes. I looked like I'd been roasted on a spit. I scratched at my cheek.

"Try not to scratch," said the nurse as she left the exam room.

Easy for her to say.

Once she returned with the scrubs, some pills, and ointment, she helped me slather up and dress. Afterwards, she poked her head out the door and said, "She's ready."

A moment later, Marlowe entered, Phillips right behind him. "Up for some questions?" asked Marlowe, taking a notebook out of his pocket and flipping it open to a pristine page.

"Absolutely." Now that I knew I had the rest of my life ahead of me, I wanted to make sure Sheri and Maxine spent the rest of their lives producing nothing more than license plates at a federal facility.

I sat on my hands to keep from scratching until the antihistamine kicked in. "Ask me anything."

"Let's start with what you've been up to," said Marlowe, pencil poised to write.

I didn't like the way he'd phrased that, or the way he eyed me, but I took him and Phillips step-by-step through the last few days, leaving nothing out, other than the fact that I knew Vince wasn't dead. I'd promised Zack I'd keep that to myself. Besides, Phillips and Marlowe already knew Vince was alive and cooling his heels over on Rikers Island.

As I told them about Sheri's hidden cameras, something occurred to me. "When I first met Sheri, she told me one of the show's techies had written a program to bypass Trimedia's spy ware."

"Spy ware?" asked Phillips.

"A computer program they use to monitor employees' Internet usage. We're not allowed to use the web for anything that's not work related. Doing so gets you fired."

He nodded. "And?"

"I half-jokingly asked her if the guy could do the same for us at the magazine. She said he'd recently won the lottery, quit his job, and was island-hopping around the Caribbean.

"But I don't think that's the case. Maxine said it was a good thing Sheri set up the spy cameras. Then she said, 'God bless your tech skills.' I don't think there was ever a tech guy who quit. I think it was Sheri all along."

Phillips and Marlowe exchanged knowing looks, like I wasn't telling them anything they hadn't already figured out for themselves.

"Hmm," said Phillips.

"Got any other insights?" asked Marlowe.

"As a matter of fact, I do. Sheri was behind everything. I'll bet she planted that e-mail from Monica on Vince's computer so you'd seize it as evidence and discover the kiddie porn. She set Vince up to get rid of him without having to pay out on his contract. Maybe Vince really isn't a pervert." Although I found that hard to believe.

The more I thought about it, the more everything jelled. "And the security tapes. Sheri volunteered to check them after the vandalism. But she didn't check them; she erased them. She said killing Lou was an accident. He probably found out about the tapes and confronted her, and she panicked."

Marlowe scrawled a few more notes on his pad, then said, "Thank you for your time, Mrs. Pollack. We'll have a uniformed officer drive you back to New Jersey."

He and Phillips turned to leave the room.

"Wait!"

They both turned back. "Something more you remember?" asked Marlowe.

"Aren't you going to tell me if I'm right?"

They shook their heads in unison, like some programmed robocops. "Sorry," said Phillips.

"Ongoing investigation," added Marlowe, spouting the company line. "We're not at liberty to discuss it."

With that, they left the room and left me with my mouth hanging open.

TWENTY-THREE

I was surprised to find Cloris waiting at my house. "Are you all right?" she asked, eyeing my reddened arms and cheeks.

"Thanks to you. What made you call Marlowe?"

"You can thank Janice. She wasn't in the office this morning. I figured maybe she had a doctor's appointment or something and didn't give it another thought. But when she arrived around noon, she stopped off at my cubicle and started telling me a Sheri story. She'd been at the studio, taping a segment all morning. I knew right then that something was wrong because how could Sheri be at the studio and on a location shoot at the same time?"

"You literally saved my life, you know."

"What do you mean—literally."

"Just what I said. They were planning to kill me."

"They?"

"Sheri and Maxine, her lover." I looked around the living room. "Where's Mama?"

"Out getting her hair done. I figured someone should be here to tell your mother and the kids that you were missing, and better me than the cops."

"So she doesn't know anything?"

"Not yet. I gave her some song and dance about needing to borrow the boys when they got home from school. I wanted to stall as long as possible. When Marlowe called to let me know you were safe, I decided to hang around to see for myself." She gingerly touched my cheek with her index finger. "Painful?"

"More itchy than anything. The hospital gave me some ointment and pills. They're helping."

"If you change into long sleeves and a pair of slacks and put on some make-up, you might be able to get away with not telling your mom and kids anything."

I liked that idea. Mama and the boys didn't need to know someone had tried to kill me. Again.

———

Zack wasn't as easy to fool. Or more likely, an inside source had alerted him to the day's events. An inside source who works for the Manhattan D.A. He sped into the driveway as Cloris and I waited for Mephisto to fertilize the curb.

"Shouldn't you be off photographing indigenous meerkat colonies or something?" I asked as he jumped out of the car.

"That was last week. I'm between assignments."

I didn't buy that for a New York minute, but instead of pressing the topic, I proceeded with introductions. "Cloris, Zack. Zack,

Cloris." To Cloris I said, "Zack is my tenant." To Zack I said, "Cloris is—."

Zack shook Cloris's hand. "Watson to your Sherlock. I've heard."

I sighed. "Is there anything about me my mother and sons haven't told you by now?"

"Doubtful." He grabbed the leash and pooper scooper from me. "Why are you out here walking the dog after nearly getting yourself killed?"

"Hmm ... let me think. Because I don't want dog poop on my carpets?"

He turned to Cloris. "Can't you make her lie down?"

"Can you make her do something she doesn't want to do?"

Now it was Zack's turn to sigh. "Glad it's not just me."

"Three's a crowd," said Cloris. "I'm out of here."

"You don't have to go," I said.

"Yes, she does," said Zack.

I opened my mouth to tell him to stop being so damned bossy, but stopped dead—no pun intended—before uttering the first syllable. The man had what romance writers refer to as a smoldering look in his eyes, something I'd previously dismissed as pure fiction, and that smolder was directed straight at me. Up to this moment, no one had ever *smoldered* at me before. Not my husband. Not any of the guys I'd dated prior to meeting Karl.

So much for telling Zack off. If only I didn't itch so much ... I carefully rolled back one loose-fitting sleeve to show him my left arm. "The right one makes for a matched set. Same for my legs."

"What the hell did they do, drop you in a patch of poison ivy?"

"Duct tape. The nurse at the hospital said I might have a latex allergy." I rolled my sleeve down.

Zack reached out to cup my face in his hand. I cringed and pulled away. "Face, too. Hidden under the make-up."

He let loose with a couple of choice expletives better left deleted. "Where else?"

"That's about it. My clothing protected the rest of my skin."

"Does it hurt?"

"Itches mostly. I'm on oral and topical antihistamines and trying not to think about it too much, so let's change the subject, okay?"

Cloris uttered one of those hey-guys-remember-me? throat clearing sounds. "As I was about to say, I need to get home, anyway." She directed an index finger toward me. "You should take tomorrow off."

"Can't. No more sick days left this year."

"Excuse me?" She raised both eyebrows. "A Trimedia employee tried to kill you a few hours ago. Not only are you entitled to some time off, you should think about filing for workman's comp."

"Forget that," said Zack. "She should sue the pants off Trimedia."

"For what?" I asked.

"For hiring a certifiable nut job and setting her loose on all of you."

"Nice idea," I said, "but I can't afford to lose my job, and what are the chances of Trimedia continuing to employ someone who is suing them?"

"Actually," said Cloris, "If they fire you for suing them, I think you can also sue them for that."

"Tempting but not worth the risk, and what would I do while these lawsuits were slogging their way through the courts? I'm already living from paycheck to paycheck and barely making ends meet." Not to mention making next to no dent in my Mount Everest of inherited debt.

Cloris offered me a rather devious smile. "Find a rich boyfriend?"

"It's a good thing you just saved my life," I told her. "Otherwise, you'd be in serious trouble right now."

Cloris left for home, and Zack and I headed up to his apartment. Over glasses of wine, he helped me concoct a story for Mama and the boys. As much as I hated lying to them, I didn't want them worrying that my name had been drawn out of a hat by every killer and psychopath in the tri-state region. In the last several months I'd had two attempts made on my life. Those were damn high odds, even for CIA operatives, let alone suburban moms. Best they didn't learn of the second one.

"I've got it! You developed a sudden allergy to Mephisto," suggested Zack after downing a glass of chardonnay and mulling ideas around in his head for a few minutes.

"I wish."

"Then how about this: you got tangled in his leash and tripped face first into a patch of stinging nettles."

"More plausible, but where's the patch? The boys will want to know to steer clear of it."

Zack poured us both more wine. "If you had dumber kids, they wouldn't think to ask."

"True. Smart kids are such a parental burden."

The conversation went downhill from there, helped along by several additional glasses of what turned out to be an excellent chardonnay. However, by the third glass, it really didn't matter. The wine and Zack were taking my mind off my itchy face and limbs, not to mention my near-death experience.

I finally settled on something mundane but semi-believable if no one looked close enough to notice the almost surgical-like precision delineating my affected skin from my unaffected skin. I suffered an allergic reaction to some organic body cream samples our beauty editor Nicole Emmerling had received and passed around at the office.

———

By the next morning, the rash had faded considerably, and the itching bordered on bearable. Ignoring Cloris's suggestion to take a few days off, I headed into the office. Had I stayed at home, I'd have nothing to do other than catch up on housework. At the office, I could catch up on the work that came with a deadline and resulted in a paycheck.

On my way to my cubicle, I grabbed a cup of coffee from the break room. Halfway down the hall, Naomi's assistant Kim caught up with me. "Naomi wants to see you in her office."

"Now?"

"Right now."

That sounded ominous. "What's going on?"

Ignoring my question, Kim continued walking toward the break room. I headed down the corridor, past my cubicle, to Naomi's office.

I poked my head around the slightly ajar door and found Naomi engrossed in some papers on her desk. I rapped once. "You wanted to see me?" I asked when she lifted her head.

"Yes. Come in, Anastasia. Close the door behind you and have a seat."

"You heard what happened yesterday?"

She nodded. "How are you feeling?"

"I'm beginning to think I'm some killer magnet. First Marlys. Then Lou."

"And Vince."

I shrugged without saying anything, not sure whether I still needed to keep that bit of information to myself. "I'm not Nancy Drew. I didn't ask to get thrown into the middle of their murders."

"Yet you were."

"Hopefully, that's all behind me now. And behind the rest of us. I'd like nothing better than to get back to normal." Or the new normal, given the other recent, unwelcome changes to my life. Thanks to Dead Louse of a Spouse, normal had flown the hacienda for good.

"As would I." Naomi dropped her eyes to the papers in front of her.

"Is that all?" I asked.

"No, I'm afraid not." She picked up the papers and tapped them into a neat pile. "I spent the better part of last evening in an emergency meeting with the board of directors and the legal department."

"Regarding the cancellation of the show?"

"Among other things. The show won't go on. It's part of the settlement I negotiated on your behalf."

"On my behalf? I don't understand."

"Cloris called me after she saw you yesterday. She mentioned a lawsuit—"

"Naomi, that was all Cloris's idea. I can assure you I have no plans to sue Trimedia."

"Yes, you do."

"No, I—"

"Anastasia, how the hell can I negotiate a settlement for a suit you don't plan to file?"

"But—"

Naomi held up her hand. "I'm going to do the talking, and you're going to do the listening. Understood?"

I nodded.

"Good. Now, in exchange for you not suing Trimedia, Trimedia has agreed to all your demands." She pushed her glasses farther up her nose and checked the papers she held between her hands. "There's the usually legal mumbo-jumbo concerning the parties of the first part and the parties of the second part and so forth. I'll skip all that if you don't mind."

"By all means." I didn't understand legal mumbo-jumbo, anyway.

"Good. First, Trimedia will cancel *Morning Makeovers* as of today. Secondly, all editors will be fairly compensated for the additional time they spent preparing for and taking part in the taping of the now defunct show. Compensation to be the standard time-and-a-half of each editor's hourly salary."

Stunned, my mouth dropped open, and I stared at Naomi. "Have they really agreed to this?" In my mind I rapidly calculated a rough estimate of how many additional hours I'd worked over the last six weeks, then sent up an extremely grateful silent prayer to the Goddess of Cash-Strapped Single Working Parents.

Naomi lifted her head. "Don't interrupt me." Then she immediately lowered her head and continued with her summation, "Secondly, effective immediately, all editorial staff contracts will be amended to include payment for any and all promotional activities for which said staff takes part."

And to think certain members of the staff thought Naomi had sold us out over the show. I never doubted her. Naomi had our backs. At heart she was one of us, having no love for the media conglomerate that now ran what used to be a family-owned business.

I smiled my thanks, but her nose was once again buried in the papers. If she saw me, she ignored me and continued reading. "Finally, Trimedia employee Anastasia Pollack agrees to accept the sum of fifty thousand dollars as full and complete restitution for the pain and suffering inflicted upon her by former Trimedia employee Sheri Rabbstein."

Naomi passed the papers and a pen across her desk to me. "If you agree to the terms, sign the last page of both copies where indicated and initial the other pages."

This went seriously above and beyond watching her editors' backs. This was Naomi stepping into the role of my Fairy Godmother. "You did this for me?"

She removed her reading glasses, placed them on the desk, and rubbed her temples. Naomi always looked like she stepped off the pages of *Vogue*, not a hair out of place, not a wrinkle in her outfit nor a worry line on her face. Not today. Today she looked every one of her fifty-nine years and then some. I wondered just how long those negotiations had taken last night and what toll they'd personally cost her. Naomi wasn't a lawyer, and she'd been up against a notorious gang of sharks and barracudas. Trimedia was used to strong-arming, not being strong-armed.

"I wasn't entirely successful," she said. "I wanted to hold out for a hundred grand. When they balked, I added the other stipulations. Of course, if you want, you can still sue. The courts might award you considerably more. If successful, you'd stand to recoup everything your husband lost and then some."

"Or not." I flipped to the last page and signed my name without bothering to read the document. Then I did the same for the second copy. My lawyer, if I had a lawyer, would freak. However, since only Naomi and I were in her office, she simply arched a brow.

"This settlement is about more than just me," I said as I initialed each page. "Trimedia took advantage of all of us, and you've made sure that never happens again. Thank you." I passed the papers back to her.

"Don't thank me," she said, handing over a check. "This is all your doing. I was merely the go-between."

I got the message. "So I can't let the rest of the staff know what you did for them?"

"You can let them know what *you* did for them. No one can ever know that you and I weren't in talks last evening each time I stepped out of the conference room. Understood?"

"Absolutely."

"Good. I've scheduled a staff meeting for noon to announce the changes. Now get back to work. We have a magazine to put to bed."

Fifty thousand dollars! I folded the check and placed it in my purse. Fifty thousand dollars wouldn't refill all the coffers Karl had pillaged, but it would make a huge dent in the home equity line of credit he'd maxed out and gambled away.

Boy, did I ever owe Cloris big time for her big mouth. Too bad I couldn't tell her why.

I was leaving Naomi's office when Kim flew down the hall, grabbed my arm, and rushed me back inside. "You two better see this," she said, grabbing the remote and flipping on Naomi's television.

TWENTY-FOUR

ABOVE A *BREAKING NEWS* banner the screen showed an ongoing high speed chase across Route 80. A traffic helicopter broadcast in real time as an NYPD police car, flying at breakneck speed, zipped around and through traffic. Accident after accident followed in the car's wake as it clipped vehicles and spun them into the paths of other vehicles. Traveling a distance behind them, county and local police cars dodged pile-ups in their pursuit of the runaway squad car.

"We now have confirmation of the identities of the two women who allegedly overpowered their police escorts and commandeered their vehicle," said the voiceover reporter. Mug shots of Sheri and Maxine flashed across the screen. "Sheri Rabbstein and Maxine Hailes were arrested yesterday in the Bronx on charges of kidnapping and criminal restraint. Unnamed sources tell me other charges are pending in Manhattan as the pair is linked to the murders of Trimedia television producer Lou Beaumont and morning television host Vince Alto."

"Holy Thelma and Louise!" I said.

"This can't end well," said Naomi. "Aren't they supposed to be behind bars? How the hell did those two commandeer a patrol car?"

"Somehow they managed to overpower the cops escorting them from the precinct to arraignment," said Kim. "No one knows how, and from what I heard earlier, no one was aware of the escape until they didn't show up at the courthouse. They managed to make it all the way into Jersey before anyone knew what was going on."

"And they're heading right toward us," I said. "They'll take 80 to 287."

"Why?" asked Kim.

"Revenge?" suggested Naomi.

"Against Anastasia?"

"Or all of us," I said. "Sheri and Maxine felt Trimedia had stolen their show from them."

"Who is this Maxine person?" asked Kim.

"I know her," said Naomi. "She's the former editor of *Popular Woman*."

"Which no longer exists," said Kim. "Hasn't for years, right?"

Naomi nodded. "Maxine lost her job when Trimedia leveraged a hostile takeover of Syndicated Features years ago. As soon as the deal was inked, Trimedia folded all the unprofitable monthlies. Last I heard, Maxine had gone into real estate."

Which explained how she had access to an empty house. I picked up Naomi's phone and dialed 9-1-1. "The police won't put two and two together and realize they're coming after us."

"9-1-1. State your emergency."

"That police chase on Route 80?" I said. "I know where the suspects are headed."

"How is that, ma'am?"

"Because I'm the person they're accused of kidnapping." That got the dispatcher's attention. I proceeded to give him the necessary details.

"Stay on the line," he said, then started issuing directions, which I relayed to Naomi and Kim.

"Police are on the way. We need to lock all the entrances and get everyone up to the top floor."

"I'll get the maintenance guy to take care of the doors and everyone on the first level," said Kim, pulling out her phone.

"Good. Head up to the fourth floor and alert everyone after you do that," said Naomi. "Anastasia, you take the second floor. I'll handle the third floor." She pulled out her cell phone and began dialing as Kim and I raced for the elevator.

"How many occupants in the building?" asked the dispatcher.

I had no idea. "How many people work here?" I asked Kim.

"Beats me," she said. "We've got five magazines here plus all the suits upstairs. Maybe two or three hundred?"

"We're not sure," I told the dispatcher. "Maybe three hundred. More or less."

"Shit!" Someone else was now on the line and not very happy. "This is Detective Batswin."

"Batswin? Boy am I glad to hear your voice." Batswin and I had history. She once thought I killed our former fashion editor Marlys Vandenburg. When I'd proven my innocence and presented her with the real killer, we'd formed a truce of sorts.

"Mrs. Pollack? Is that you? Jeez! Don't tell me *you're* the kidnap vic."

"Small world, huh?"

"Maybe you need to go into a safer line of work. Like bomb disposal."

"Is that your way of telling me you care?"

"Just round up all those people and get them up to the fourth floor, okay? We'll have the building surrounded before that NYPD car arrives."

"Working on it."

Within five minutes everyone in the building was crammed in front of the east-facing windows, awaiting a showdown. The Morris County S.W.A.T. team arrived. Local police blocked the road leading to our office building and the train station across the street. In the distance we could see a road block of police vehicles at the Route 287 off-ramp. Several helicopters circled overhead.

"There they are!" shouted a guy from the production department.

We watched as Sheri and Maxine flew down the ramp, directly at the road block, but at the last minute, the driver cut the wheel sharply. The stolen police car flew off the ramp and landed in the adjacent field. A moment later the driver sped around the road block, heading right toward us.

"They didn't stop them at the ramp," I told Batswin, but she was busy screaming at someone on her end. I guess she already knew.

At the next roadblock Sheri and Maxine pulled guns and started firing.

"How the hell did they get weapons?" Batswin screamed.

Good question from Batswin.

Dumb move by Sheri and Maxine.

The cops fired back, and unlike Sheri and Maxine, they didn't miss. The squad car spun out of control, flipped into the retention ditch, and a moment later burst into flames.

———

Three days later, Zack and I had our first official date. Two brushes with death in the last few months had made me realize that life was too short to mourn Dead Louse of a Spouse any longer than the time I'd already devoted to him. Protocol be damned. Given what Karl had done to me and our kids, I owed him nothing. As a matter of fact, because of Karl, I owed nearly half the world.

Besides, had I declined Zack's invitation, Mama and the boys might have hogtied me and dragged me to the restaurant. I'd been tied up enough lately, thank you very much. So I dressed up and planned to enjoy myself at dinner in Manhattan with my drop-dead-gorgeous, drool-worthy hunk of a tenant.

"I've arranged for us to have drinks with someone before dinner," said Zack as we sped up the New Jersey turnpike in his silver Porsche Boxster.

I often wondered if he ever felt embarrassed parking that sexy sports car next to my mud-brown eight-year-old used Hyundai. Then I remembered it was Zack, not Karl, parking alongside me. Zack, who gave up the glamour of Manhattan to live above a garage in Westfield, New Jersey. Zack, a man who had his priorities screwed on straight.

"Does this someone have a name?" I asked.

"Doesn't everyone?"

"You're not going to tell me, are you?"

"Nope."

I shrugged. I could think of only one person Zack would want me to meet, the only person he'd ever mentioned to me, and I was definitely interested in meeting her.

We parked at a garage on the East Side near Forty-second Street, then walked toward Grand Central Terminal. "Is this where we're having dinner?" I asked.

"Just drinks. The location is convenient and the atmosphere conducive to conversation."

Zack led me inside the terminal and up to the Campbell Apartment, a cocktail lounge from a long-gone era. *Elegant* and *luxurious* didn't begin to describe the place. Once the office and salon of early twentieth-century tycoon John W. Campbell, the space with its intricately hand-carved woodwork, immense leaded-glass window, and massive stone fireplace nearly defied description.

I tried not to gape and ogle. I'd heard about the Campbell Apartment, of course. What New Yorker—or in my case, bridge and tunnel New Yorker—hadn't? I just never expected to find myself sipping cocktails here. One drink probably cost as much as a meal for four back in Westfield, and Westfield isn't cheap.

The lounge was relatively empty. "I expected this place to be much busier," I said as a hostess led us toward a secluded nook with a loveseat and a couple of upholstered chairs surrounding a cocktail table. In the dimly lit ambience, I barely made out the profile silhouette of a woman seated at one of the chairs.

"Mostly during the week," said Zack. "They cater to a certain fat-cat commuter crowd."

The woman in the chair stood as she saw us approach. "Darling!" She kissed Zack—on the lips—then offered me a huge smile and her hand. "You must be Anastasia. I've been looking forward to meeting you. I'm Patricia Tierney, Zack's ex-wife."

Patricia towered over me, only partly due to her four-inch stilettos which brought her nose to nose with Zack. She wore a gray pantsuit over a white silk shirt. With her severely short, spiky brown hair, high cheekbones, and size 0 figure, she looked like she'd just stepped off a Fashion Week catwalk. However, her eyes told a different story, one that announced her true profession, a don't-mess-with-me prosecutor.

I shook her hand and forced myself to return her smile. "Pleased to meet you." I think. That certainly was more than a friendly quick peck she'd planted on Zack.

"Sit," she said, waving an arm toward the remaining seats as she settled back into her chair. Zack led me over to the loveseat and sat down beside me.

"I took the liberty of ordering us Prohibition Punch," said Patricia. She turned to me. "If you've never tried one, Anastasia, you'll love it. It's the Apartment's signature drink. Champagne, Grand Marnier, and rum with a splash of this and that."

"Sounds potent."

"The best kind of drink."

The waitress arrived with three brandy snifters filled nearly to the top. Patricia raised her glass and looked directly at me. "Shall we drink to staying alive?"

"Absolutely!" Under the circumstances, I couldn't think of a better toast. We clicked snifters.

"Which is why I told Zack I wanted to meet you," she said. "After your ordeal, I'm sure you have questions, and you deserve to hear all the details, something you'll never get out of Phillips and Marlowe or anyone else at the NYPD."

I took a sip of my drink and sat back. "Go ahead." Although I had already fit most of the puzzle together on my own, I was still a few pieces shy of a complete picture.

"Rabbstein was too guilt-ridden to request legal counsel," she began. "Once she and Hailes were brought to the Bronx precinct and separated, Rabbstein couldn't wait to unburden her soul." Patricia sighed. "How I wish I'd been present to hear that jailbird sing. Unfortunately, I've had to settle for the transcripts."

"I overheard Sheri mention something about Lou's death being an accident," I said.

Patricia nodded. "So she claimed. I'm more inclined to believe she lost control and killed Beaumont out of fear and desperation."

"Because Lou discovered the security tapes had been tampered with?"

"Not exactly. I'd better start from the beginning." Patricia took a sip of her drink, then continued, "Some years ago, Rabbstein and Hailes had planned a show similar to *Morning Makeovers*."

"Back during Maxine's stint as editorial director of *Popular Woman*?"

Patricia quirked an eyebrow. "You know about that?"

"Naomi, our editorial director, recognized Maxine's name. Anyway, I always suspected Sheri came up with the idea for the show years ago."

"Why?"

"Based on the crafts projects she wanted to feature," I explained. "Many of them were once popular trends that had come and gone ages ago."

Patricia nodded, then continued. "Anyway, the show died in the planning stages."

"Because Trimedia folded *Popular Woman*?"

"Right. This was back before Beaumont came aboard to helm *You Heard It Here First with Vince and Monica*. Rabbstein worked for the previous producer and stayed on after Beaumont took over eight years ago. She said she tried to get him to sign onto the idea, even though Hailes never landed another magazine gig. Or maybe because of it. The two lovebirds desperately wanted to work together.

"Anyway, Beaumont hated the idea, and that was that. The rejection festered in Rabbstein, and she grew to hate Beaumont. Then your mother came along and basically suggested the same format."

"And Lou was so head-over-heels for Mama," I said, "that he'd agree to anything to make her happy."

"Rabbstein went ballistic. She and Hailes decided to get even. They trashed the set out of spite."

Which explains why Sheri had volunteered so quickly to check the security tapes. She knew they'd show her and Maxine entering the building sometime between Friday evening and Monday morning.

"Apparently, at some point either later Monday or early Tuesday," continued Patricia, "Beaumont realized Rabbstein never viewed the tapes."

But according to Hector, no one had asked about the security tapes for that time period. "Do you know how Lou found out?"

Patricia shook her head. "We'll probably never know. Rabbstein didn't say, and Beaumont's dead. Anyway, when he confronted her, she panicked."

"Stabbing him with one of my knitting needles."

"She claimed she was only threatening him with it, that he reached to grab it out of her hand, and somehow wound up stabbed through the heart."

"Somehow?" asked Zack, joining the conversation for the first time.

Patricia smiled at him. "Some people are just delusional, darling. You should know that."

I quickly glanced at Zack, who was smiling back at his ex-wife. I decided to ignore whatever can of worms lay between them. Best to turn the conversation back to the original subject. "Sheri must have hacked into the security system to sabotage the tapes after she killed Lou. I overheard Maxine say it was a good thing Sheri was so tech savvy."

"Yes, she was worried that the police would seize the tapes as evidence in the murder, and she didn't want them questioning why she and Hailes had entered the building after hours that weekend."

"Can I assume Sheri hacked into Vince's and Monica's computers to plant that incriminating e-mail that Vince claimed he never wrote?"

"She did. That's how she learned Alto was blackmailing Monica Rivers. Alto kept a detailed journal on his computer, along with a spreadsheet of Rivers's payments to him."

"How did Alto find out Rivers is a junkie?" asked Zack.

"He caught her in the act. She'd been jonesing for a hit so badly one day on the set that she forgot to lock her dressing room door. He walked in on her shooting up."

Talk about being trapped between a rock and a hard place! Monica not only had to turn tricks to support her drug habit but to keep Vince quiet. "So when Sheri discovered the blackmail and the porn, she came up with a way to get rid of both of them without having to pay out their contracts."

Patricia nodded, then downed the remains of her punch before continuing. "Rabbstein confessed to being the anonymous source who phoned in the tip that led us to the Kips Bay brothel."

"But why try to kill Vince?" I asked. "That's one piece that doesn't make any sense to me. She'd already set everything in motion to get rid of him."

"Panic," said Patricia. "When Alto was released on bail, Rabbstein told Hailes she was afraid Alto's lawyers would find some way to get him off. She worried she'd not only have to take him back on the show but that he'd turn around and sue everyone connected with the show. Rabbstein and Hailes were too close to getting what they wanted. A lawsuit might force Trimedia to cancel the show. Hailes took matters into her own hands."

"So Sheri killed Lou, and Maxine tried to kill Vince."

"Killed, not tried to," said Patricia. "Vince died late last night."

No one said anything for what seemed like an eternity. I stared into my drink, Zack sipped his, and Patricia twirled the bowl of her snifter between her palms. I suppose I should feel sorry for Vince, but I couldn't work up an iota of sympathy toward him.

"Good riddance," Zack said, finally breaking the silence. I nodded in agreement. I'm sure we'd all been thinking a variation of the same thing: With kiddie porn all over his computer, how could anyone know for certain that Vince's perversion had been confined to jacking off in front of computer images? The world was better off with one less pervert.

"I still don't understand why Sheri and Maxine tried to frame me for everything by planting the mop dolls at the scene of each crime."

"I wish I knew," said Patricia. "I was looking forward to questioning both of them. I was also looking forward to trying them in court." Her eyes sparked with excitement for a moment. "What a case that would have been!"

Then she sighed, and the spark disappeared. "Now I'll never have the chance. Although, dying the way they did, Rabbstein and Hailes definitely saved the taxpayers of New York a pile of cash."

"I think I know why Sheri singled you out," Zack said to me.

Patricia and I both turned to him. "Why?" I asked.

"You were a surrogate for Flora," he said. "Sheri couldn't lay the blame on the one person she wanted to hurt the most, so she picked you as the next best thing."

"By casting the blame on me, she did hurt Mama."

"In the only way she could short of doing her physical harm," said Patricia. "Good one, Zack."

"I do have my moments," he said.

They exchanged a look that I couldn't interpret and wasn't sure I wanted to.

"What about the note I found in Lou's apartment?" I asked. "Who sent that?"

Patricia waved away the question. "Totally irrelevant to the case. One of Beaumont's ex-wives harassed him periodically because he owed her quite a bit in alimony."

"Francine? I met her at Lou's funeral."

"That's the one." Patricia stood up. "Time for me to catch a train. The little darlings will be wondering where I am."

"Little darlings?" I asked.

She pulled an iPhone from her jacket pocket, pressed the button, and held the phone up. An image of two blond toddlers in matching lace pinafores filled the screen. "Mia and Chloe. I thought I was born lacking any maternal genes," she said. "Turns out they were only lying dormant for four decades."

She planted another overly friendly kiss on Zack's lips. "I'll tell the girls their Uncle Zacky sends them hugs and kisses."

"Always," said Zack.

"You should bring Anastasia with you the next time you drive up for a visit," she added.

Patricia then did something totally unexpected, at least as far as I was concerned. She wrapped her arms around me as if we were the best of friends and whispered in my ear, "You go, girl!"

I was far too stunned to do anything but smile as she headed toward the exit. "Well," I said finally. "So that's your ex-wife."

"That's my ex-wife."

My phone rang at that moment. I checked the display. "The hospital," I said, flipping the phone open. "Hello?"

"Mrs. Pollack?"

"Yes?"

"Dr. Pavlochek wanted you to know that your mother-in-law has stabilized. He's scheduled her brain surgery for eight o'clock Monday morning."

THE END

© Robert Winston

ABOUT THE AUTHOR

Lois Winston straddles two worlds. She's an award-winning author published in mystery, romantic suspense, humorous women's fiction, and non-fiction.

She's also an award-winning designer of needlework and crafts projects for magazines, craft book publishers, and manufacturers. Like Anastasia, Lois worked for several years as a crafts editor. A graduate of the Tyler School of Art, she often draws on her art and design background for much of the source material in her fiction. She and her husband live a stone's throw from Manhattan (assuming you can throw a stone across the Hudson).

Lois loves to hear from readers. Visit her at www.loiswinston .com, and check out Anastasia's Killer Crafts & Crafty Killers blog at www.anastasiapollack.blogspot.com.

If you enjoyed reading *Death By Killer Mop Doll*, here's an excerpt from the next book in the series ...

Revenge of the Crafty Corpse

EXCERPT

"IF THAT DAMN WOMAN doesn't shut up, I'm going to strangle her!"

My mother-in-law had been settled into the Sunnyside of Westfield Assisted Living and Rehabilitation Center for all of ten minutes before she began carping about the accommodations. Uppermost on her list of complaints was her roommate, a woman we'd so far only heard, due to the mauve and burgundy floral print curtain separating their beds and a one-sided phone conversation detailing the latest episode of some cable soap opera—in a syrupy sweet southern accent quite at odds with her blunt vocabulary. At least, I hoped she was summarizing a soap opera. I'd hate to think, given the X-rated play-by-play, that she was gossiping about actual people.

"Shh. Lower your voice, Lucille. They can hear you in Hoboken."

"Don't you shush me! And I don't care if that prattling twit or anyone else hears me. This is unacceptable. I want a private room." She tightened her hand into a fist and pounded it against the arm of her wheelchair, but given her weakened state, the punctuating gesture left negligible impact.

"Medicare won't cover a private room," I told her, forcing my voice to remain calm as I unpacked her suitcase.

Three weeks ago Lucille had suffered a minor stroke. Subsequent tests revealed a brain tumor, which may or may not have accounted for some of her more bizarre behavior over the last few months. With my mother-in-law, it was hard to tell.

Lucille had weathered the stroke and surgery remarkably well for an eighty-year-old. The tumor proved benign. After a brief hospital stay, she was now ready for some minor rehab to help her regain her strength and coordination. Hence, today's resettlement.

"If my son were alive, he'd never let you dump me in this hell hole."

She should only know that her son had tried to kill her to get his hands on her life's savings—which he then proceeded to gamble away, leaving me to clean up the mess after he conveniently dropped dead at a roulette table in Las Vegas. Trusting wife that I was at the time, I thought Karl was at a sales meeting in Harrisburg, Pennsylvania.

Given his knack for pulling off such a duplicitous life, Karl should have been a CIA operative instead of an auto parts salesman. At least then our sons and I would be receiving a fat government pension. As it was, Dead Louse of a Spouse left me in stratospheric debt and at the mercy of both an army of bill collectors and Ricardo the loan shark. Not to mention his mother and Manifesto, her French bulldog, AKA Mephisto the Demon Dog to the rest of the family.

Ricardo now resides in a federal facility. However, barring some philanthropic leprechaun gifting me with his pot of gold, I'm stuck with the bill collectors, Lucille, and Mephisto. The bill collectors treat me better. And yet I continue to refuse to divulge to Lucille the truth about her precious Karl, no matter how much she goads me.

My name is Anastasia Pollack, and I'm a glutton for punishment. Welcome to my dysfunctional world. I hope the universe is taking note because as far as I'm concerned, I definitely qualify for sainthood at this point.

"Hell hole?" I glanced around Lucille's half of the generous, well-appointed room, equipped with abundant creature comforts, including her own flat screen TV, a leather recliner with heat and massage, and wi-fi. "Hardly."

"You're not the one stuck here. If you possessed an ounce of consideration, you'd allow me to remain at home and drive me to rehab every day," she said. "But I know the truth. This is all part of your grand scheme to get rid of me permanently."

I wish. Sunnyside was more exclusive country club than hell hole, right down to its exclusive country club-like fees. I placed the last of her circa-1970s polyester pantsuits in the dresser, slammed the drawer shut, and spun around to confront her.

"How exactly am I supposed to shuttle you back and forth to rehab *and* go to work? Are you suggesting I quit my job? Alex, Nick, you, and I can live out of my eight-year-old Hyundai and Dumpster dive for our meals just so Lucille Pollack, the diehard communist, doesn't have to share a room with a talkative stranger for a month? Very politically correct of you, Comrade Lucille."

"How dare you mock me!"

I needed to get out of there and back to work before I did some strangling of my own. And it wouldn't be the faceless voice currently detailing her skepticism over the supposed sexploits of one Mabel Shapiro, who, according to Lucille's roommate, couldn't satisfy a man twenty years ago, let alone now.

"I told you, Lucille, between Medicare and your supplemental insurance, you're only covered for a month's stay. After that, whether you're ready to come home or not, you're back living under my roof."

"This is all your fault!" she continued.

"My fault? Just what about your situation is my fault? Did *I* force you to jaywalk across Queens Boulevard? Did *I* drive the SUV that mowed you down? Did *I* make you keep your life's savings in shoeboxes under your bed instead of in a bank? Did *I* torch your apartment building, leaving you homeless and penniless? How is any of that *my* fault, Lucille? I'm the one who opened my home to you when you had nowhere else to go."

"Charging me exorbitant rent! You're no better than a slumlord."

"You're paying exactly what you paid each month on your apartment in Queens. Not a penny more. And for that you're receiving a place to live *and* all you and your dog can eat. Besides, I only asked you for room and board *after* your son left me broke and up to my eyeballs in debt, but I suppose that's my fault, too?"

She glared straight ahead, refusing to make eye contact with me, her lips pinched into a straight line, her post-surgery shaved head making her look even more like Mephisto than usual.

Of course, she blamed me. She's been blaming me for everything since the day Karl introduced us. Hell, she probably even blamed me for her stroke and the brain tumor. So much for hoping the removal of that tumor would improve her personality. "If you don't like the arrangements, you're free to make your own at any time."

Which, unfortunately, she wouldn't because Lucille had it far better at *Casa Pollack* than anywhere else she could afford. And she knew it.

"What are you gawking at?" she demanded.

I glanced over my shoulder and followed her laser glare to the middle of the room where I found myself staring at Laura Ashley. Or what Laura Ashley might have looked like had she lived into her nineties, complete with pink-tinged white pin curls, poorly applied make-up caked into the crevices of deep wrinkles, and transplanted from Wales, UK, to Westfield, NJ.

I hadn't seen so many ruffles and such an over-abundance of Cluny lace since my cousin Susannah Sudberry's English garden-themed wedding back in 1992. The most god-awful lace-edged, pouf-sleeved floral-print bridesmaid's dress ever created still resides in my attic. However, I might have to hand over that designation to Lucille's roommate's outfit. At least my bridesmaid's gown didn't have the addition of a coordinating yo-yo cardigan sweater.

At some point the soap opera play-by-play had ended. How long Lucille's roomie had been eavesdropping on us was anyone's guess, but before Lucille could hurl another barb, I crossed the room and held my hand out to the woman. "Mrs. Wegner? I'm Anastasia Pollack." I knew her name from the nameplate tacked to the wall outside the room. Lucille's name had already been added beneath that of Lyndella Wegner.

She took my hand in a surprisingly firm grip for such a petite and elderly woman. "Pleased to meet you, sugar. And call me Lyndella. Mrs. Wegner was my mother-in-law, bless her hard-hearted soul."

Looks like I'd found another loser in the mother-in-law lottery. I nodded in Lucille's direction, "And this is my mother-in-law Lucille Pollack, your roommate for the next month."

Lyndella nodded toward Lucille. "Not too happy to be here, are you, sugar?"

A part of me (the nasty part I kept tamped down as much as possible) wanted to tell her that *happy* wasn't in the commie curmudgeon's lexicon, but she'd learn that for herself soon enough. Instead, I said, "I'm afraid Lucille has been through quite a bit the last several months."

She directed another question to Lucille. "So what's your story, sugar?"

I stifled a giggle. Lyndella Wegner's strong accent seemed right at home juxtaposed against her Laura Ashley-meets-Blanche Dubois demeanor but totally at odds with twenty-first-century Westfield.

"Mind your own business," muttered Lucille. "And I'm not your *sugar*."

Lyndella ignored the rudeness. Or maybe she hadn't heard Lucille. Modern hearing aids are so tiny, I couldn't tell if Lyndella wore any underneath her pink pin curls. She glanced at her watch and said, "I'm afraid we'll have to postpone our get-to-know-each-other chat until later, girls. It's time for my needlework class, and I can't be late. Those other women, bless their Yankee hearts, would be lost without my expert guidance." Then she ducked behind the curtain divider.

Lyndella reappeared a moment later. In one hand she held a ball of pink crochet cotton. She cradled a length of finely crocheted extra-wide pink lace and a crochet hook in her other hand.

"That's exquisite work," I said.

"Of course, it is, sugar."

I held out my hand. "May I?" She placed the delicate lace across my fingers. I examined the stitching closer. "Did you also crochet the lace on your dress?"

She executed a flat-footed pirouette to show off her workmanship. "I make all my own clothes. Always have. And they're of a far better quality than anything you'll find in any department store."

And how modest of her to say so. I had to admit, though, the dress fit her like couture, and her attention to detail rivaled anything strutting down New York's Fashion Week catwalks.

Lyndella flipped up the hem of her skirt and held it out for me to inspect. "See here, sugar. French seams. I dare say, you won't find any of those hanging on a rack at Macy's or Lord & Taylor."

"Probably not," I agreed, although I failed to see the need to French seam poplin when pinking shears worked just as well and took much less time and effort. However, I kept that judgment to myself.

"I'll tell you a little secret, sugar. Handwork keeps both the mind and body sharp." She tapped her temple with an index finger. "Mark my words, you young people will regret your store-bought ways when you get older, but it will be too late. You'll wind up doddering old fools, sipping Ensure and drooling into your mashed bananas."

I certainly hoped not, but I had no desire to engage in a debate of my generation's future with this woman....